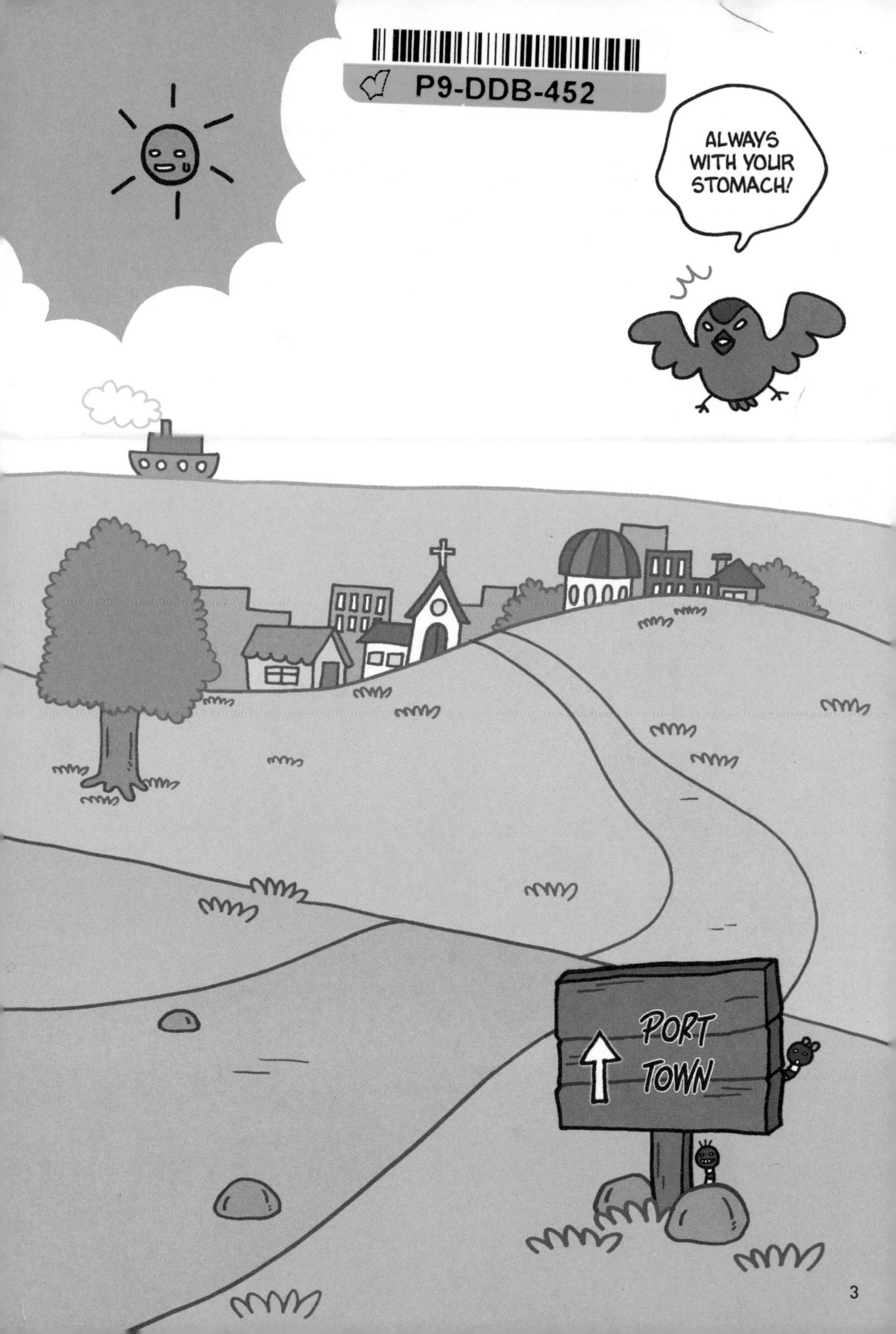
ALWAYS WITH YOUR STOMACH!
PORT TOWN

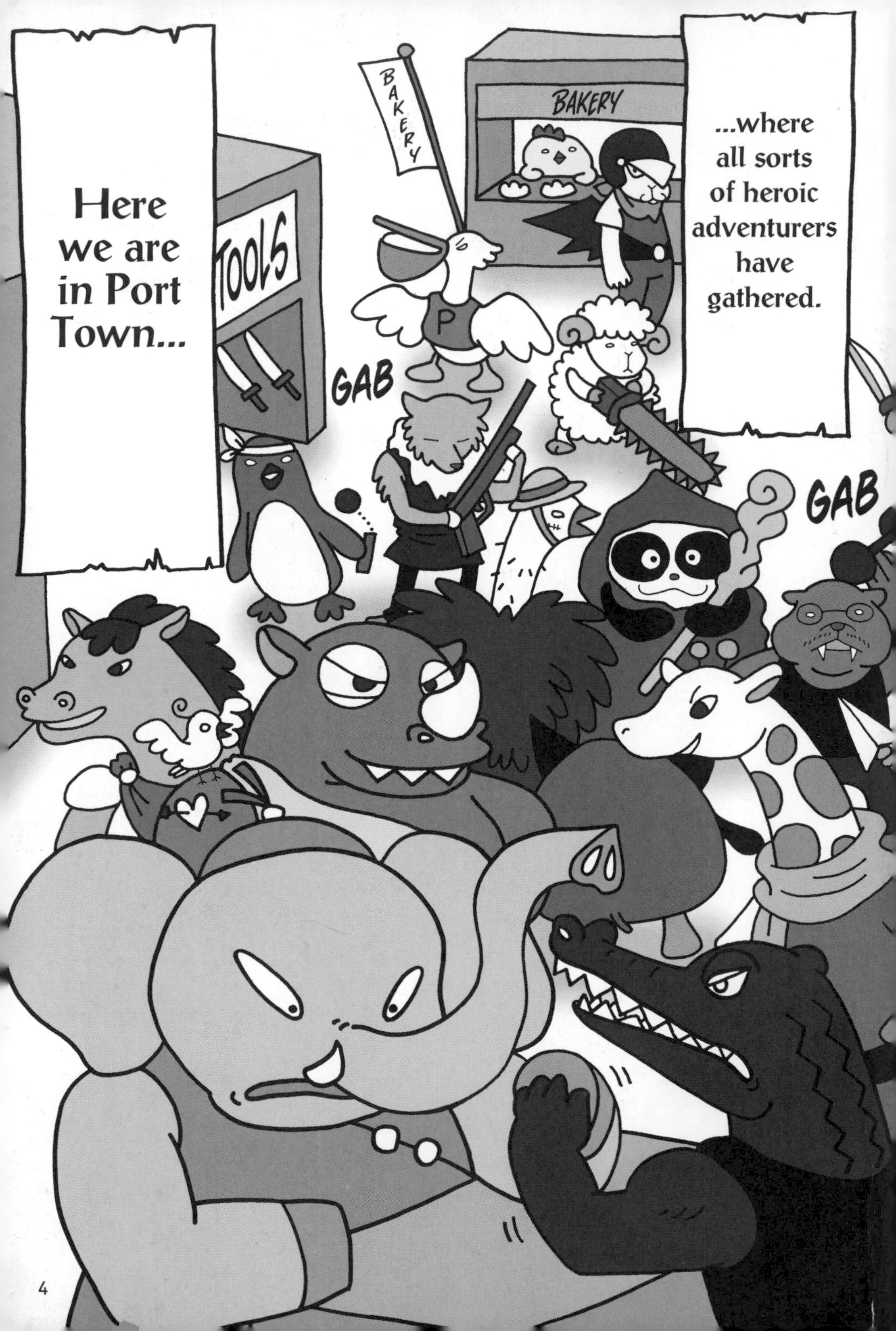
Here we are in Port Town...
TOOLS
BAKERY
BAKERY
P
GAB
...where all sorts of heroic adventurers have gathered.
GAB

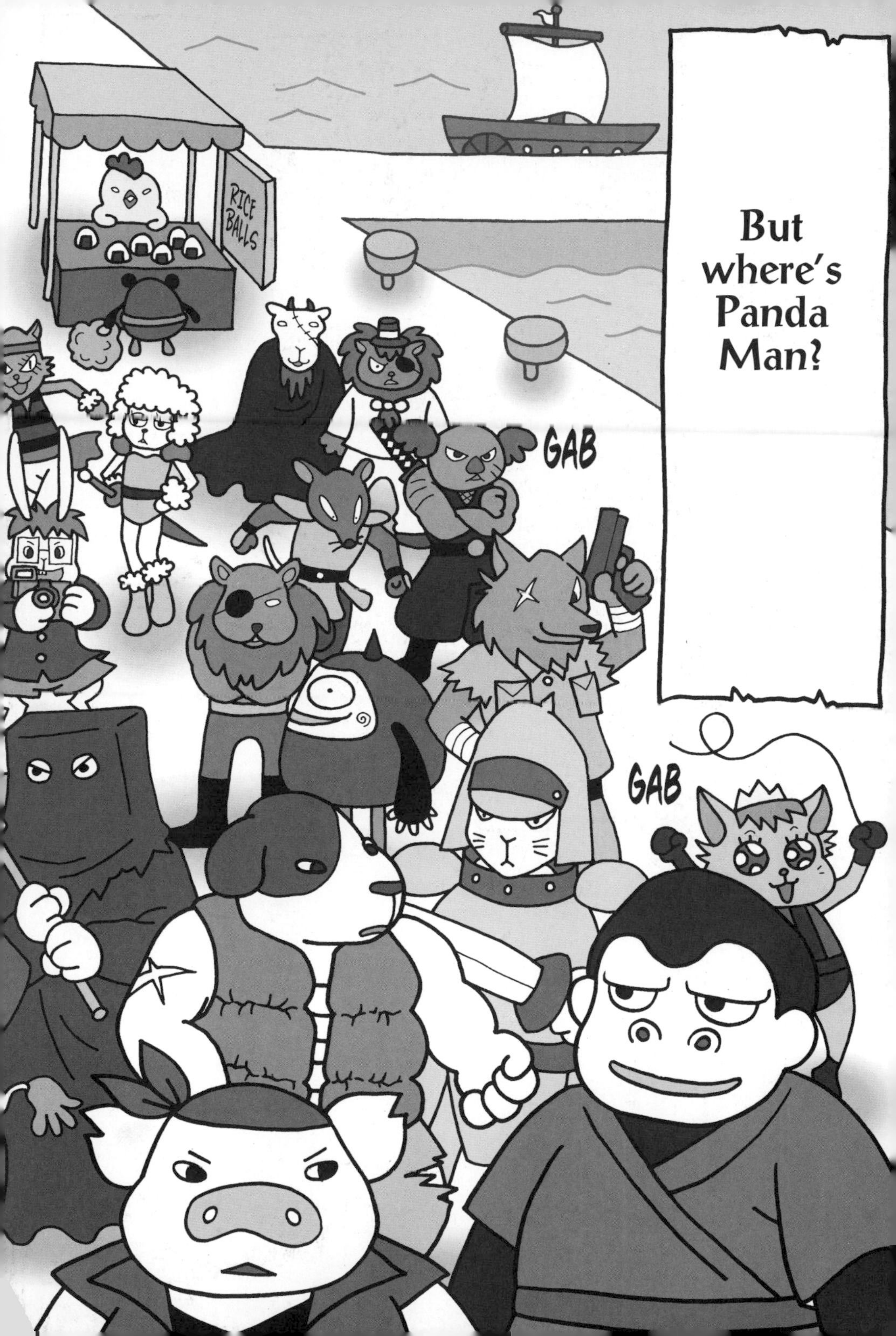
But where's Panda Man?
RICE BALLS
GAB
GAB

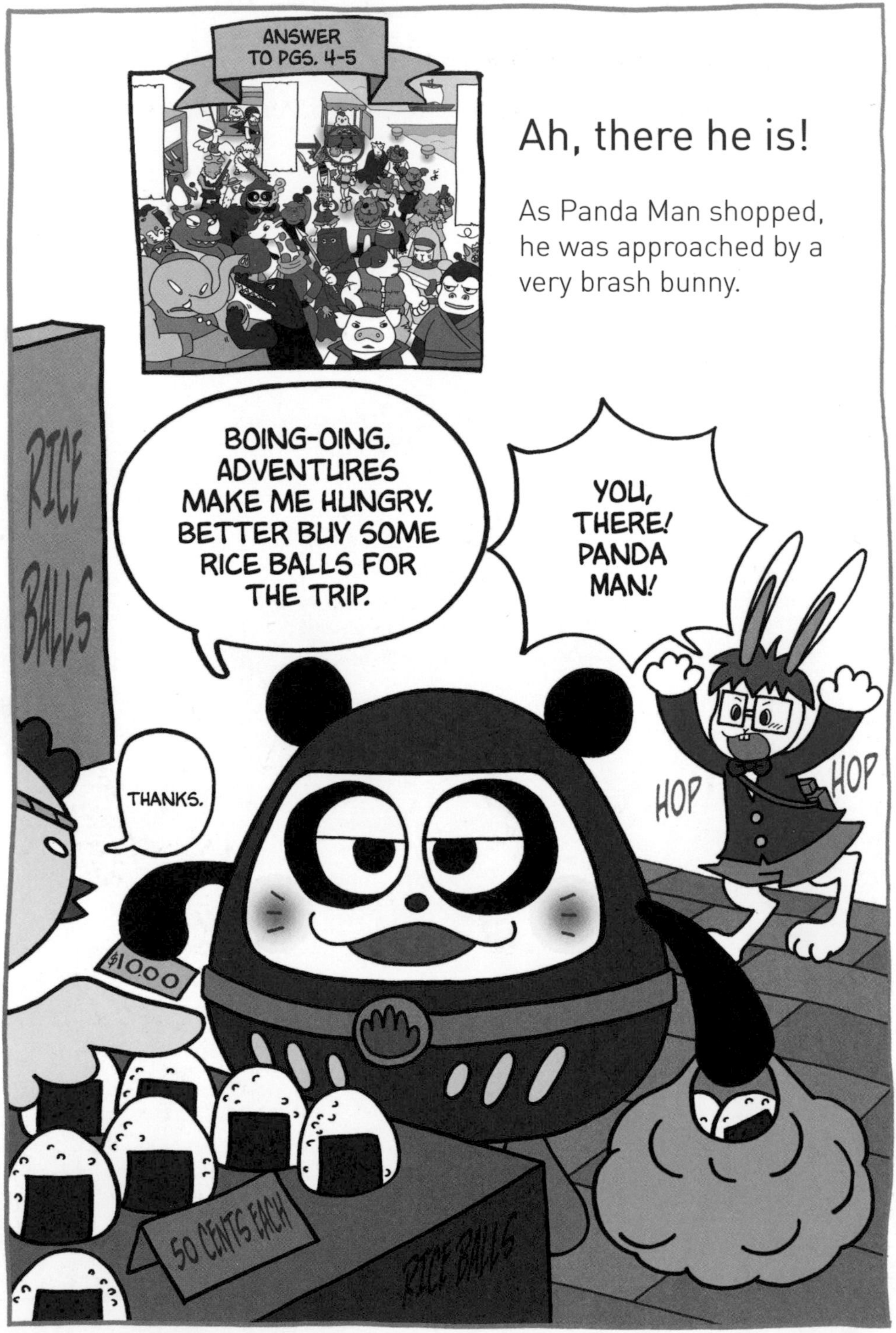
ANSWER TO PGS. 4-5
Ah, there he is!
As Panda Man shopped, he was approached by a very brash bunny.
RICE BALLS
BOING-OING. ADVENTURES MAKE ME HUNGRY. BETTER BUY SOME RICE BALLS FOR THE TRIP.
THANKS.
$10.00
YOU, THERE! PANDA MAN!
HOP HOP
50 CENTS EACH
RICE BALLS

"Boing-oing? Who're you?" Panda Man asked.

"Hutch Hutcherson, ace reporter. I'm covering the treasure hunt," Hutch replied.

"Huh."

"Panda Man, as the world's greatest martial artist, how are you feeling about the competition?" Hutch demanded.

"Naturally, the all-you-can eat pass is as good as mine," Panda Man replied.

"Just as I thought!" Hutch smiled.

"Well then, how about some photos of the winner?"

"Of course," Panda Man agreed.

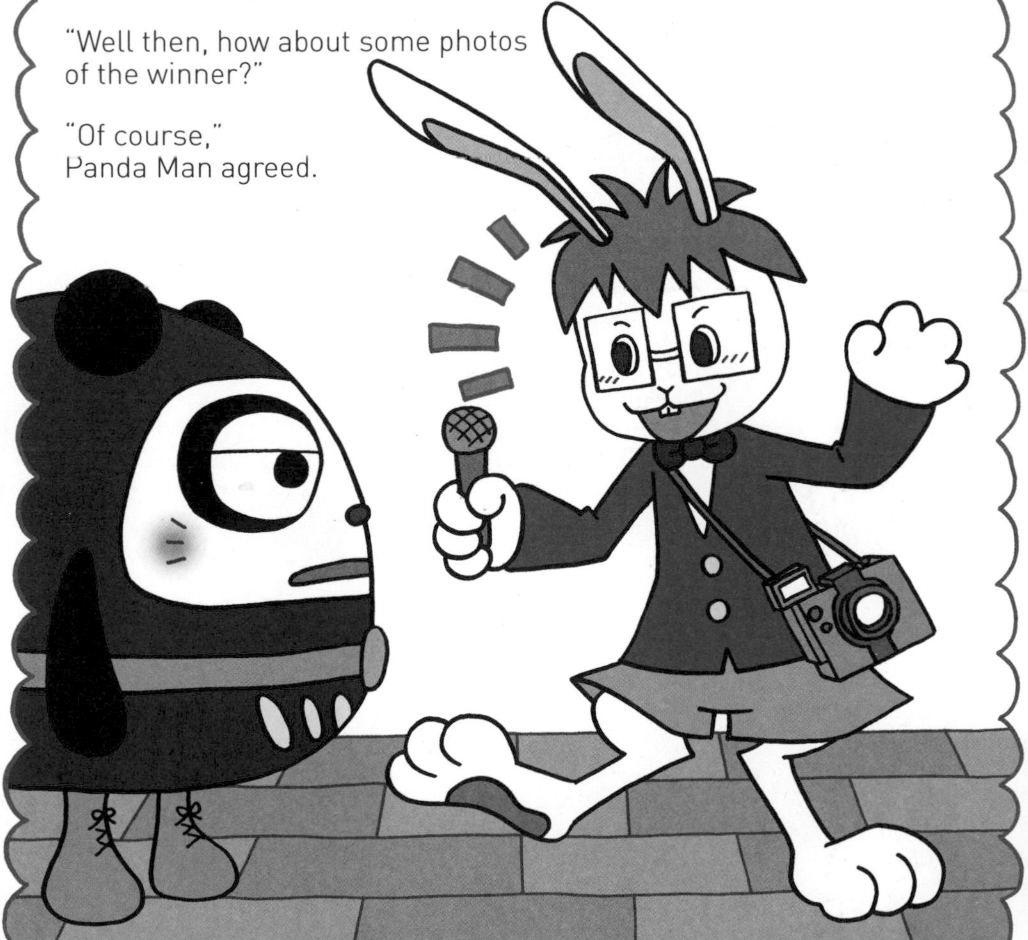

Used to having his picture taken, Panda Man was an expert at posing for the camera.

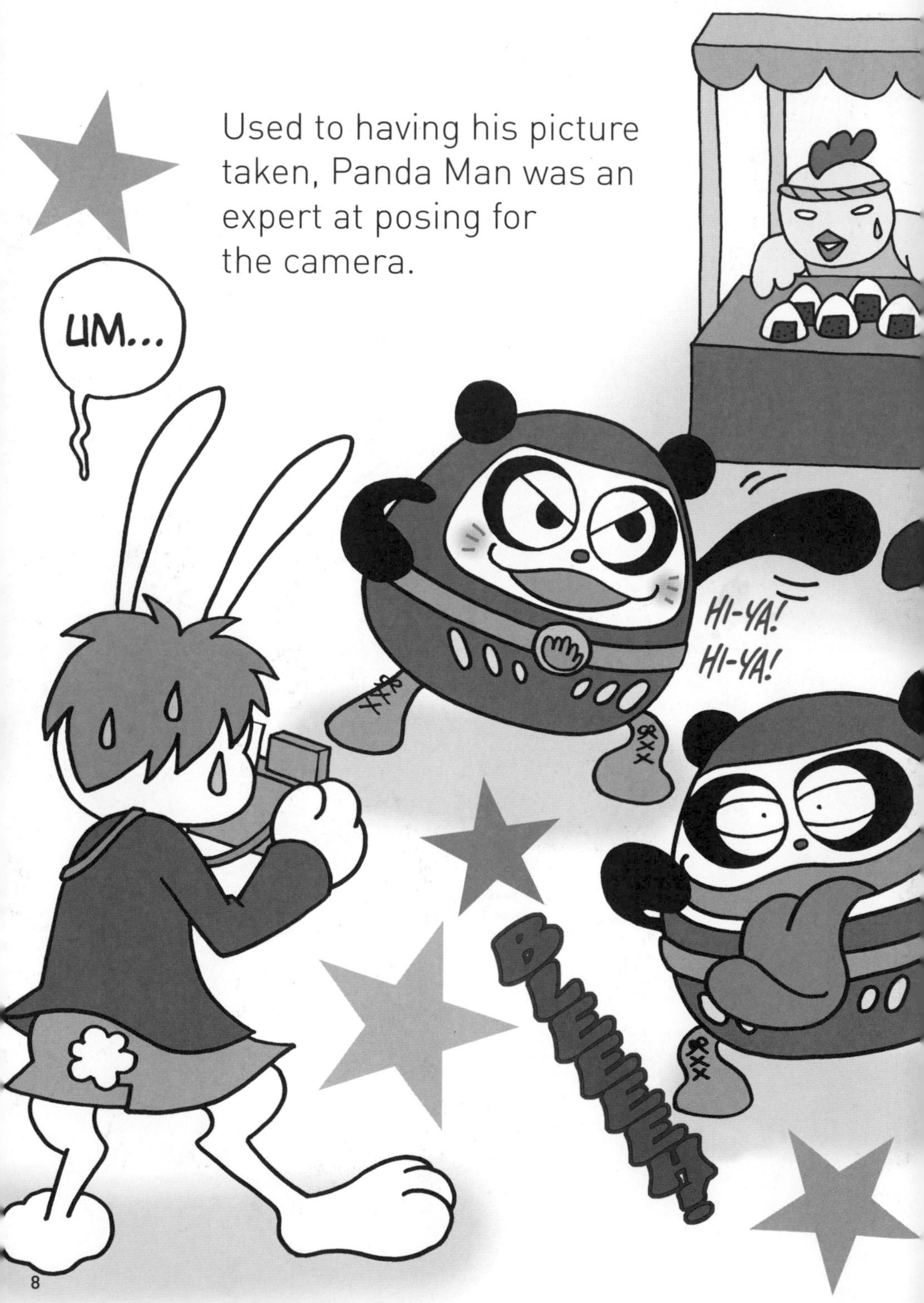
HI-YA!
HI-YA!
UM...

All eyes were on Panda Man when suddenly...

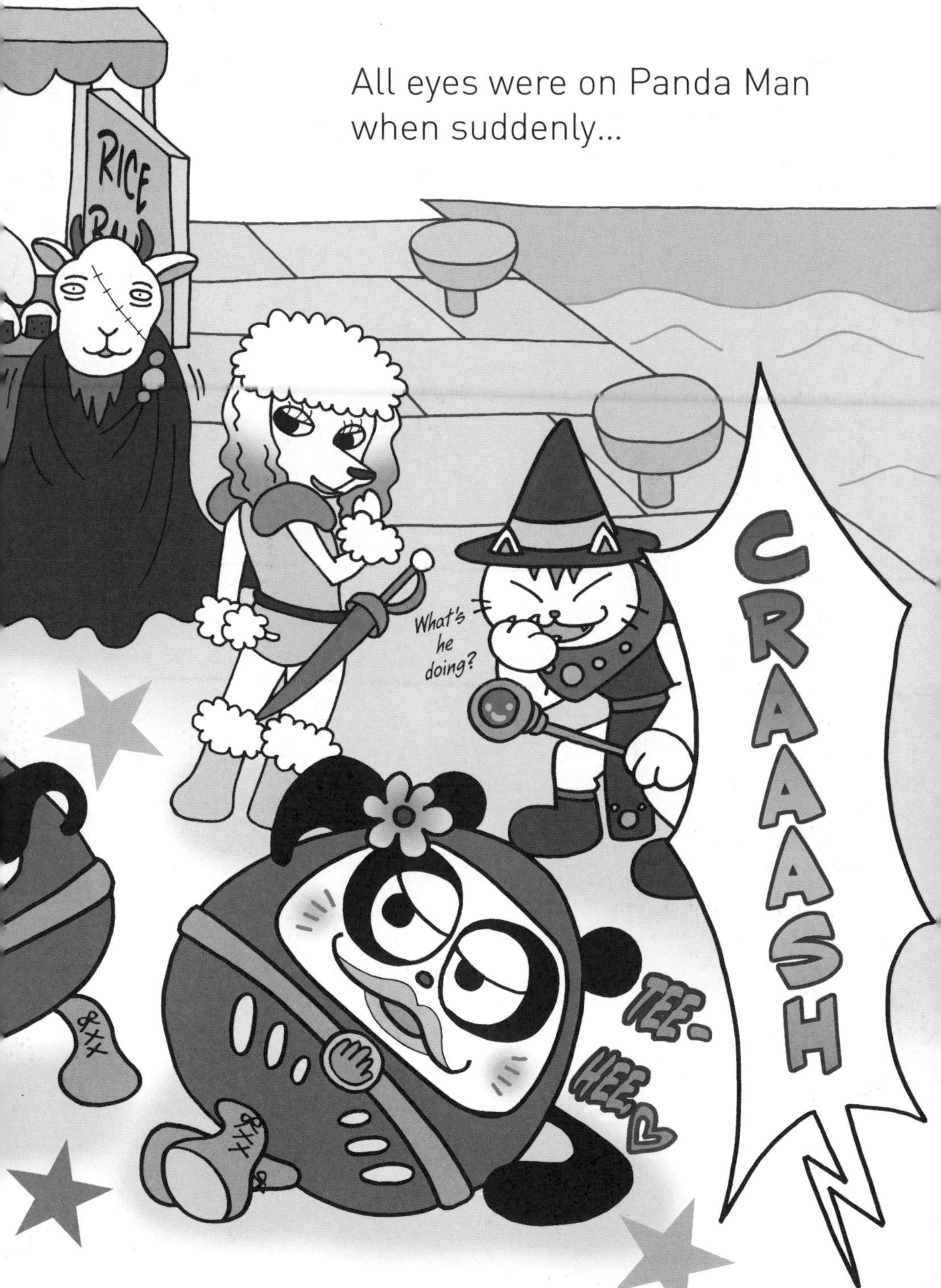
RICE BALL
What's he doing?
CRAAASH
TEE-HEE♥

A fight broke out! Unfortunately, there were a few ne'er-do-wells among the adventuring heroes. And this was one of them.

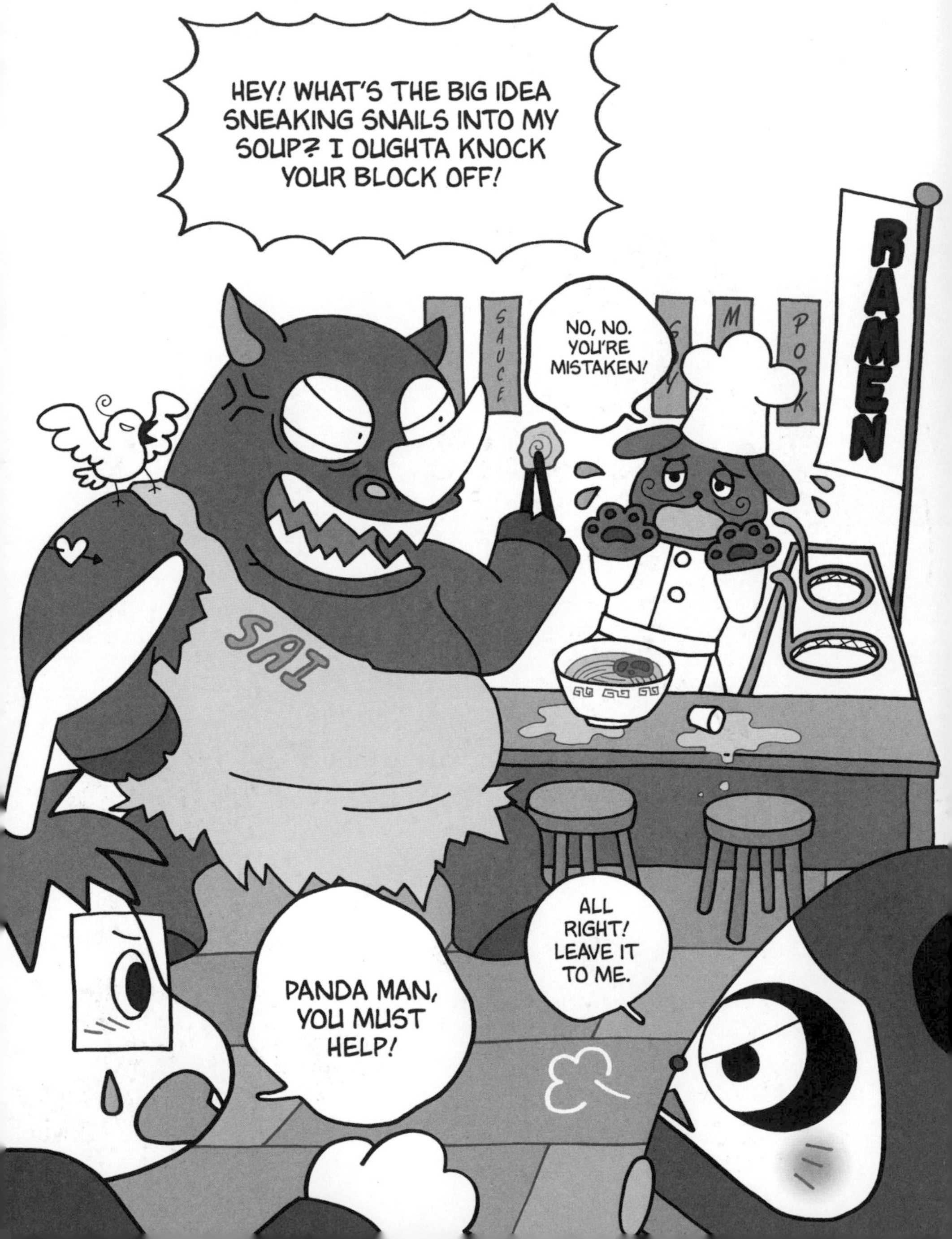
HEY! WHAT'S THE BIG IDEA SNEAKING SNAILS INTO MY SOUP? I OUGHTA KNOCK YOUR BLOCK OFF!
NO, NO. YOU'RE MISTAKEN!
RAMEN
SAUCE
SAI
PANDA MAN, YOU MUST HELP!
ALL RIGHT! LEAVE IT TO ME.

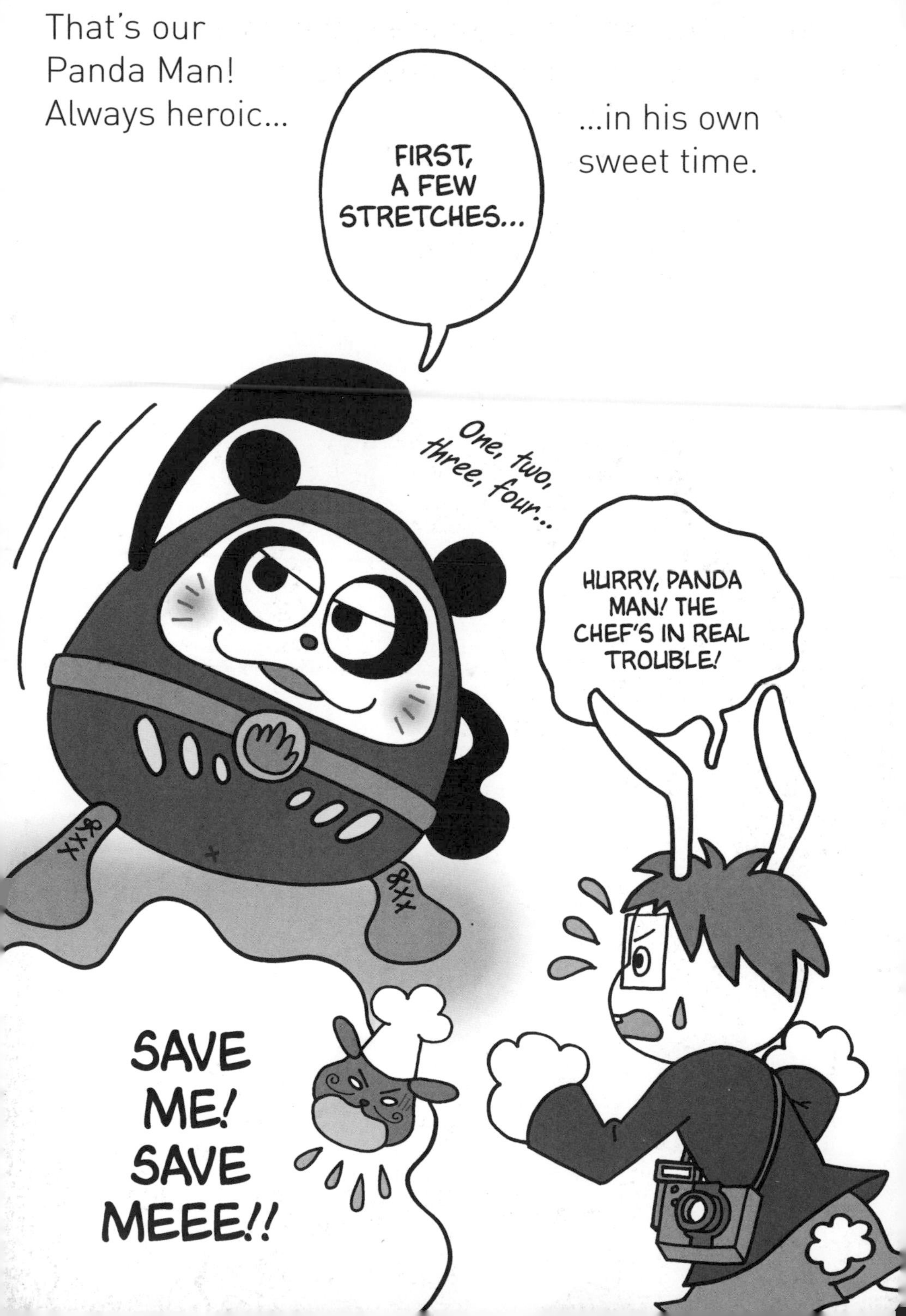
That's our Panda Man! Always heroic...
FIRST, A FEW STRETCHES...
...in his own sweet time.
One, two, three, four...
HURRY, PANDA MAN! THE CHEF'S IN REAL TROUBLE!
SAVE ME! SAVE MEEE!!

Suddenly, something *very* speedy sped toward the cranky customer...

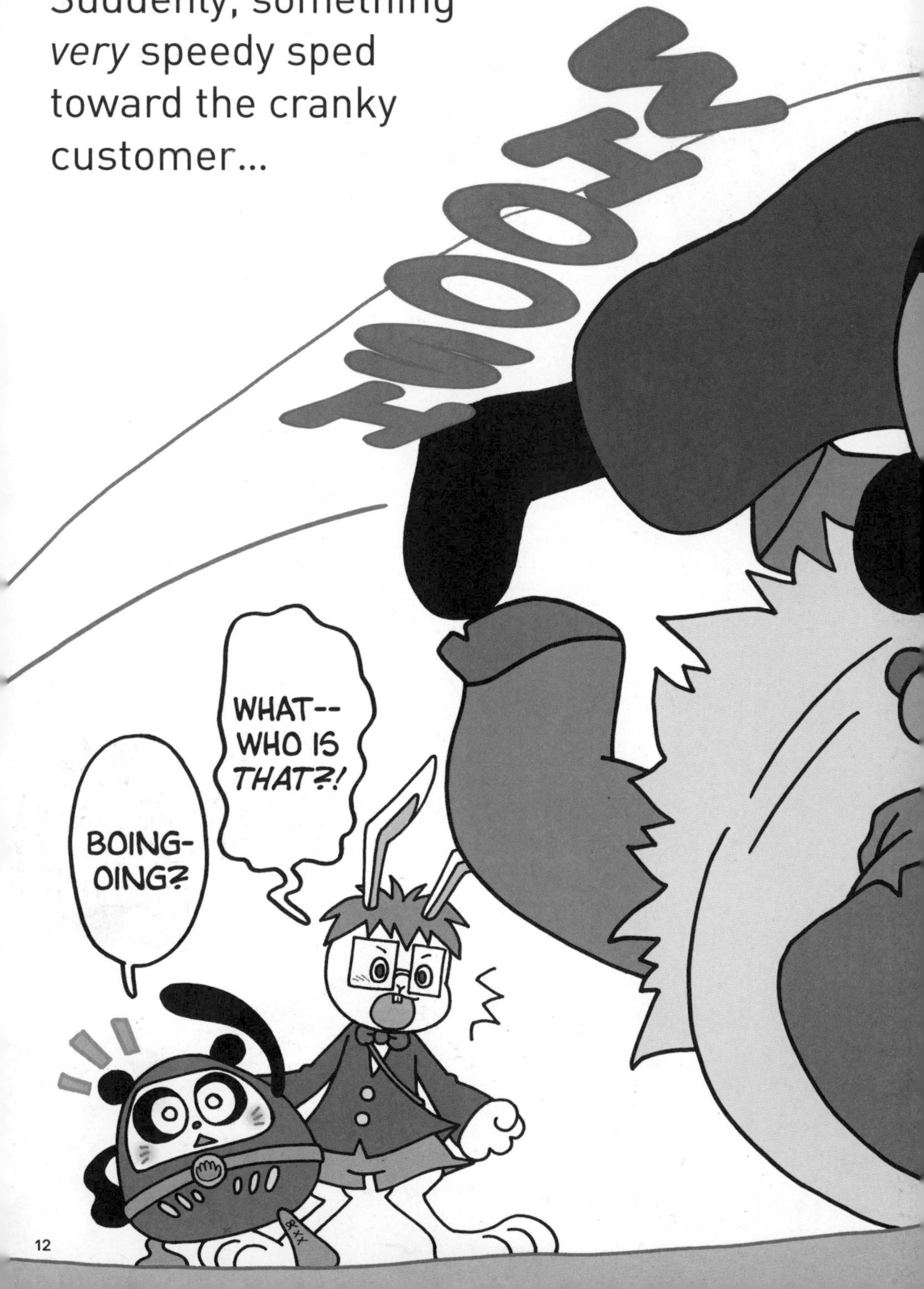
WHOOSH
WHAT-- WHO IS *THAT?!*
BOING-OING?

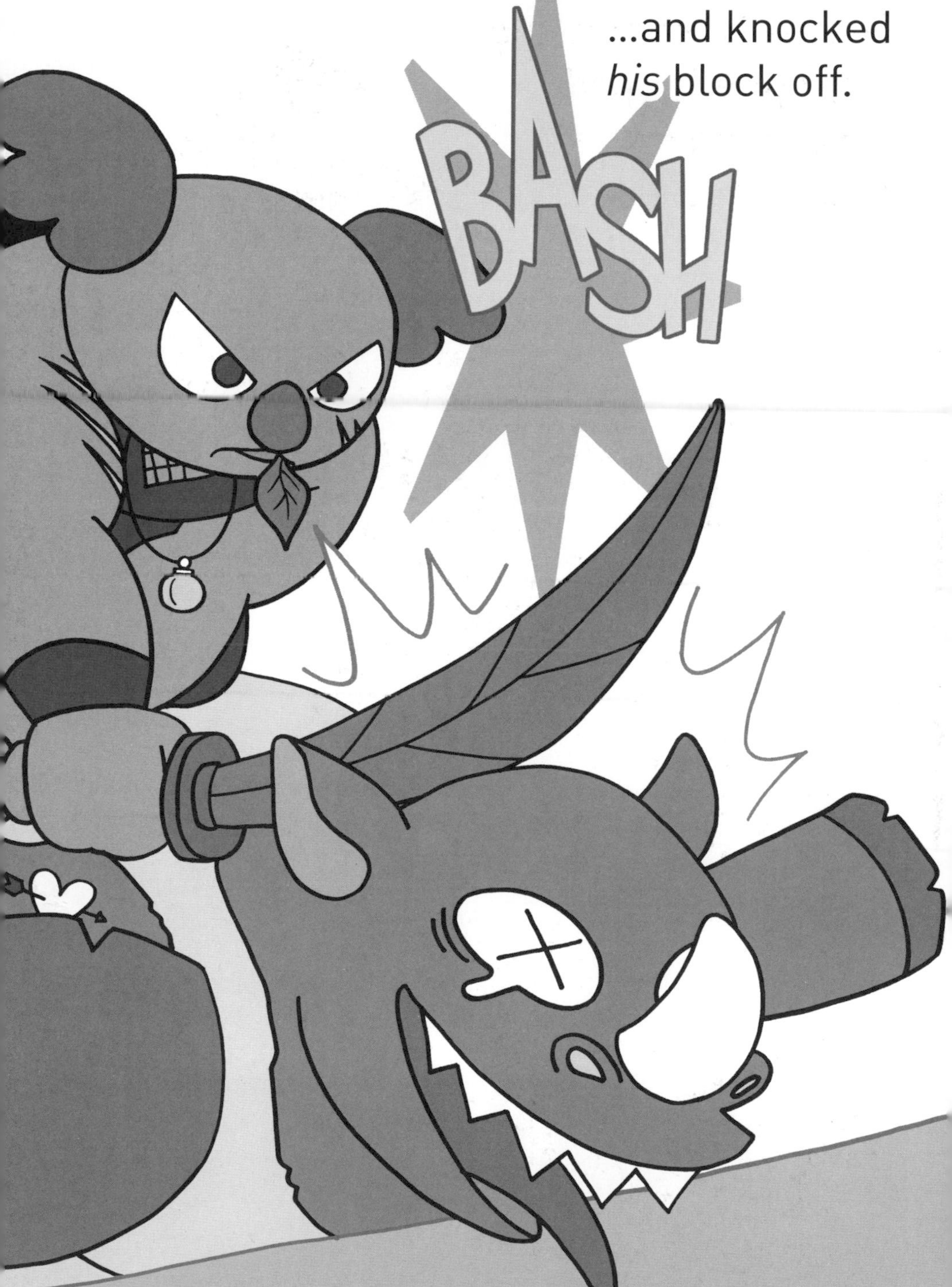
...and knocked
his block off.
BASH

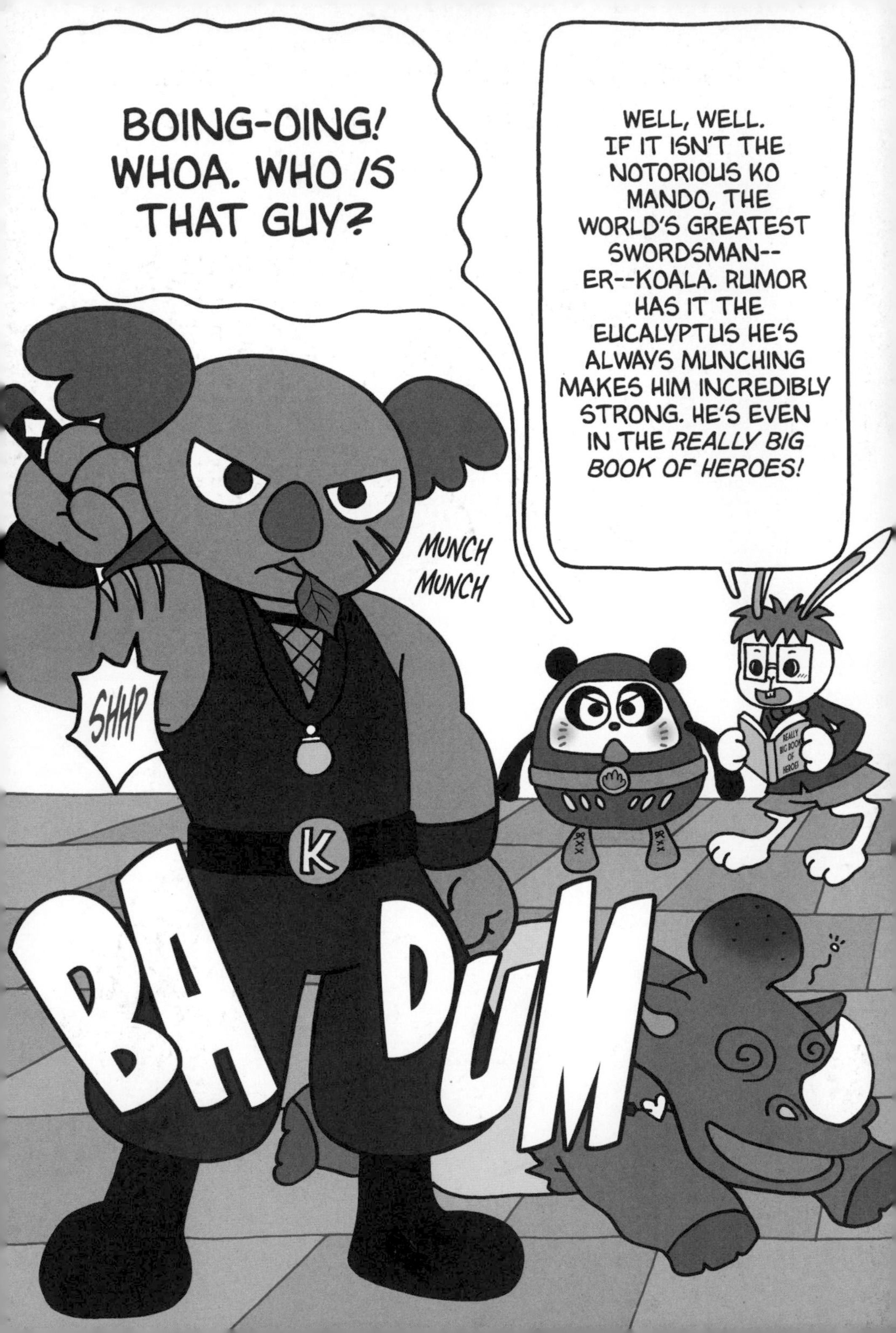
BOING-OING! WHOA. WHO IS THAT GUY?
WELL, WELL. IF IT ISN'T THE NOTORIOUS KO MANDO, THE WORLD'S GREATEST SWORDSMAN-- ER--KOALA. RUMOR HAS IT THE EUCALYPTUS HE'S ALWAYS MUNCHING MAKES HIM INCREDIBLY STRONG. HE'S EVEN IN THE *REALLY BIG BOOK OF HEROES!*
MUNCH MUNCH
SHHP
K
REALLY BIG BOOK OF HEROES
BA DUM

Ko Mando turned to Panda Man. "So, you're Panda Man, huh? I have a feeling this treasure hunt is going to come down to you and me. But in the end, I will win."

Panda Man shot back with **the world's greatest comeback.** "Boing-oing! Boing-oing!"

The sparks of competition flew.

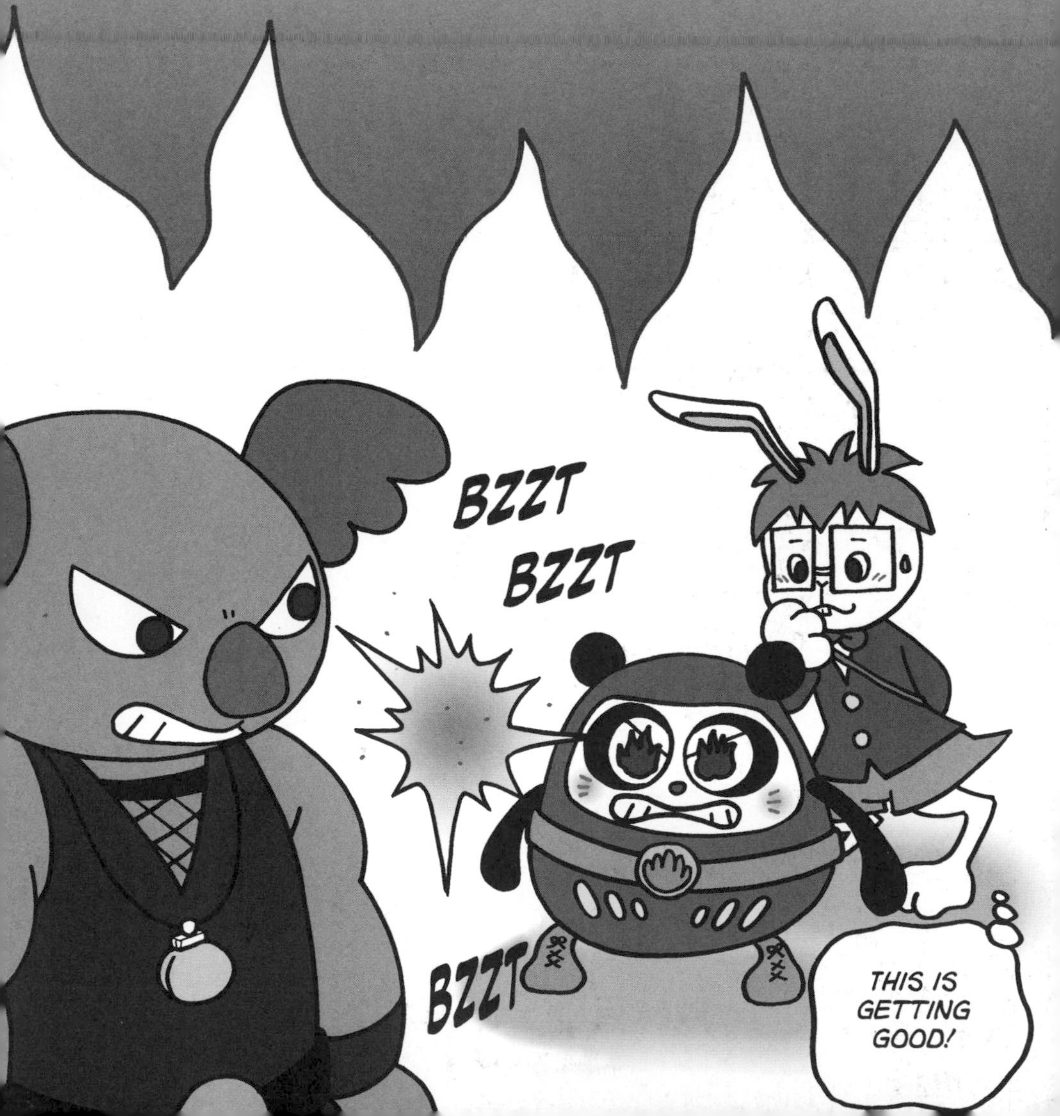
BZZT
BZZT
BZZT
THIS IS GETTING GOOD!

With a look of sheer determination, Ko Mando grasped the pendant on his chest.

Could Ko Mando have a secret?

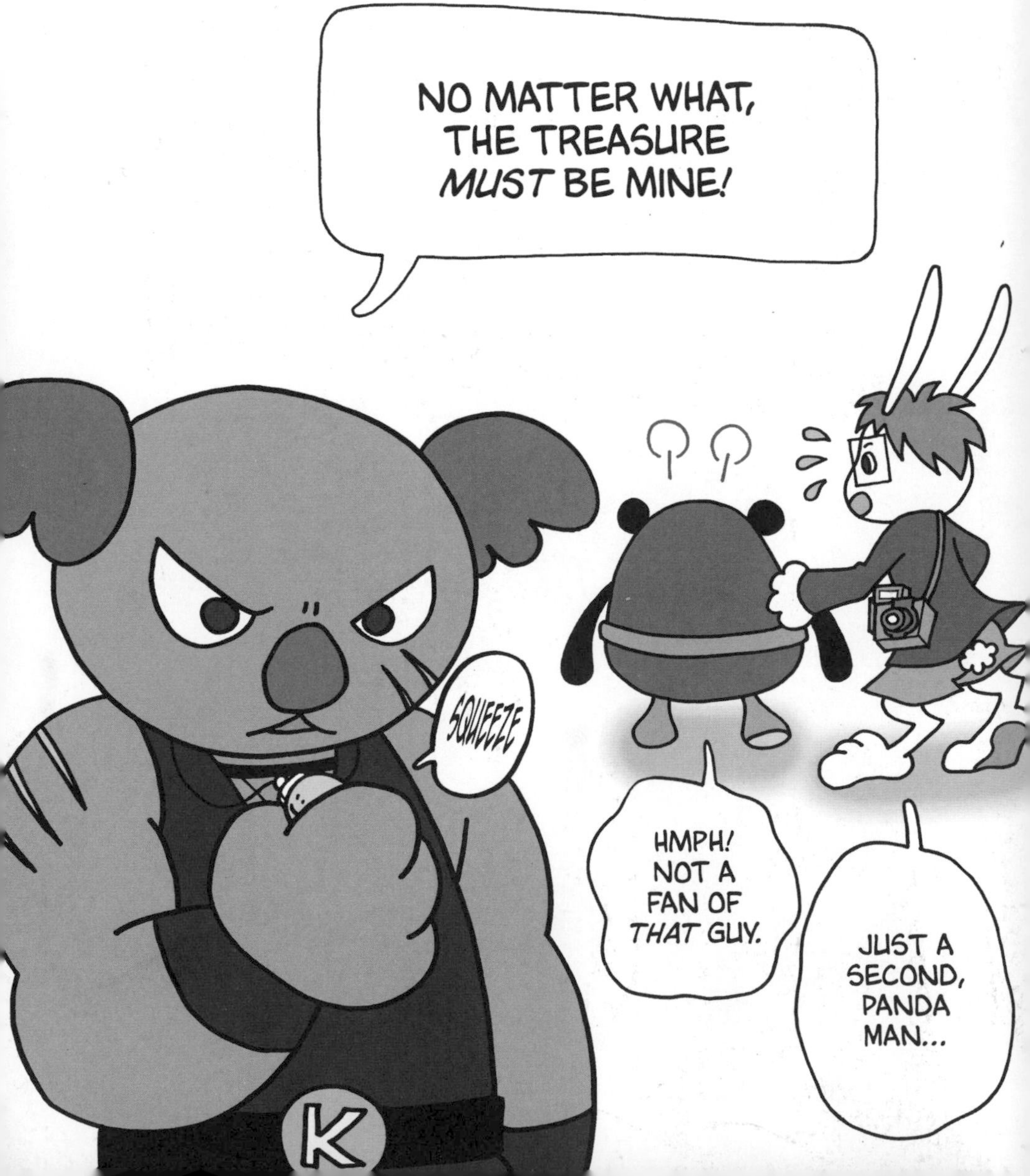
NO MATTER WHAT, THE TREASURE *MUST* BE MINE!
SQUEEZE
HMPH! NOT A FAN OF *THAT* GUY.
JUST A SECOND, PANDA MAN...

Just then the trumpets blared, announcing the arrival of the very wealthy Bill Apes.

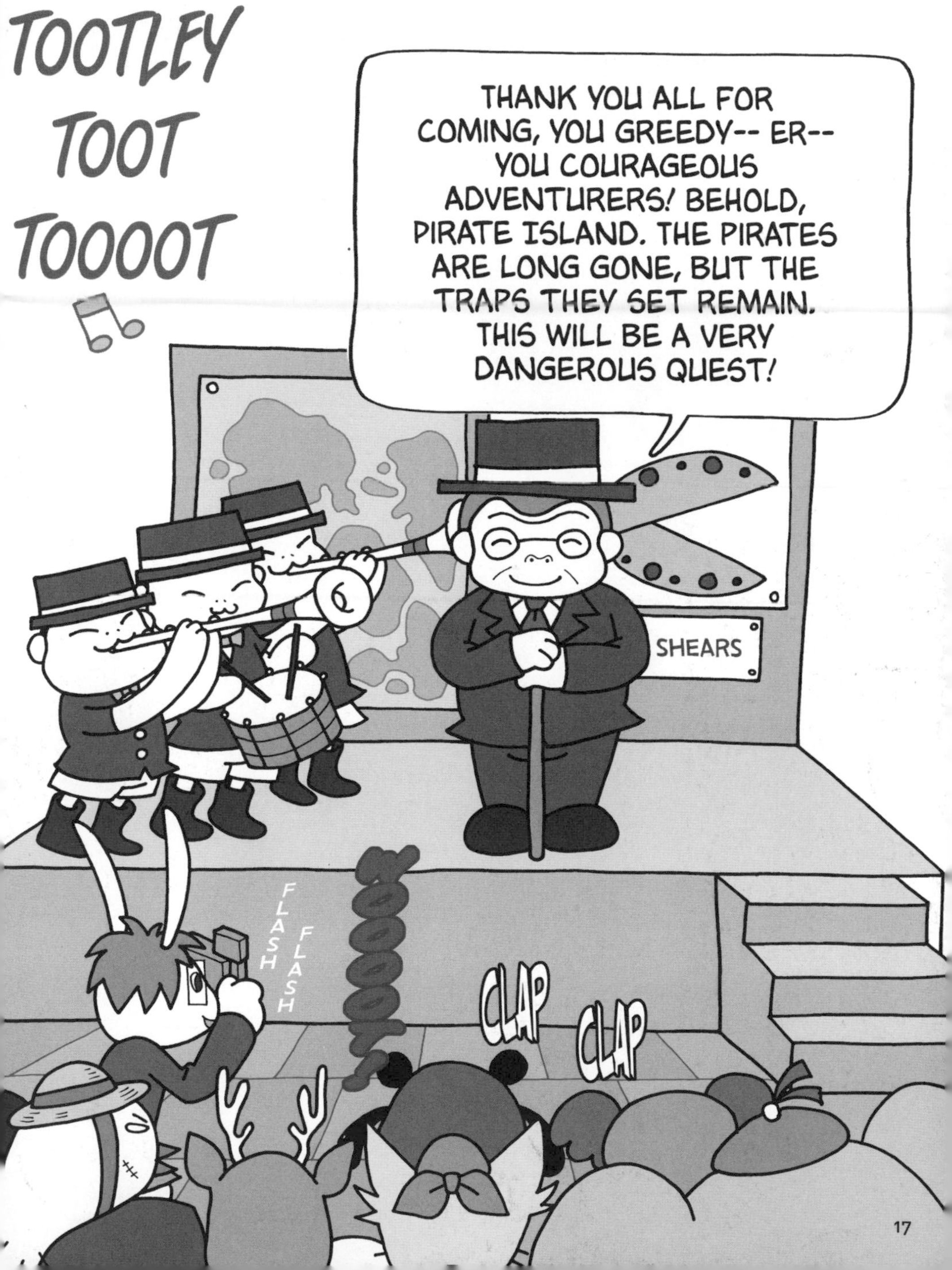
TOOTLEY TOOT TOOOOT
THANK YOU ALL FOR COMING, YOU GREEDY-- ER-- YOU COURAGEOUS ADVENTURERS! BEHOLD, PIRATE ISLAND. THE PIRATES ARE LONG GONE, BUT THE TRAPS THEY SET REMAIN. THIS WILL BE A VERY DANGEROUS QUEST!
SHEARS
FLASH FLASH
CLAP CLAP

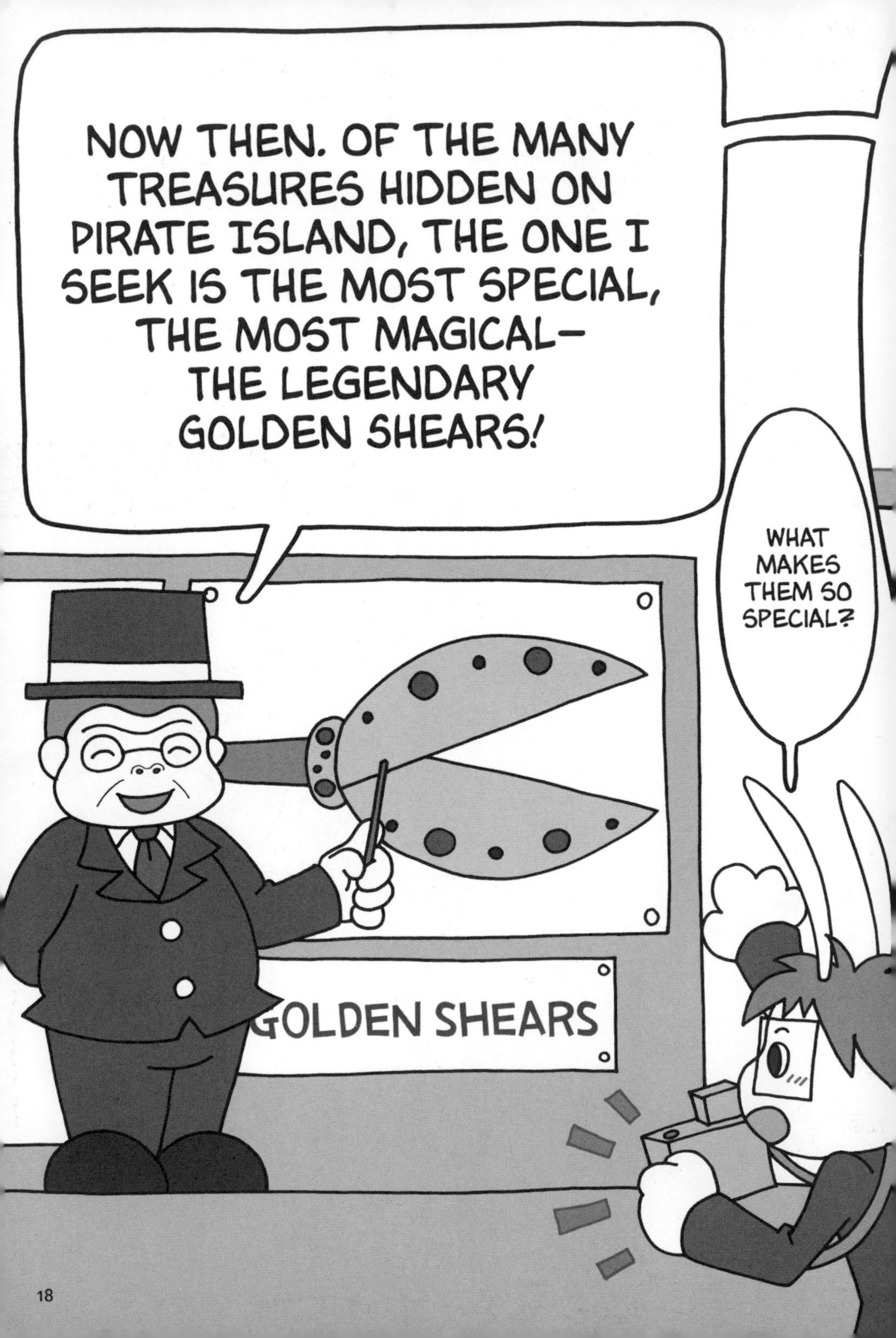
NOW THEN. OF THE MANY TREASURES HIDDEN ON PIRATE ISLAND, THE ONE I SEEK IS THE MOST SPECIAL, THE MOST MAGICAL— THE LEGENDARY GOLDEN SHEARS!
GOLDEN SHEARS
WHAT MAKES THEM SO SPECIAL?

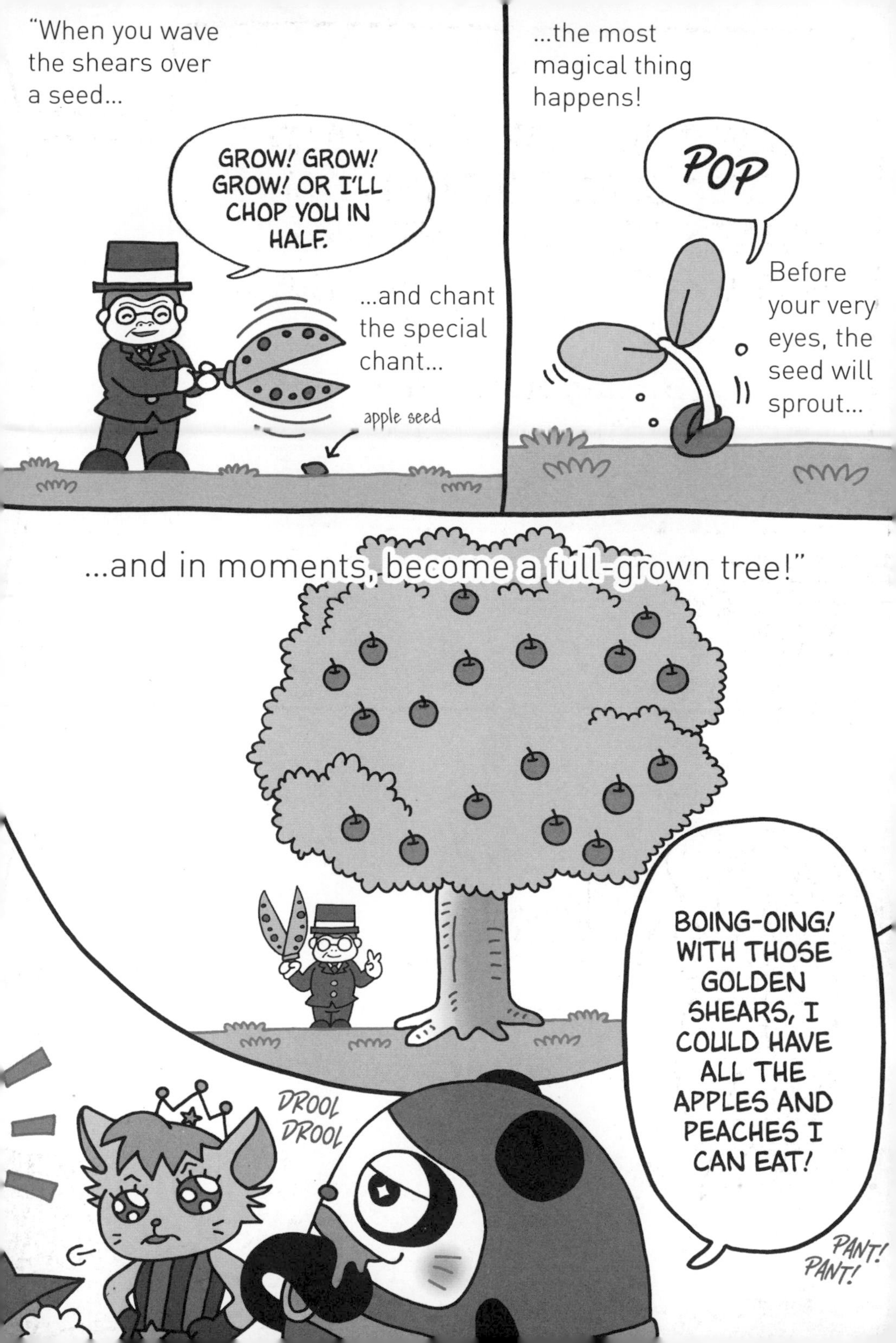
"When you wave the shears over a seed...
GROW! GROW! GROW! OR I'LL CHOP YOU IN HALF.
...and chant the special chant...
apple seed
...the most magical thing happens!
POP
Before your very eyes, the seed will sprout...
...and in moments, become a full-grown tree!"
DROOL DROOL
BOING-OING! WITH THOSE GOLDEN SHEARS, I COULD HAVE ALL THE APPLES AND PEACHES I CAN EAT!
PANT! PANT!

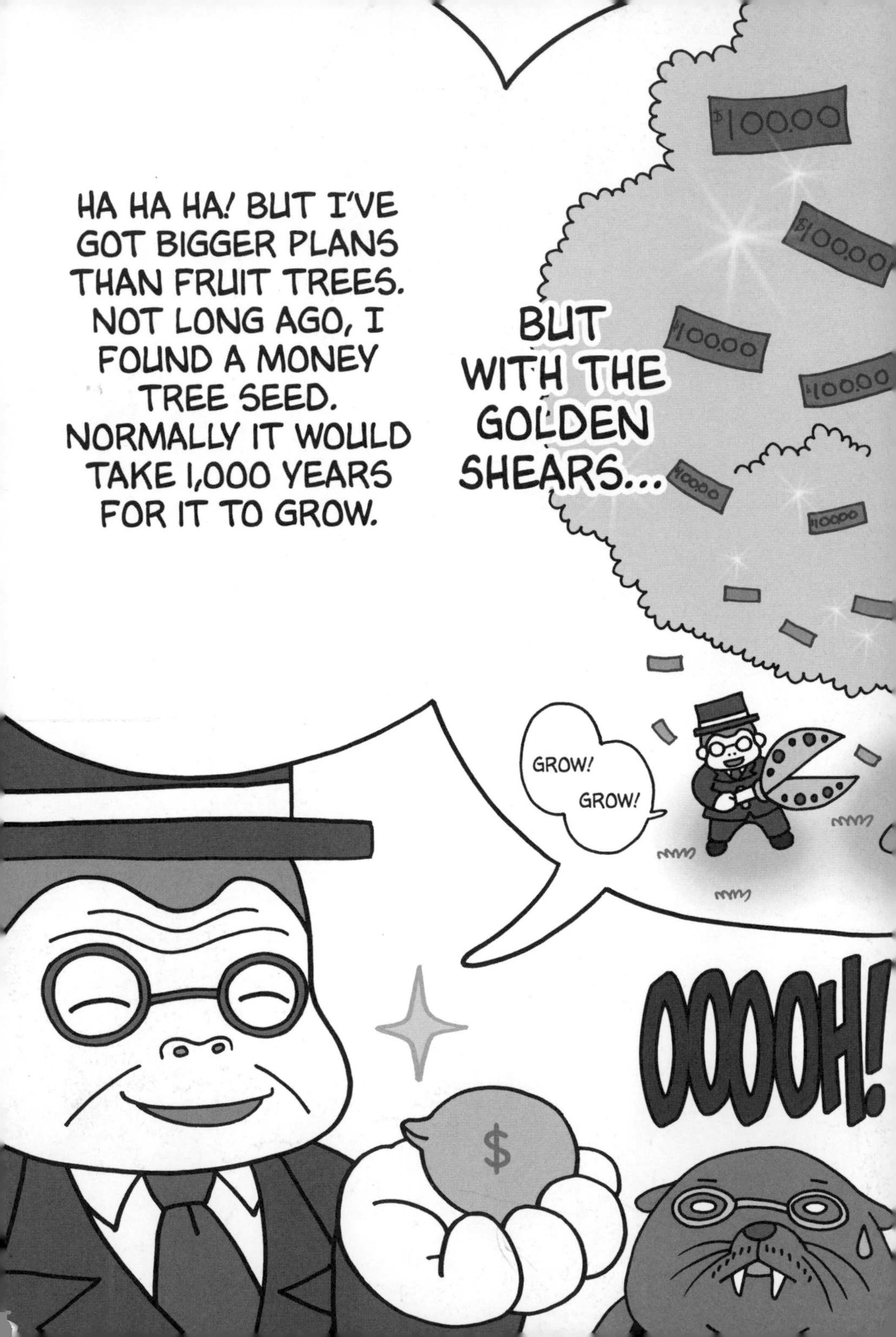
BUT WITH THE GOLDEN SHEARS...
$100.00
GROW! GROW!
HA HA HA! BUT I'VE GOT BIGGER PLANS THAN FRUIT TREES. NOT LONG AGO, I FOUND A MONEY TREE SEED. NORMALLY IT WOULD TAKE 1,000 YEARS FOR IT TO GROW.
OOOOH!

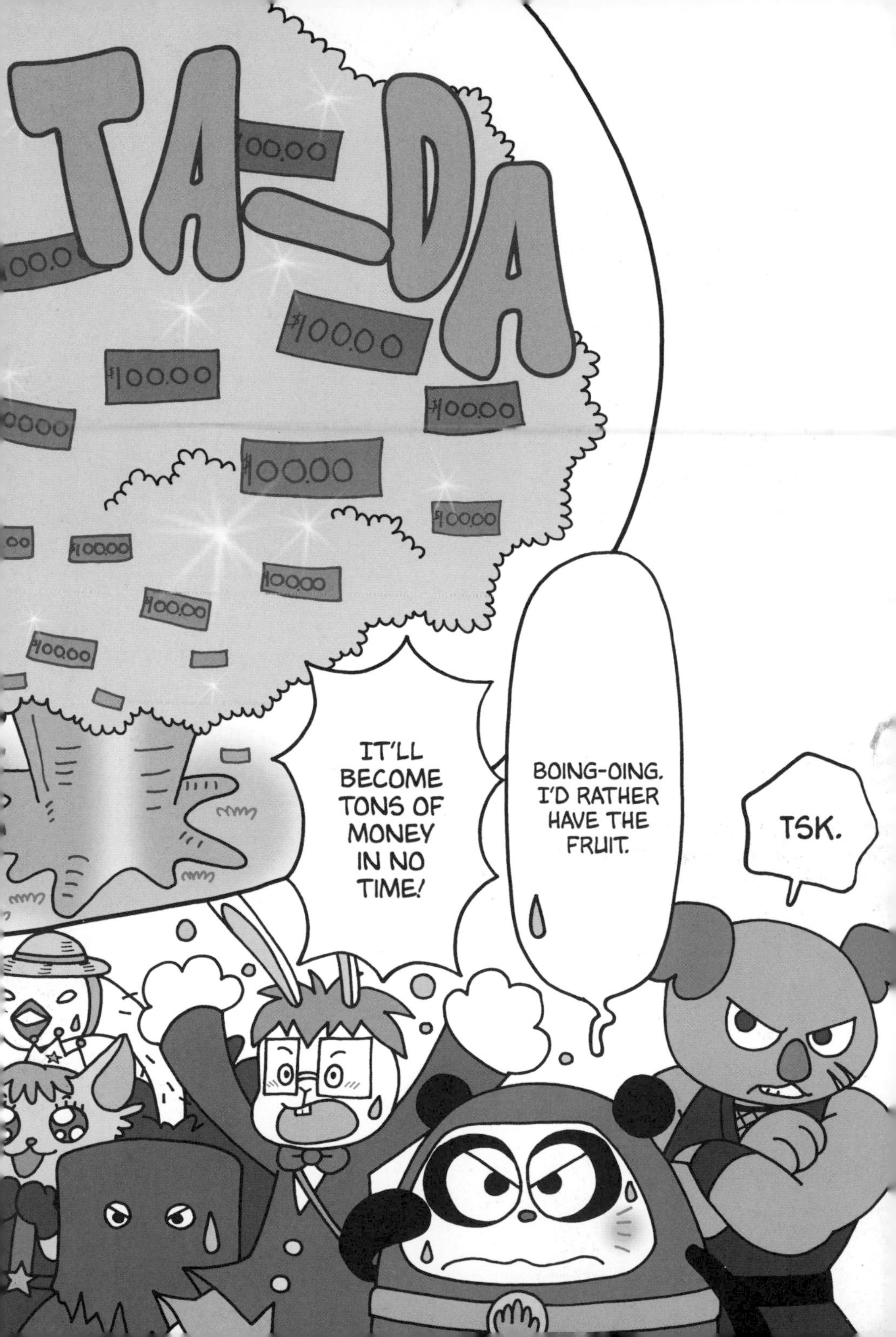
TA-DA
$100.00
TSK.
BOING-OING. I'D RATHER HAVE THE FRUIT.
IT'LL BECOME TONS OF MONEY IN NO TIME!

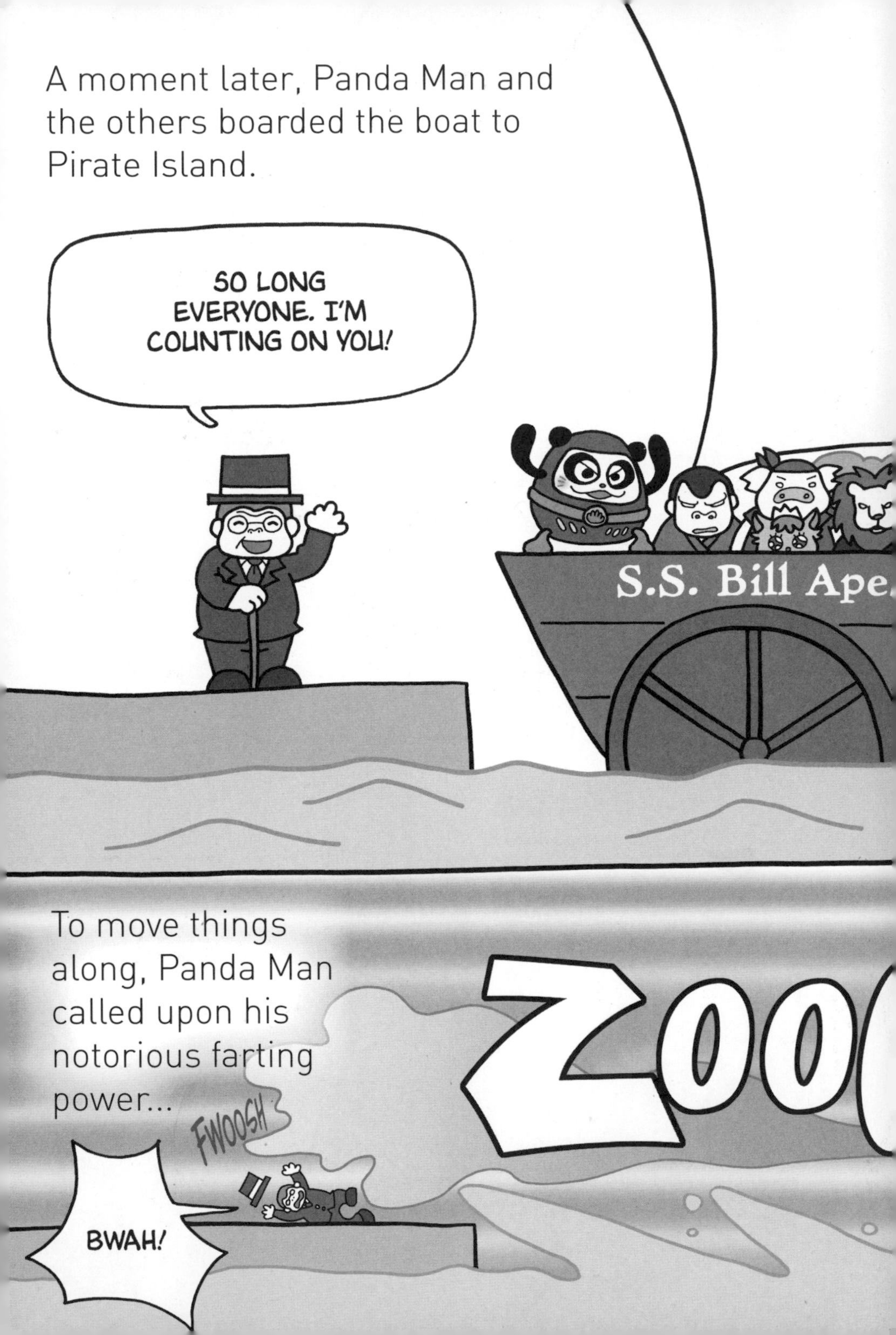
A moment later, Panda Man and the others boarded the boat to Pirate Island.
SO LONG EVERYONE. I'M COUNTING ON YOU!
S.S. Bill Ape
To move things along, Panda Man called upon his notorious farting power...
ZOO
FWOOSH
BWAH!

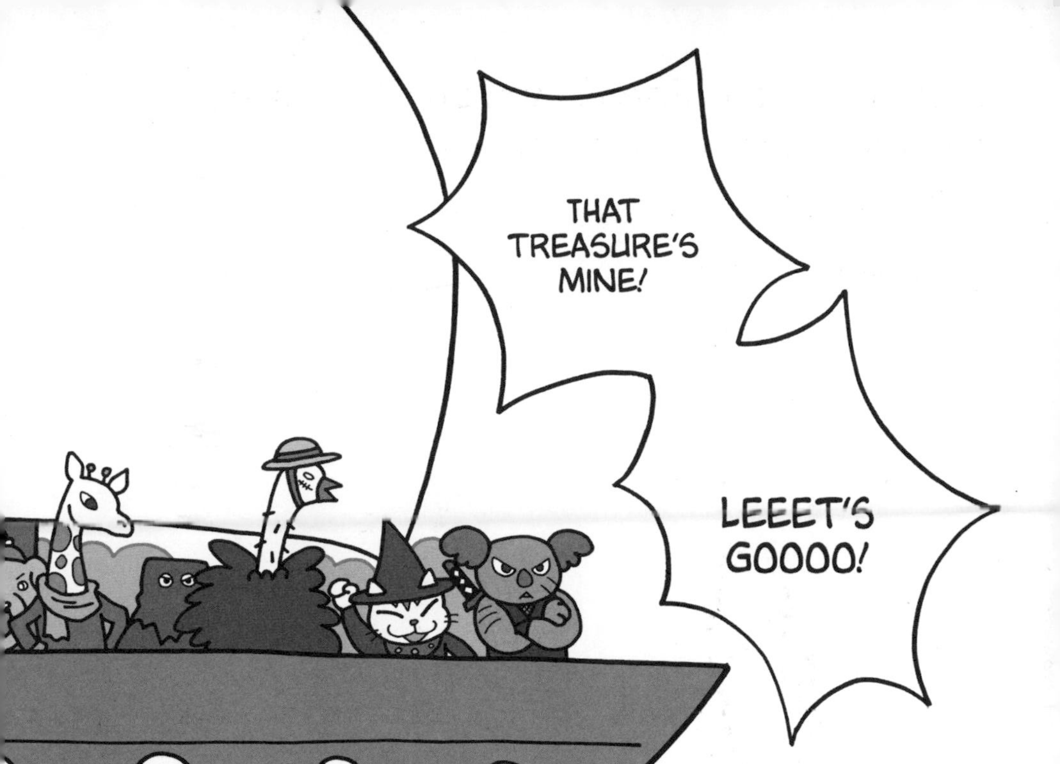
THAT TREASURE'S MINE!
LEEET'S GOOOO!
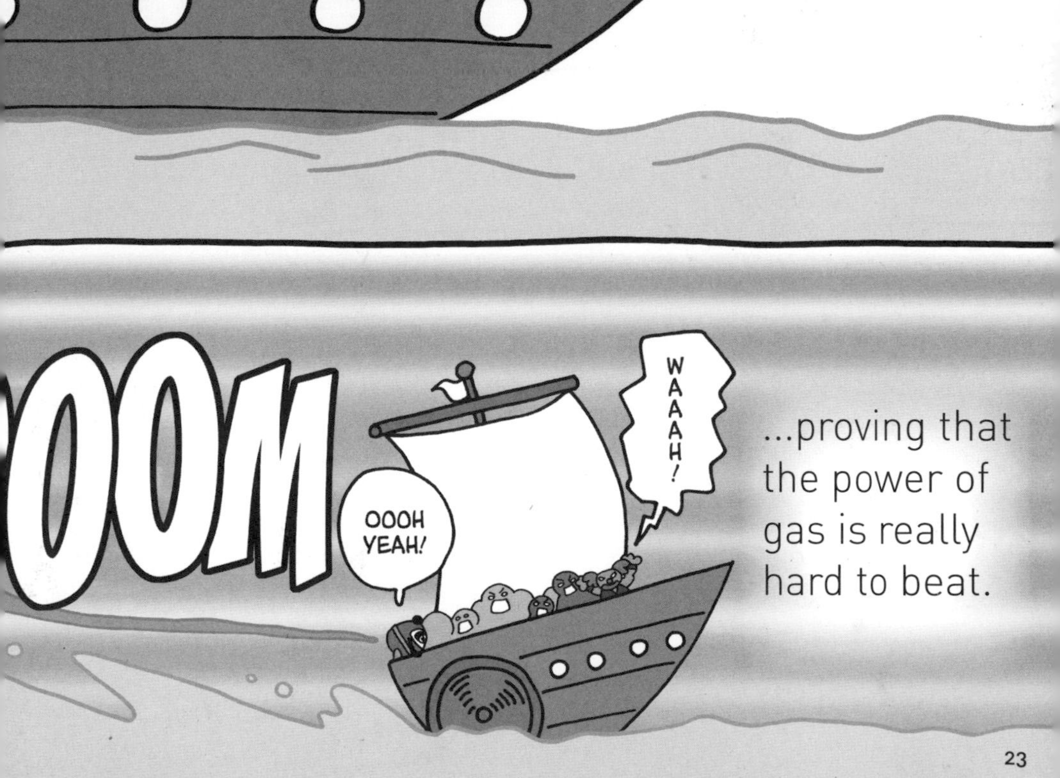
...proving that the power of gas is really hard to beat.
WAAAH!
OOOH YEAH!
OOM

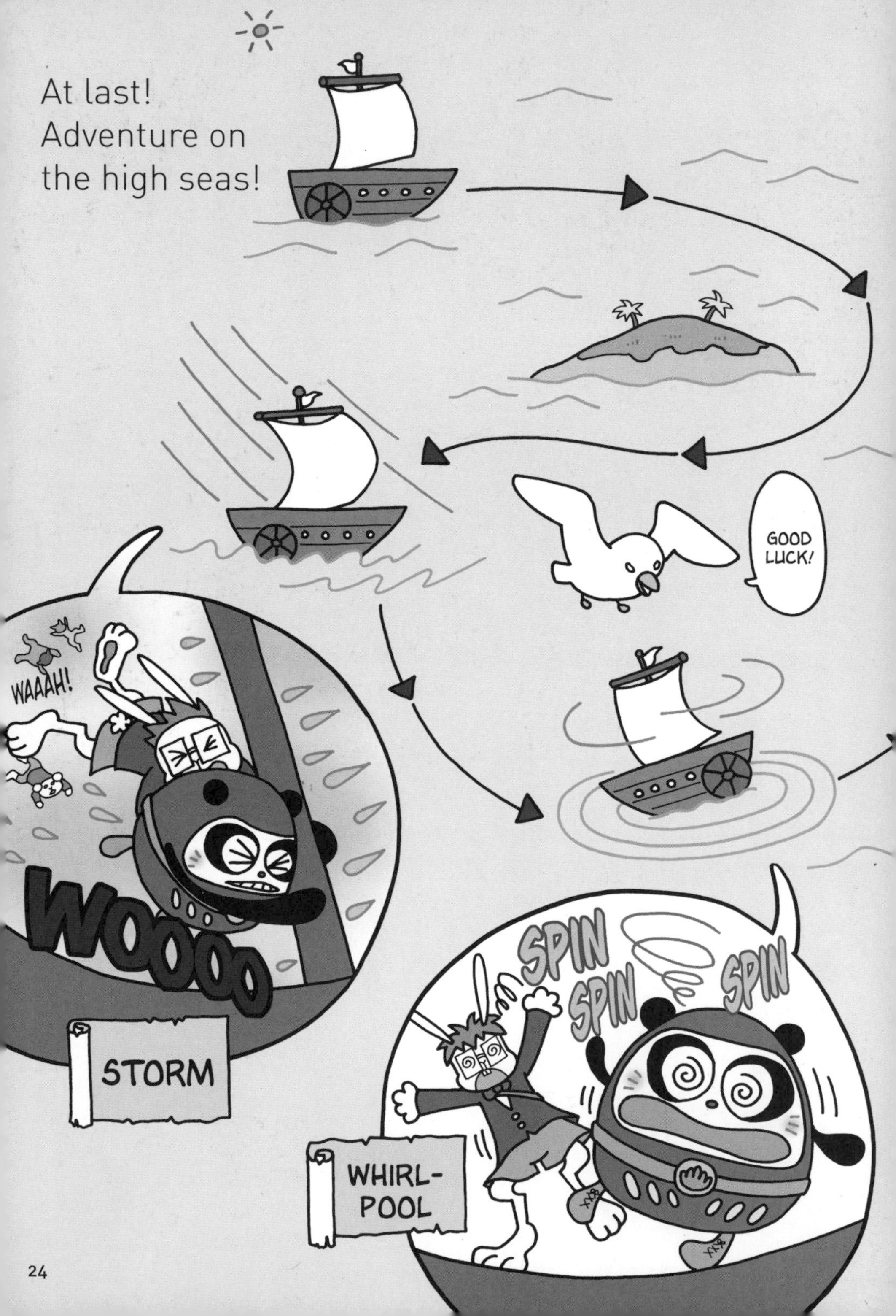
At last!
Adventure on
the high seas!
GOOD LUCK!
WAAAH!
WOOOO
STORM
SPIN
SPIN
SPIN
WHIRL-
POOL

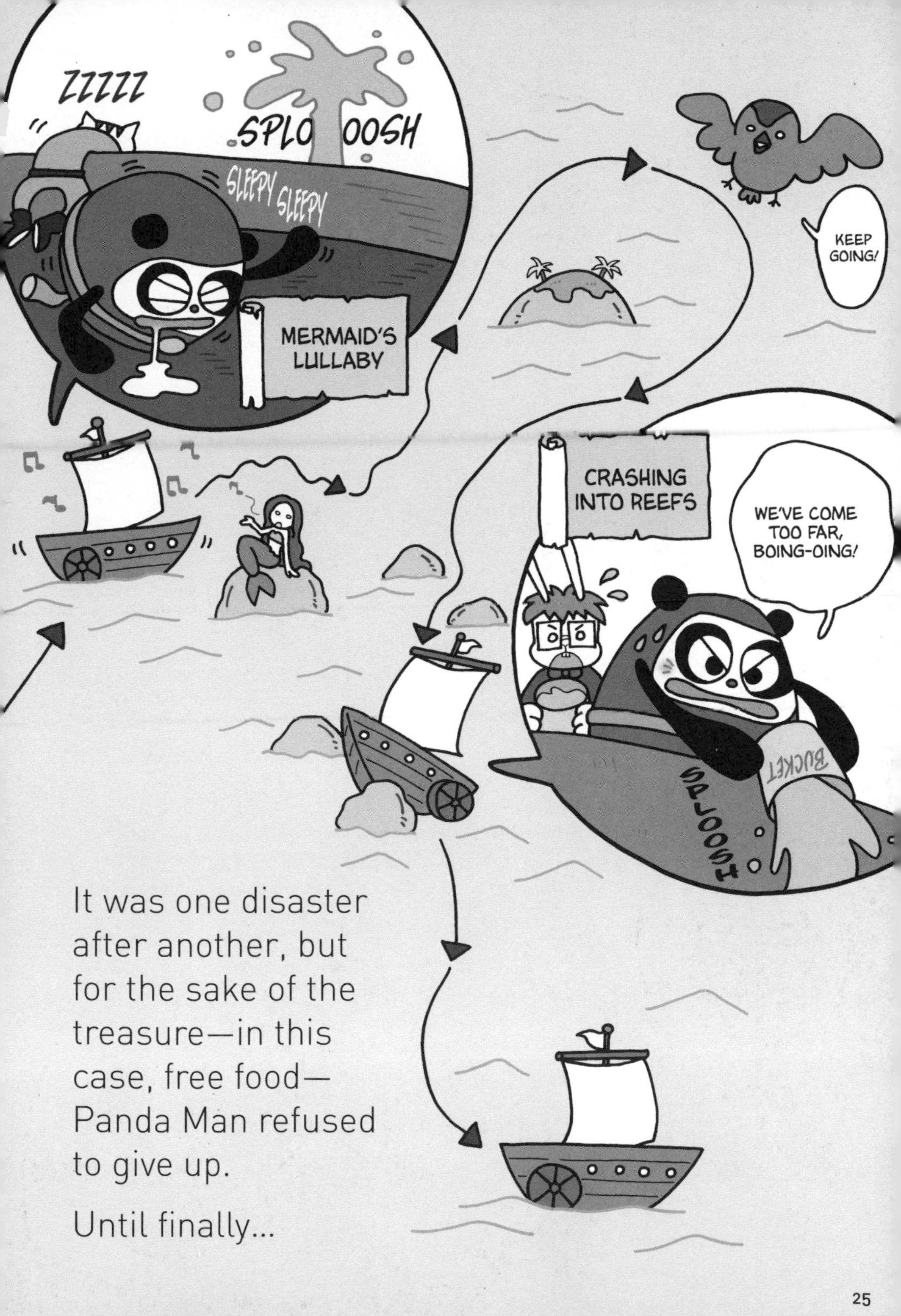
ZZZZZ
SPLOOSH
SLEEPY SLEEPY
MERMAID'S LULLABY
KEEP GOING!
CRASHING INTO REEFS
WE'VE COME TOO FAR, BOING-OING!
SPLOOSH
BUCKET

It was one disaster after another, but for the sake of the treasure—in this case, free food—Panda Man refused to give up.

Until finally...

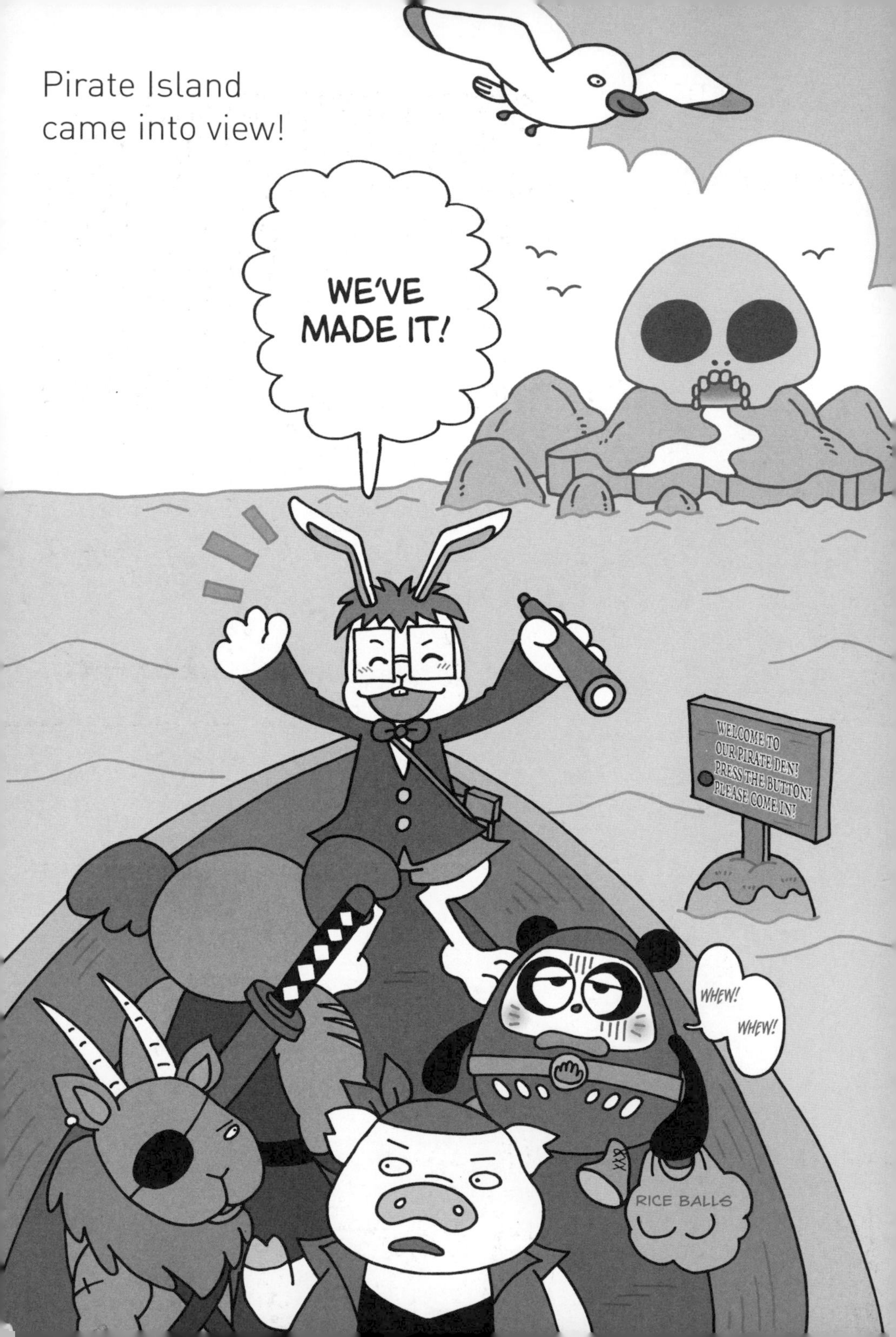
Pirate Island came into view!
WE'VE MADE IT!
WELCOME TO OUR PIRATE DEN! PRESS THE BUTTON! PLEASE COME IN!
WHEW! WHEW!
RICE BALLS

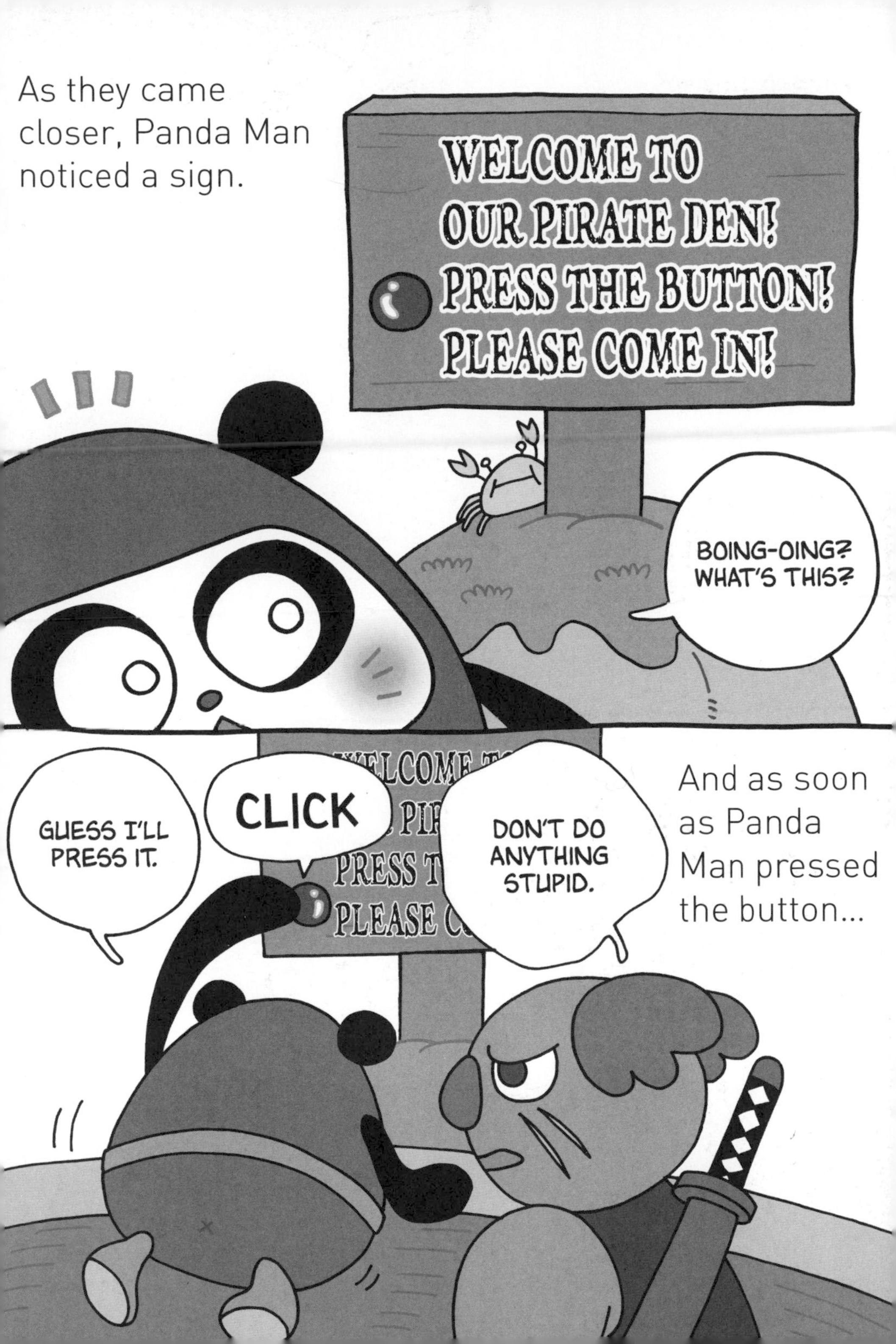
As they came closer, Panda Man noticed a sign.
WELCOME TO OUR PIRATE DEN! PRESS THE BUTTON! PLEASE COME IN!
BOING-OING? WHAT'S THIS?
GUESS I'LL PRESS IT.
CLICK
DON'T DO ANYTHING STUPID.
And as soon as Panda Man pressed the button...

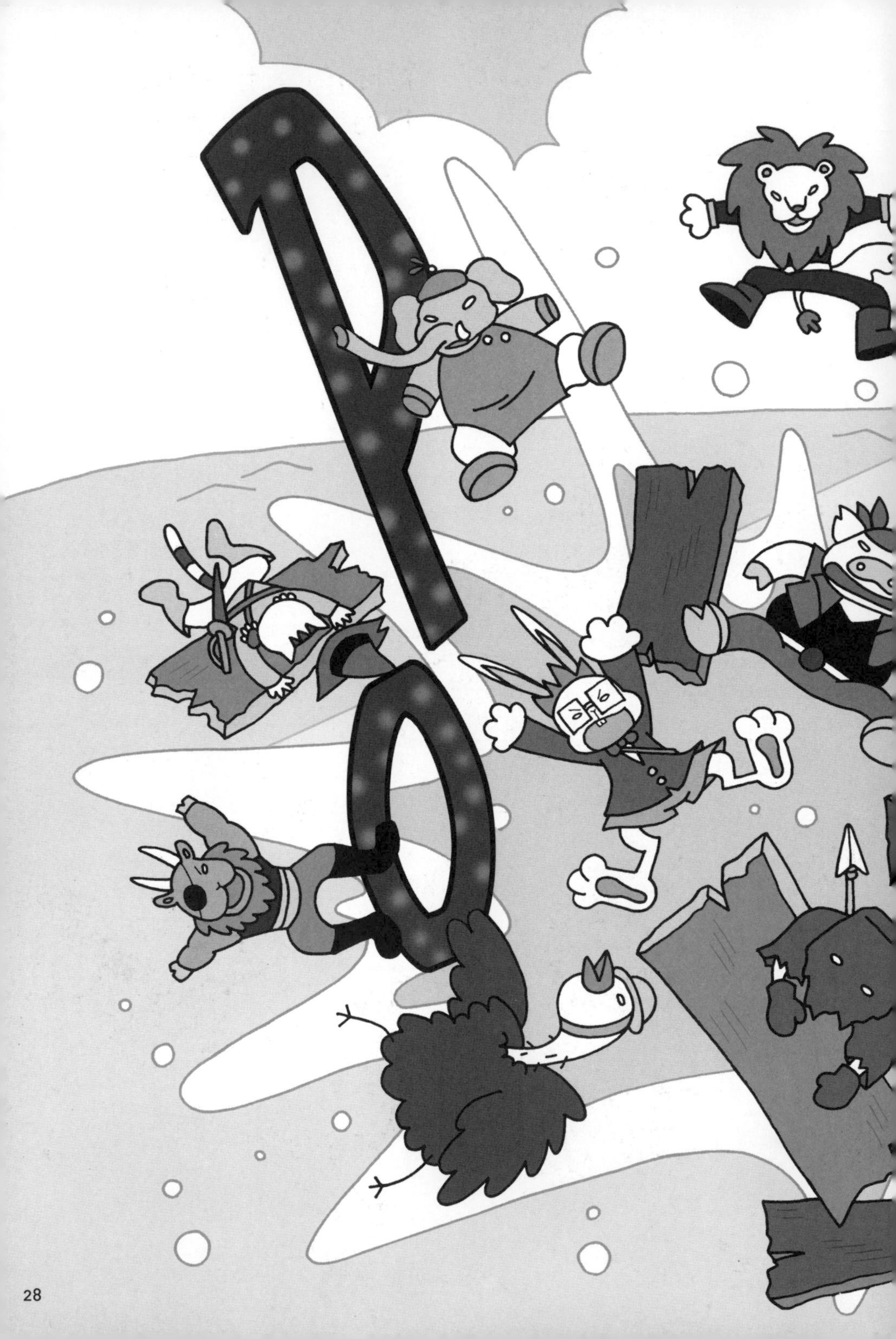

A cannon fired from Pirate Island and blew the boat to smithereens!

It was the first pirate trap!

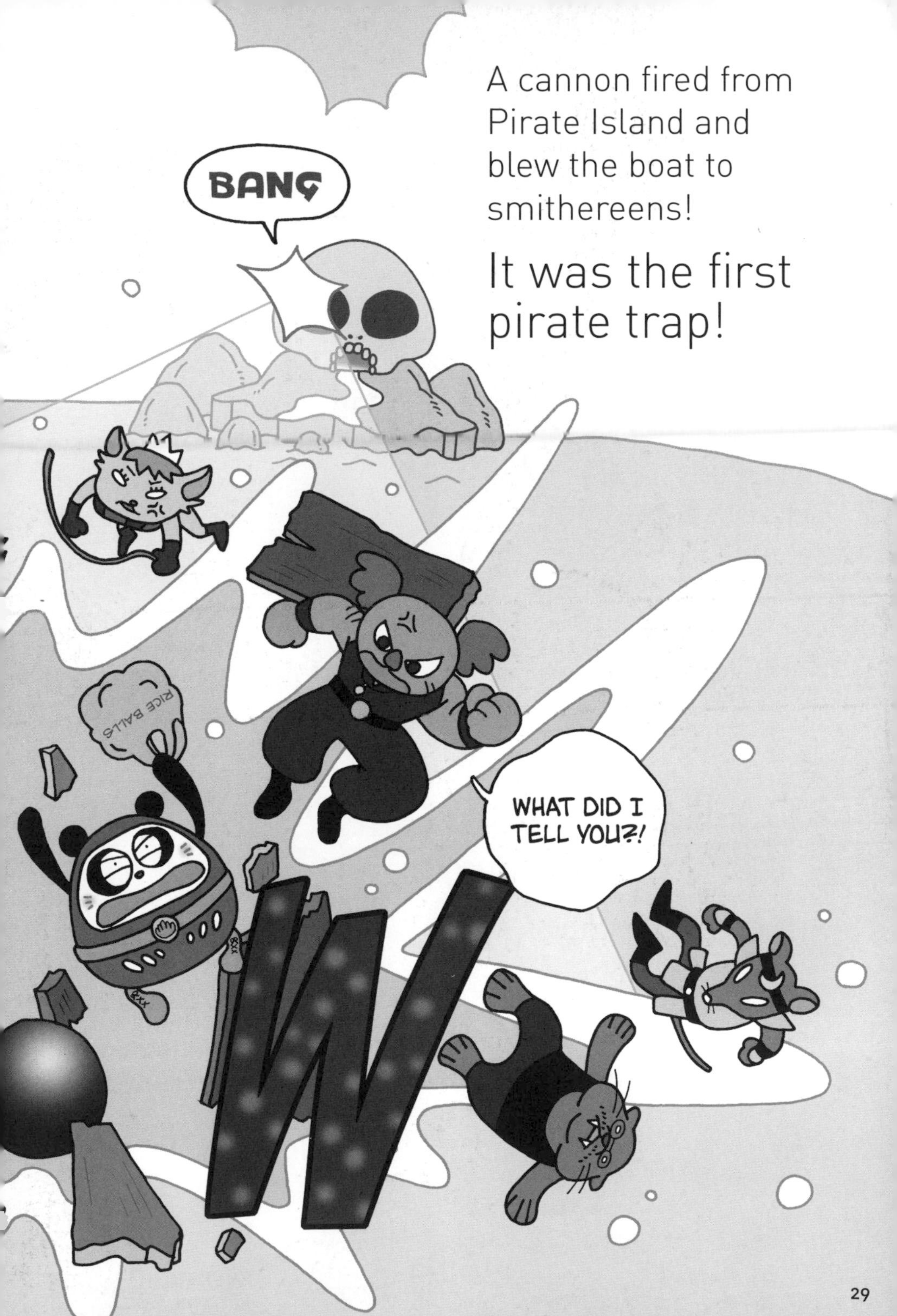
BANG
RICE BALLS
WHAT DID I TELL YOU?!

While the adventurers flailed about in the sea, a school of sharks closed in.

Everyone flew into a panic—except Ko Mando. Thinking quickly, he nibbled on a eucalyptus leaf and...

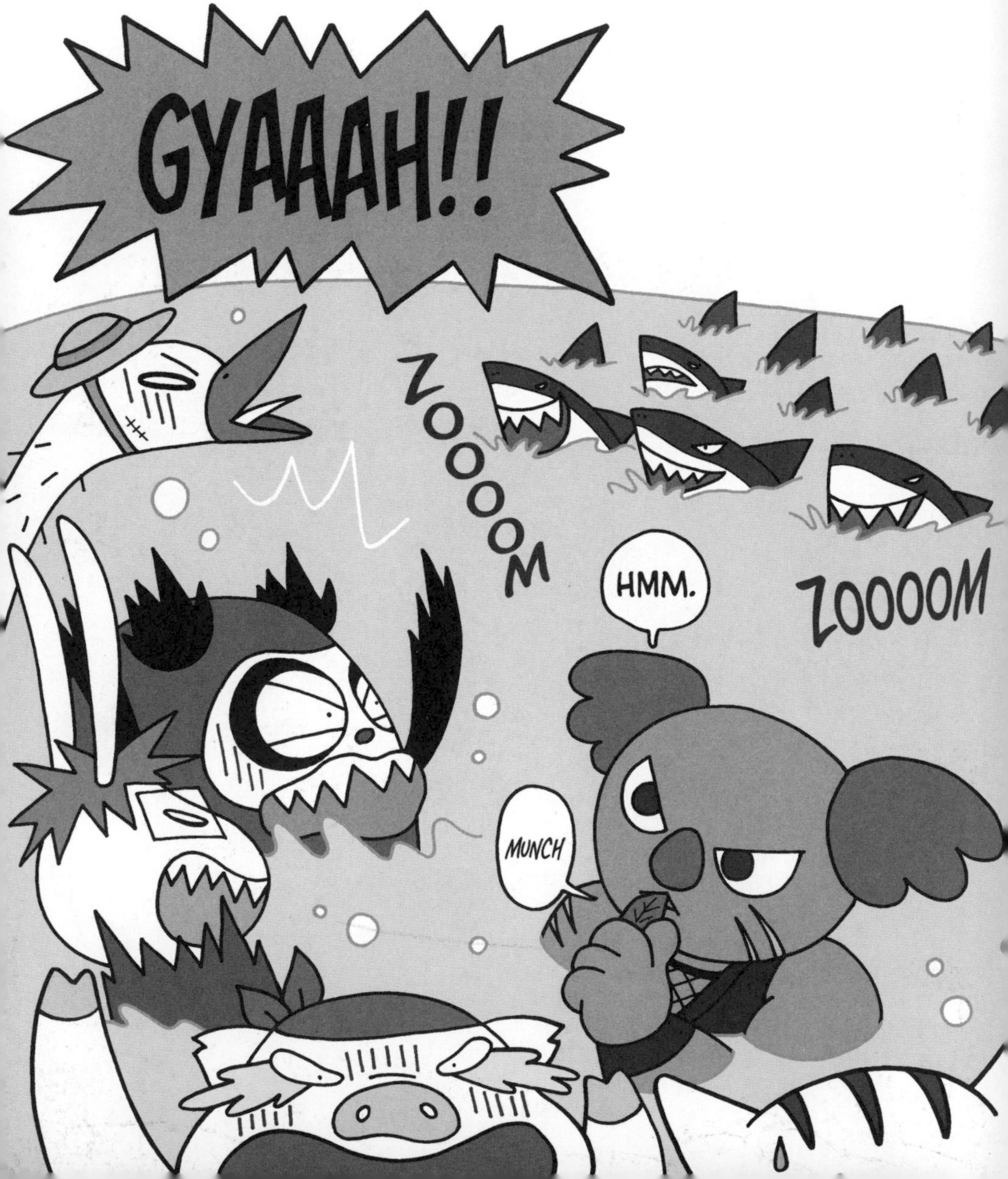
GYAAAH!!
ZOOOOOM
HMM.
ZOOOOM
MUNCH

...hopped from one shark's head to the next, making his escape. Panda Man, on the other hand, could only throw rice balls.

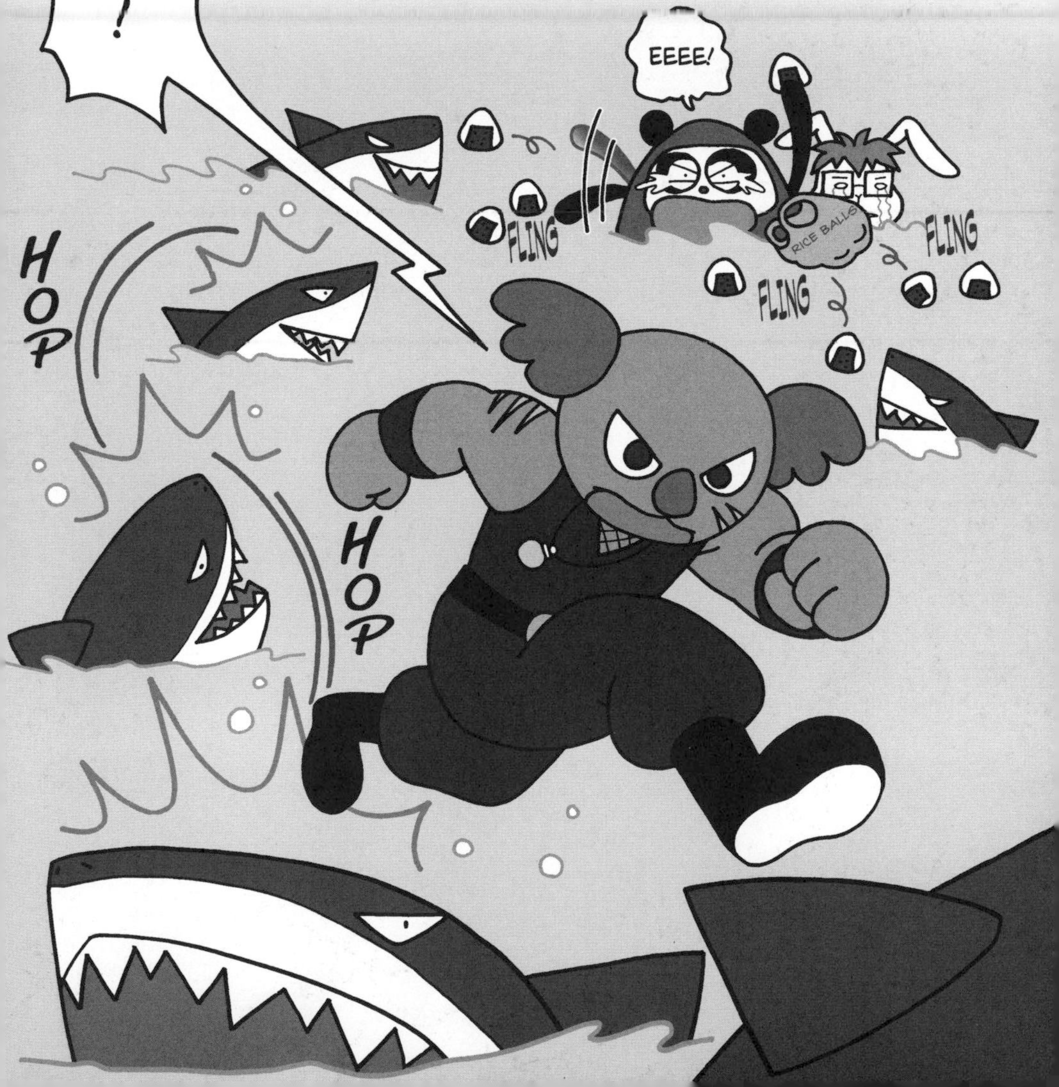

Smelling the rice balls, other creatures swam up from the depths of the sea.

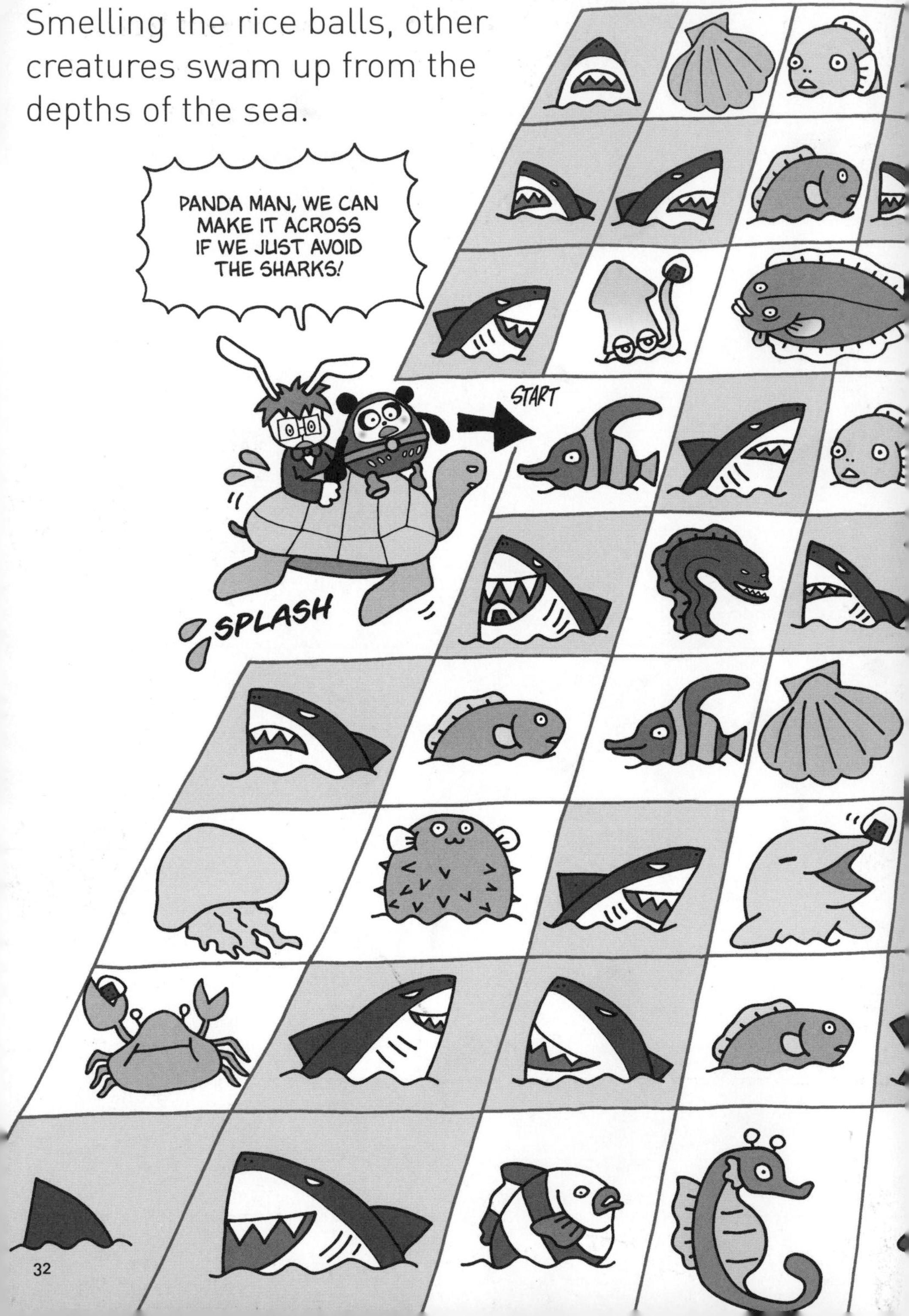
PANDA MAN, WE CAN MAKE IT ACROSS IF WE JUST AVOID THE SHARKS!
START
SPLASH

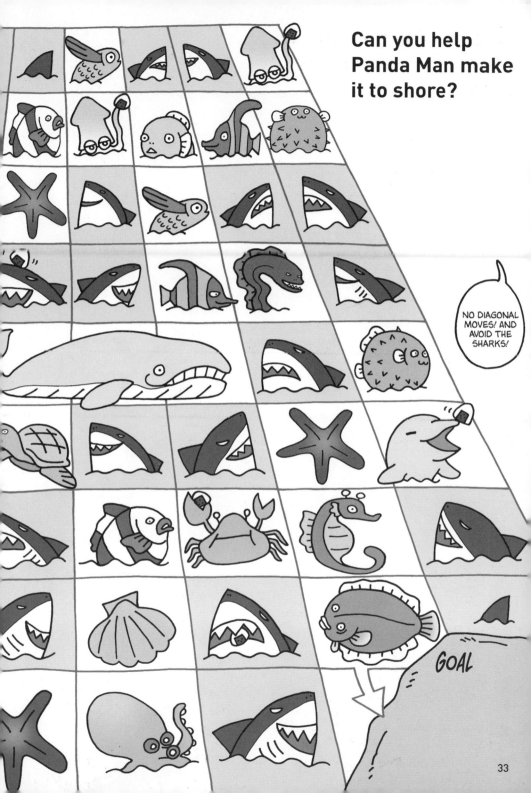

Can you help Panda Man make it to shore?

NO DIAGONAL MOVES! AND AVOID THE SHARKS!

GOAL

33

Thanks to you, Panda Man made it safely to Pirate Island! Unfortunately, the sharks chased the rest of the adventurers away.
WAAAH! RUN AWAAAY!
SPLASH
SPLASH
NOM NOM
HUFF! HUFF!
BOING-OING... THAT WAS CLOSE...
PHEW!
DRIP DRIP
ANSWER TO PGS. 32–33
PHEW, THANKS FOR HELPING.

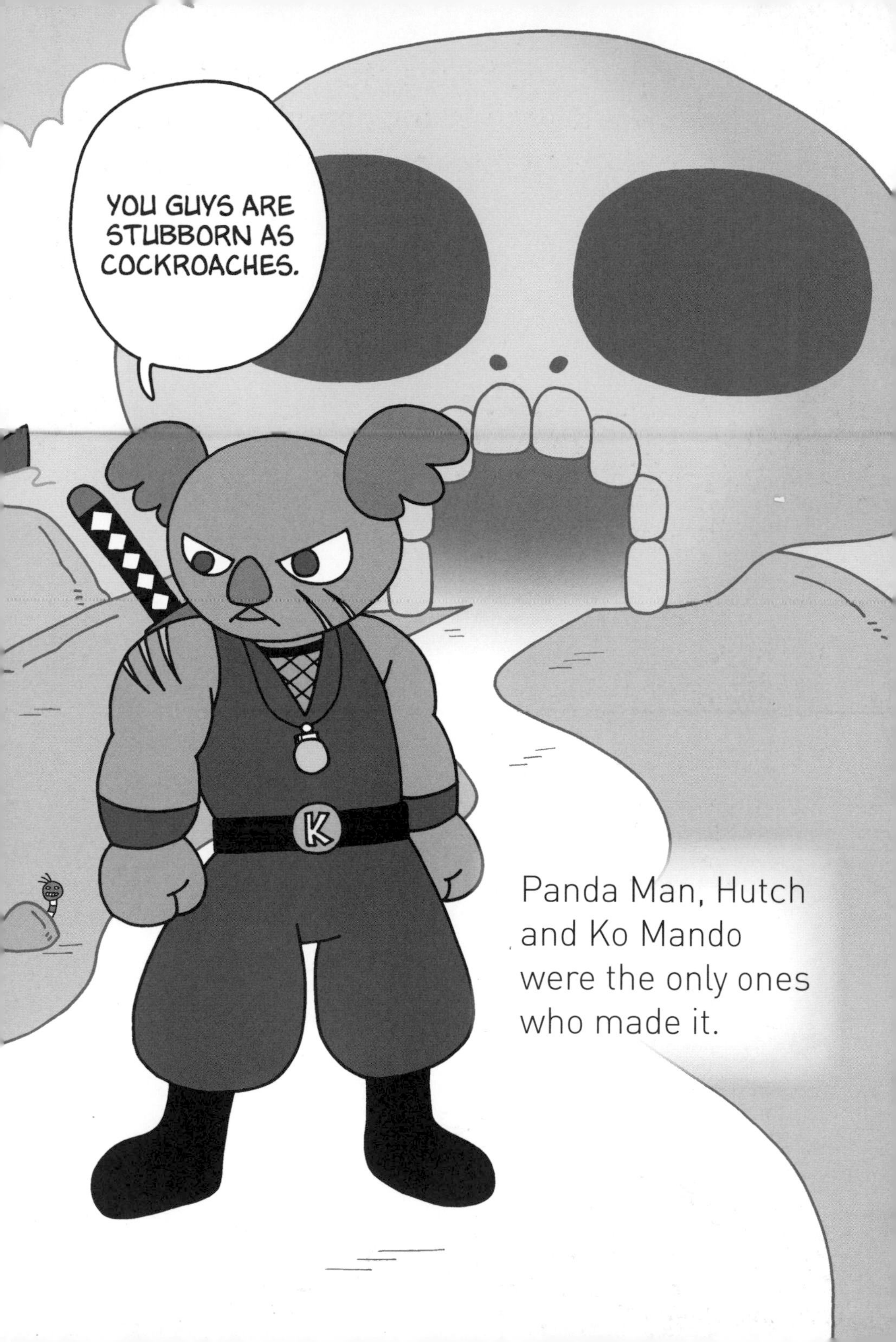
YOU GUYS ARE STUBBORN AS COCKROACHES.
Panda Man, Hutch and Ko Mando were the only ones who made it.

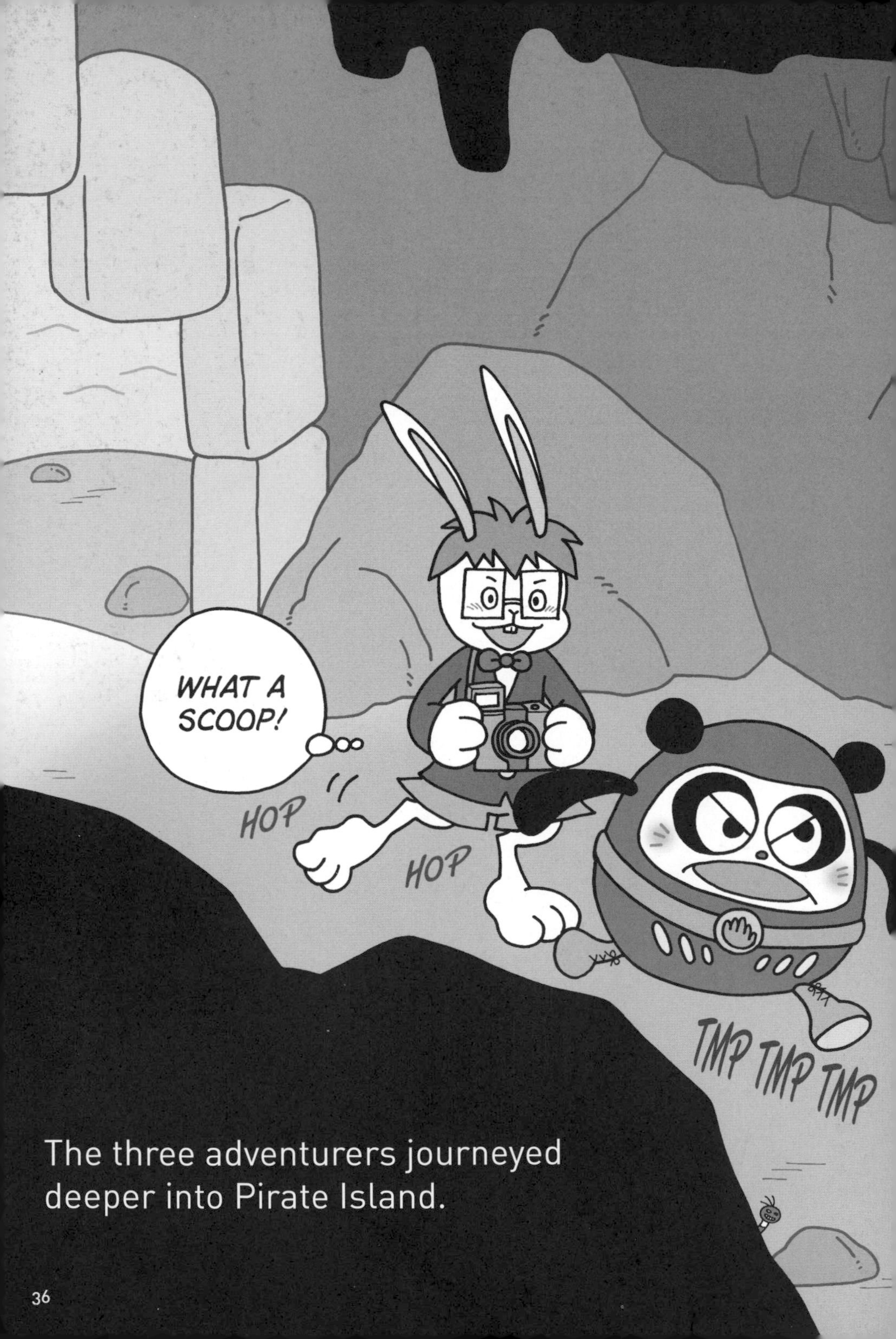
WHAT A SCOOP!
HOP
HOP
TMP TMP TMP

The three adventurers journeyed deeper into Pirate Island.

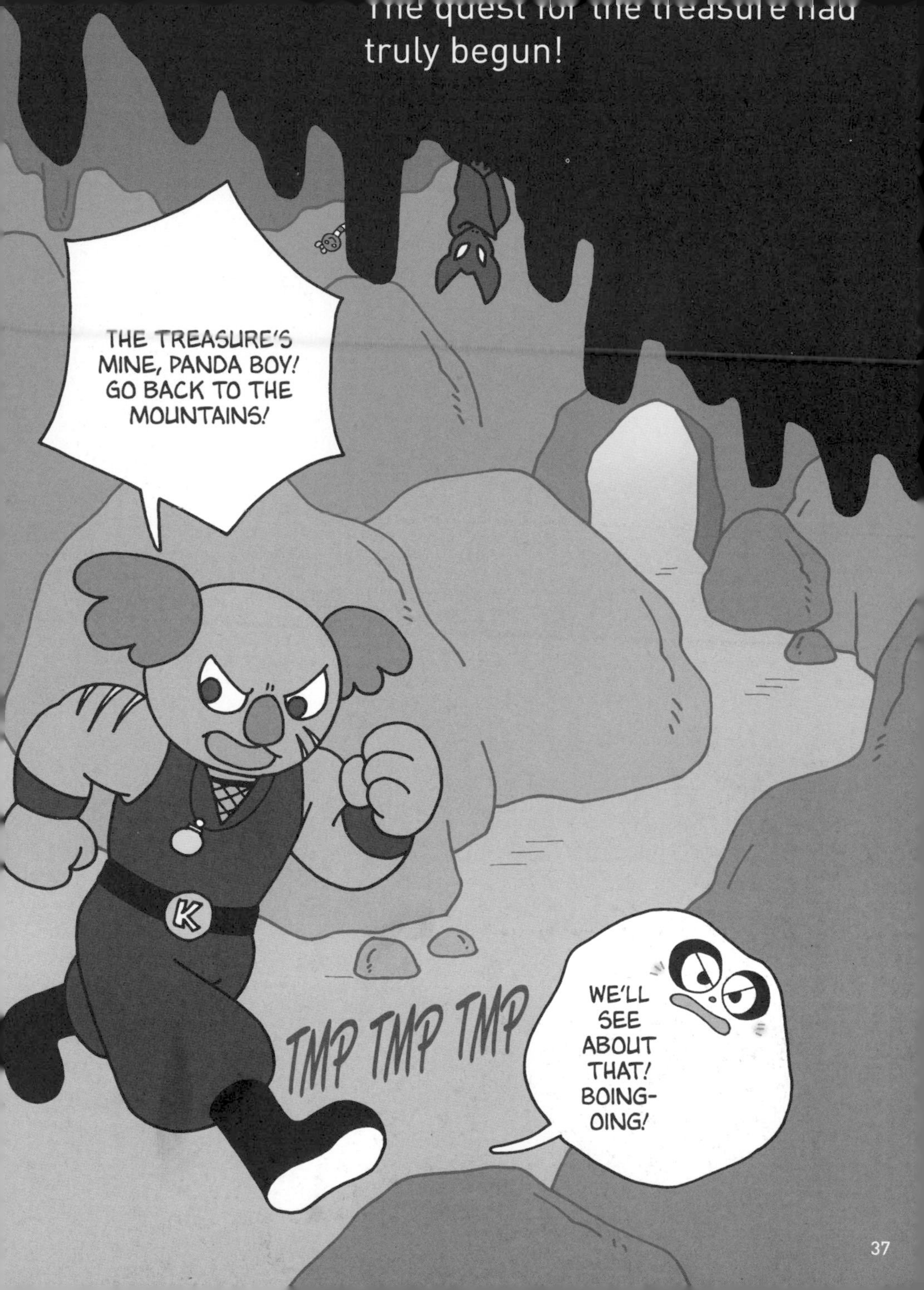
The quest for the treasure had truly begun!
THE TREASURE'S MINE, PANDA BOY! GO BACK TO THE MOUNTAINS!
WE'LL SEE ABOUT THAT! BOING-OING!
TMP TMP TMP

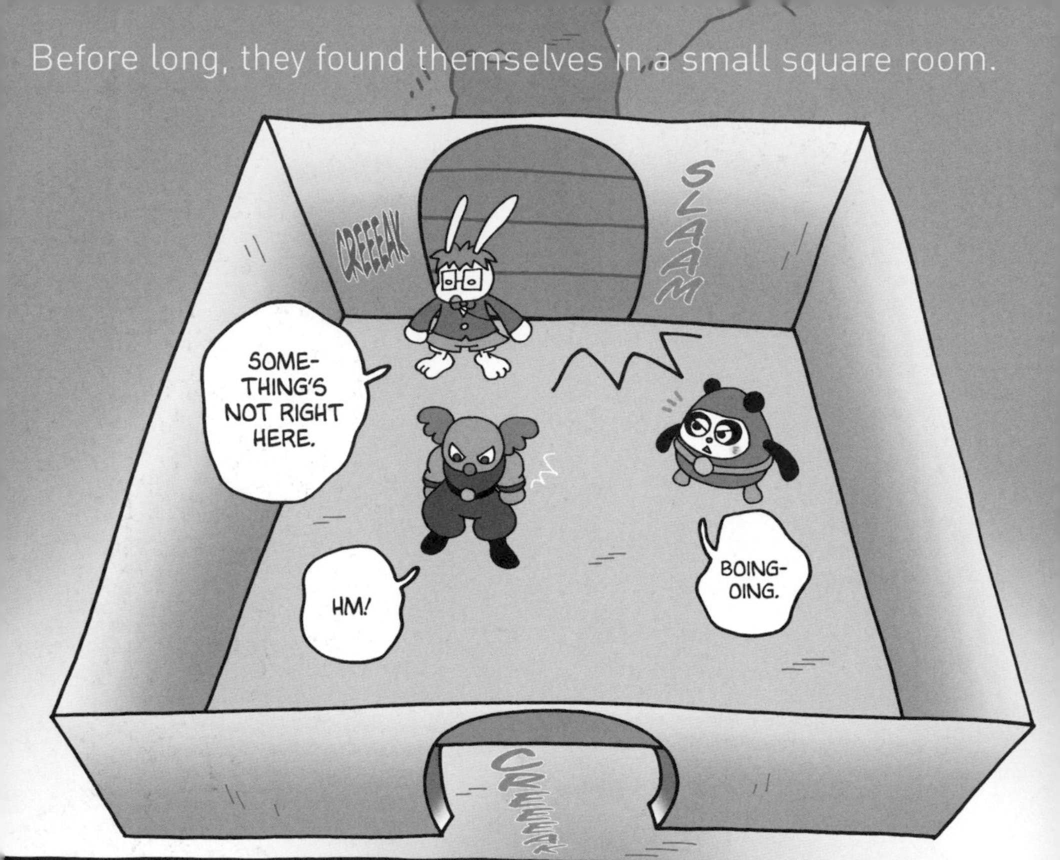
Before long, they found themselves in a small square room.
CREEEAK
SLAAM
SOME-THING'S NOT RIGHT HERE.
HM!
BOING-OING.
CREEEEAK

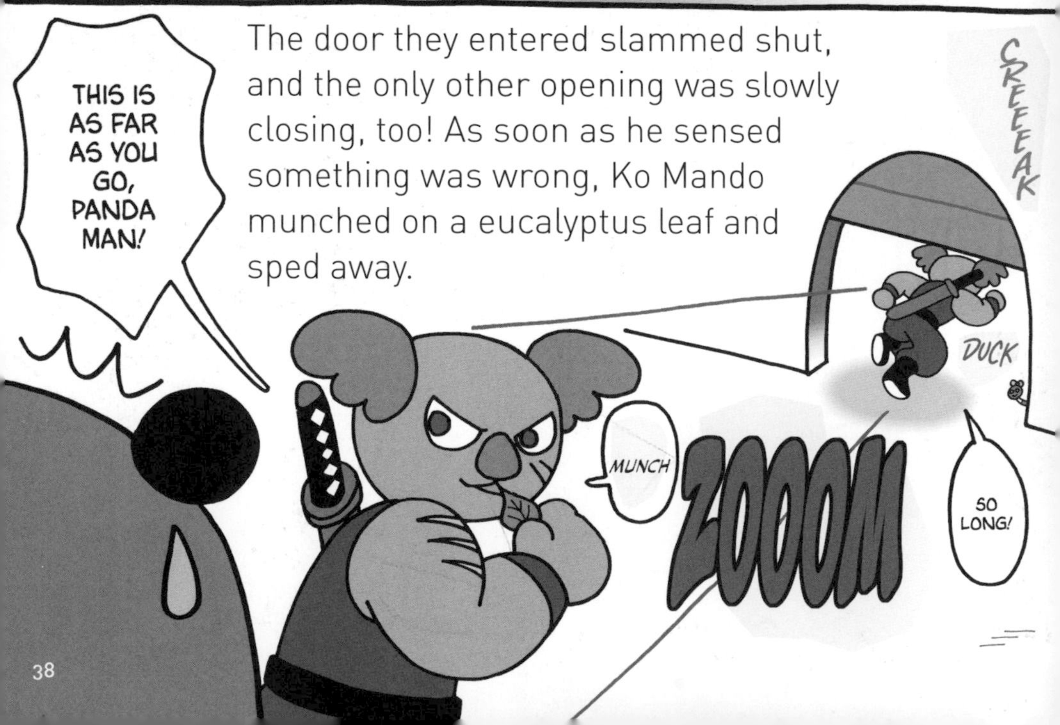
THIS IS AS FAR AS YOU GO, PANDA MAN!
The door they entered slammed shut, and the only other opening was slowly closing, too! As soon as he sensed something was wrong, Ko Mando munched on a eucalyptus leaf and sped away.
CREEEAK
DUCK
MUNCH
ZOOOM
SO LONG!

RRRR
AAAOOOOGGAAAAH!!
When the door closed completely, the ceiling began to lower!
UMBLE

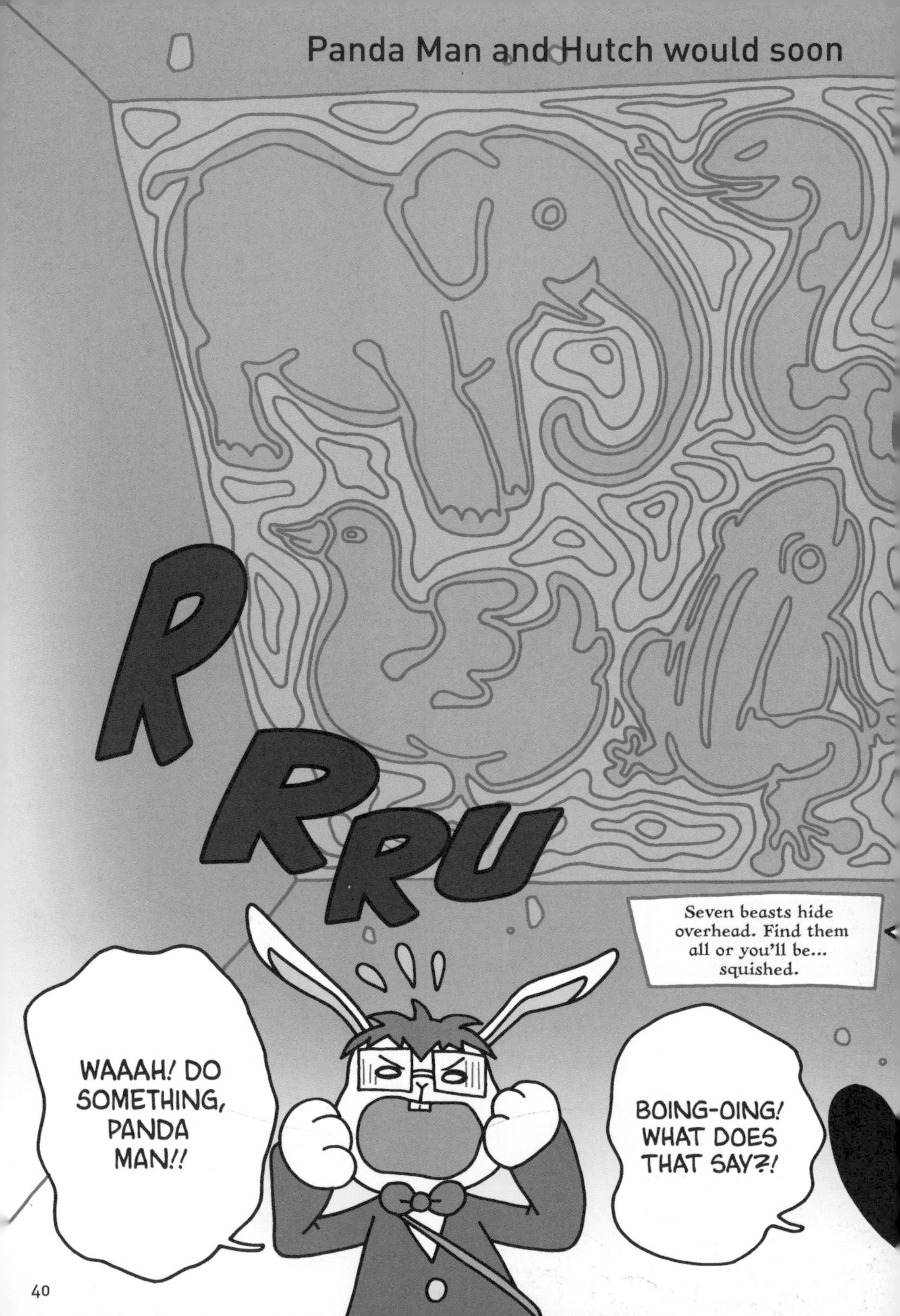

Panda Man and Hutch would soon
RRRRU
Seven beasts hide overhead. Find them all or you'll be... squished.
BOING-OING! WHAT DOES THAT SAY?!
WAAAH! DO SOMETHING, PANDA MAN!!

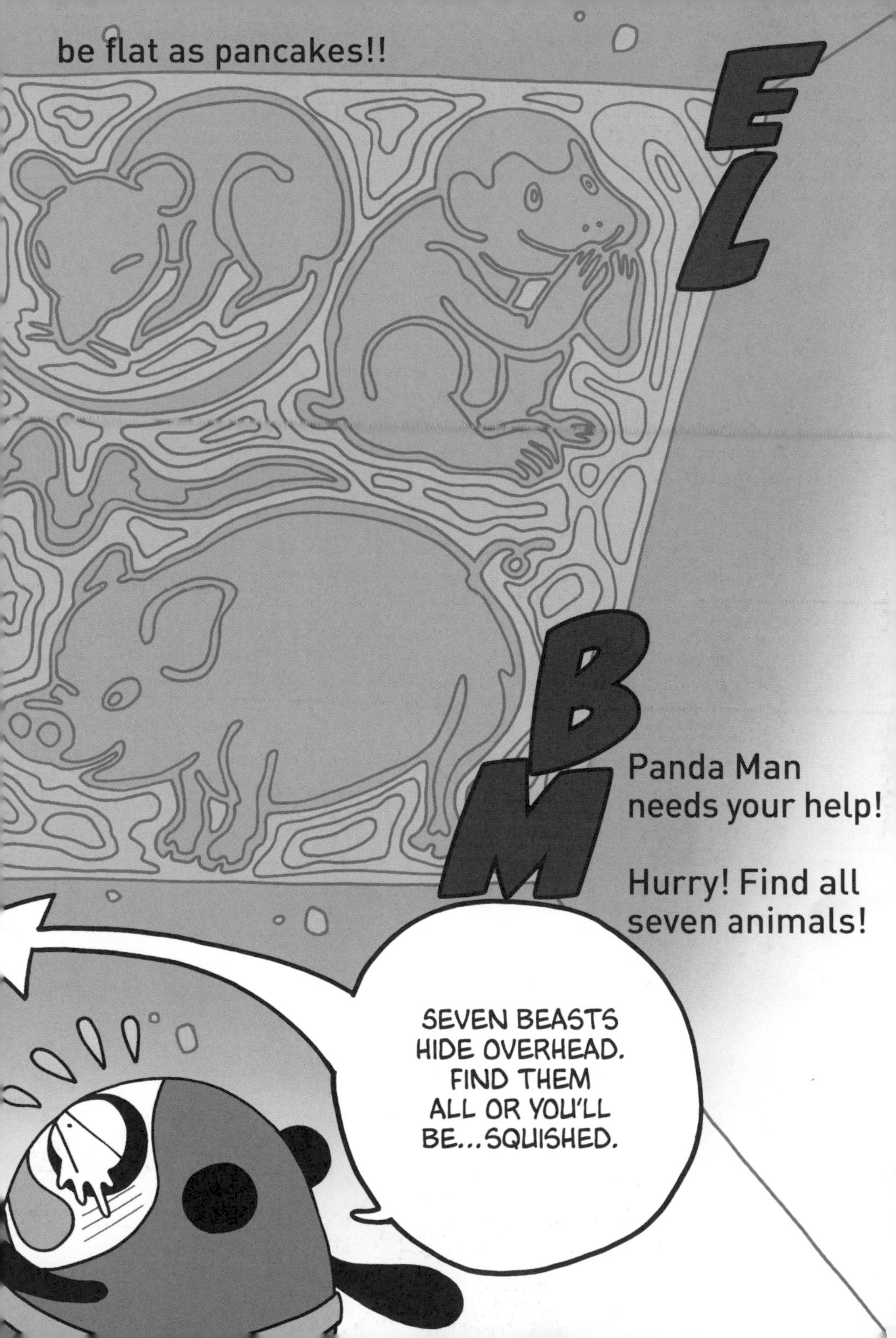
be flat as pancakes!!
EL
BM
Panda Man needs your help!
Hurry! Find all seven animals!
SEVEN BEASTS HIDE OVERHEAD. FIND THEM ALL OR YOU'LL BE...SQUISHED.

"Boing-oing! I found them all!" Panda Man cried.

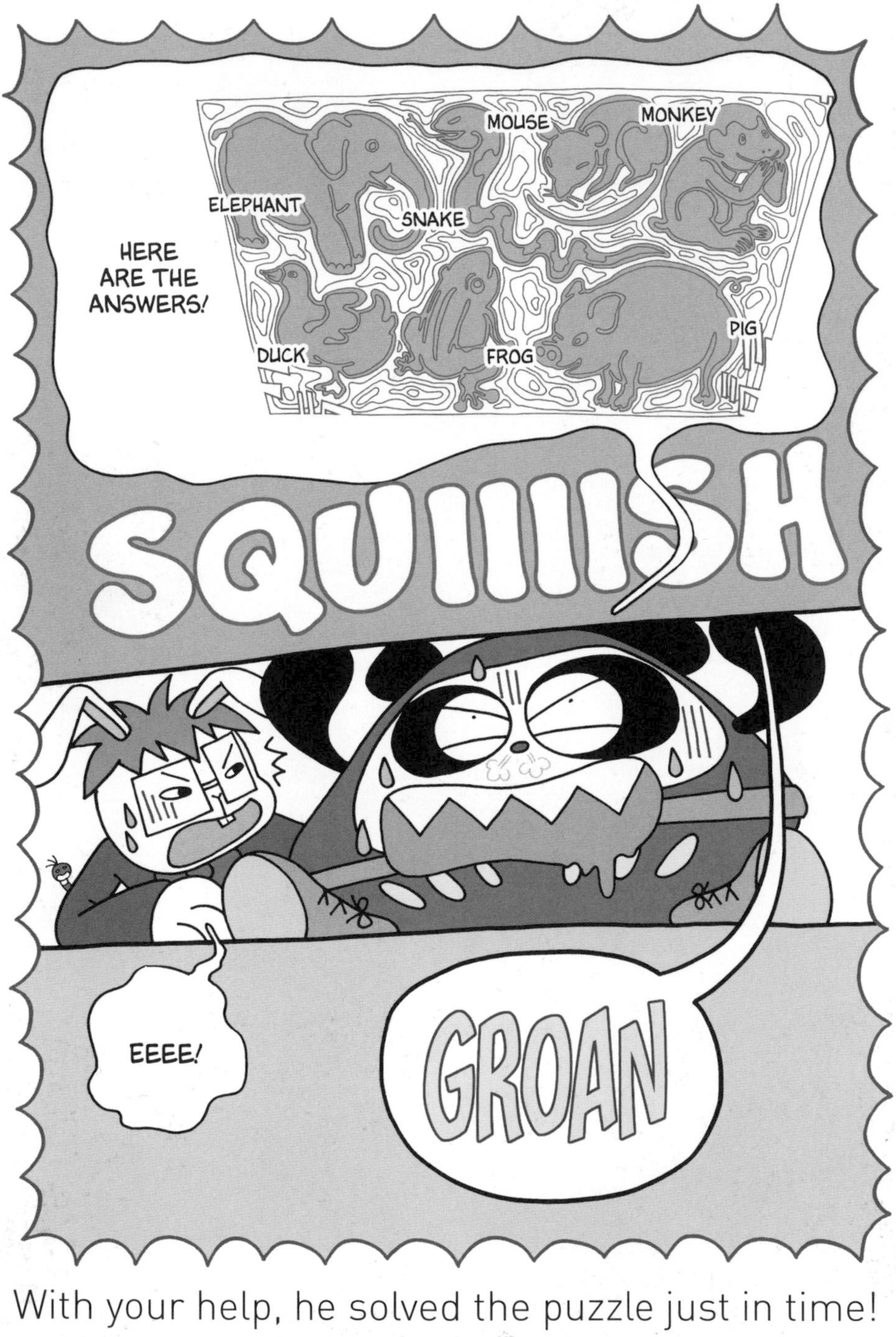
HERE ARE THE ANSWERS!
MOUSE
MONKEY
ELEPHANT
SNAKE
DUCK
FROG
PIG
SQUIIIISH
GROAN
EEEE!

With your help, he solved the puzzle just in time!

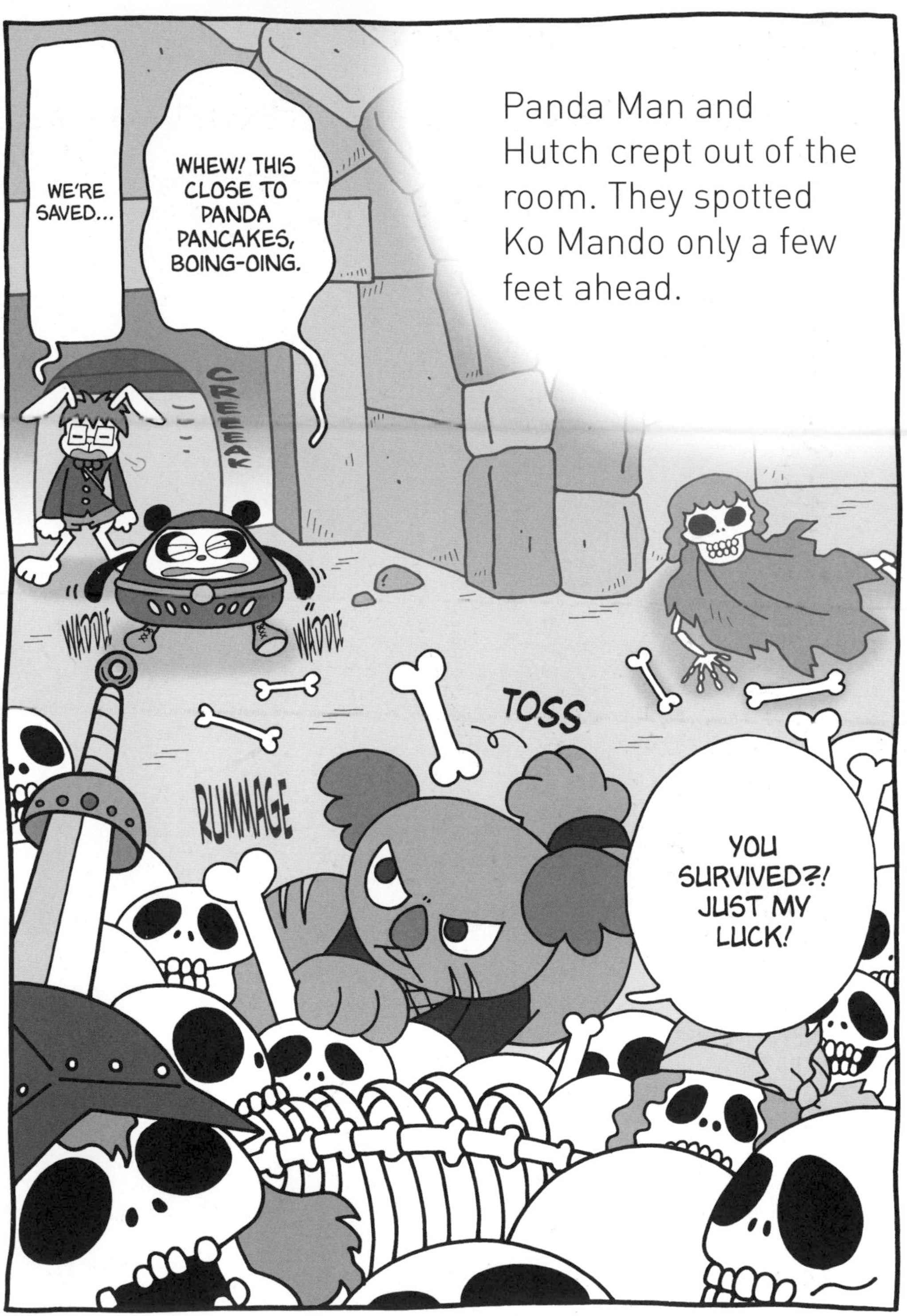

Panda Man and Hutch crept out of the room. They spotted Ko Mando only a few feet ahead.
WHEW! THIS CLOSE TO PANDA PANCAKES, BOING-OING.
WE'RE SAVED...
CREEEAK
WADDLE WADDLE
TOSS
RUMMAGE
YOU SURVIVED?! JUST MY LUCK!

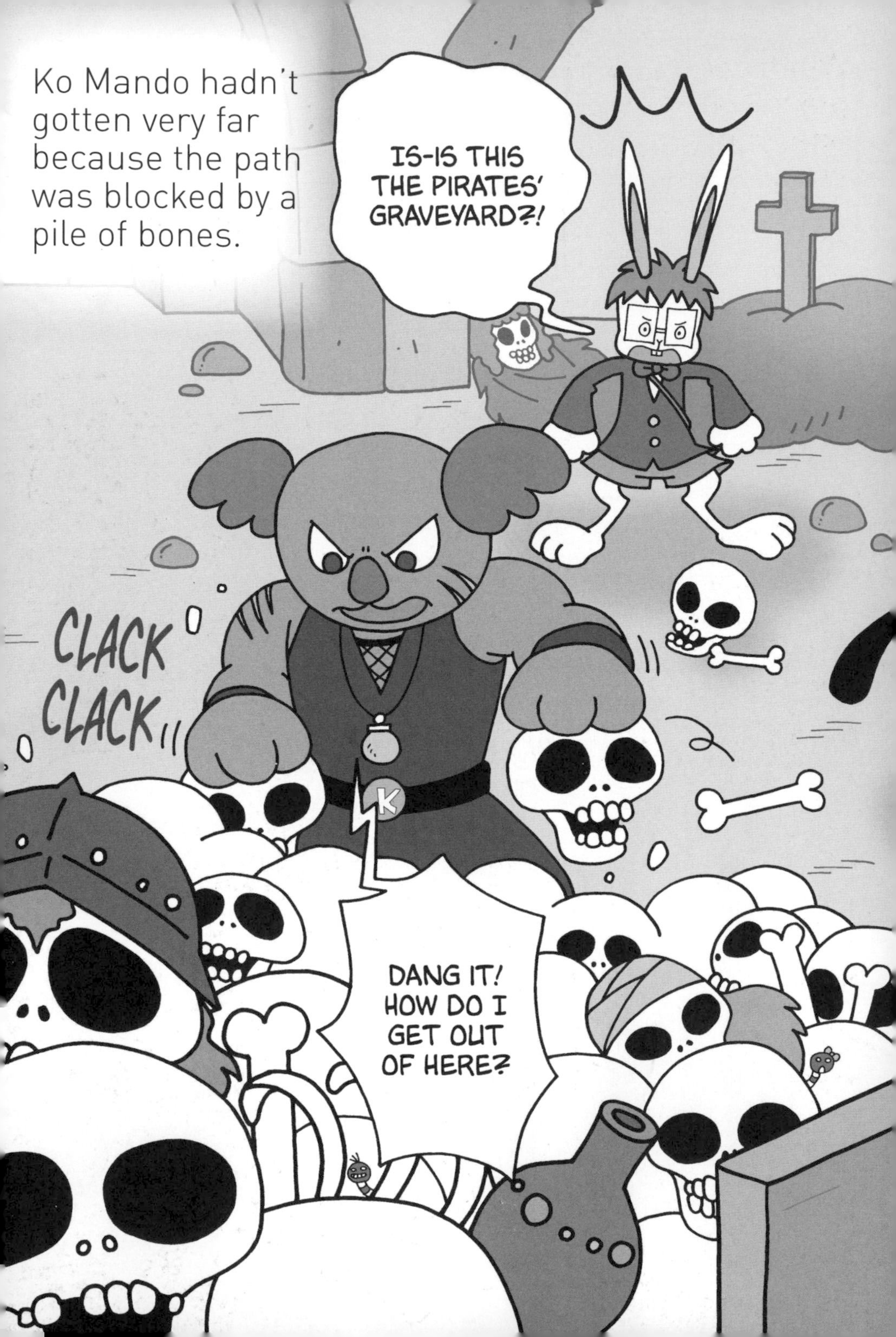
Ko Mando hadn't gotten very far because the path was blocked by a pile of bones.
IS-IS THIS THE PIRATES' GRAVEYARD?!
CLACK CLACK
DANG IT! HOW DO I GET OUT OF HERE?

Whatever the place was, no one wanted to stick around.

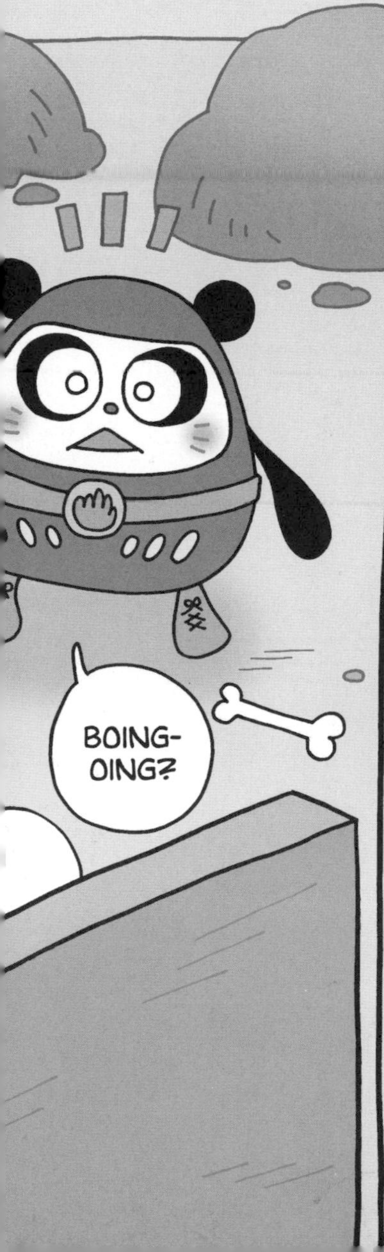
BOING-OING?

Just then, Panda Man noticed another sign.

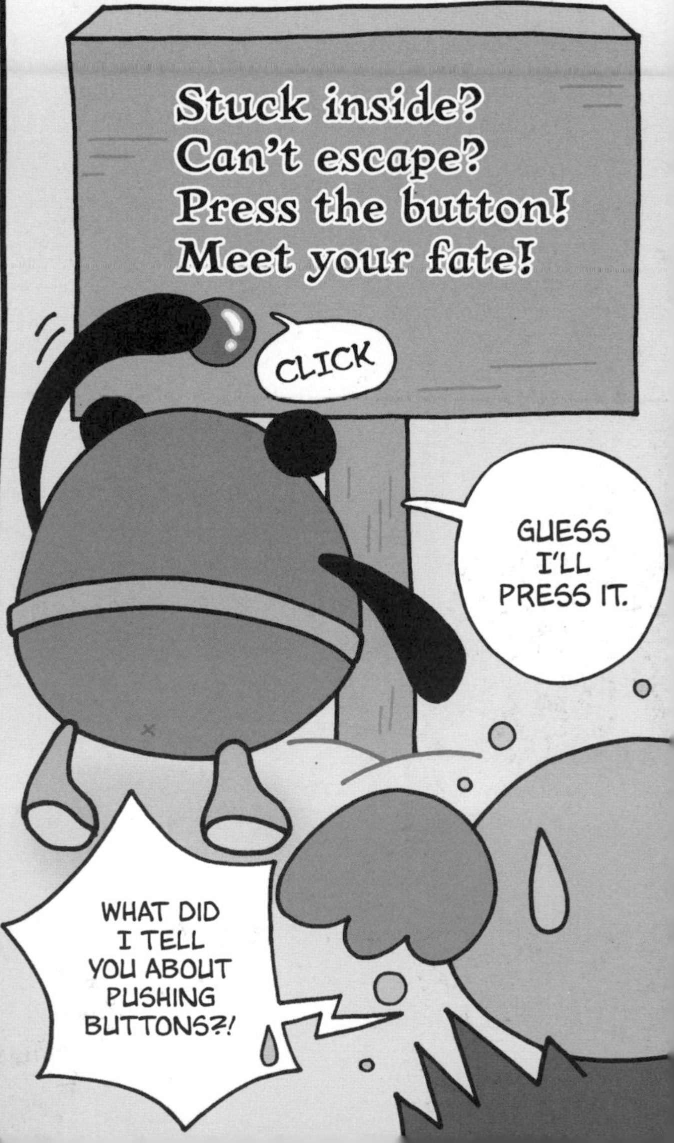
Stuck inside?
Can't escape?
Press the button!
Meet your fate!
CLICK
GUESS I'LL PRESS IT.
WHAT DID I TELL YOU ABOUT PUSHING BUTTONS?!

CLACK! CLACK!

As soon as Panda Man pushed the button, the bones rose and fit themselves together into dozens of skeletons!

The pirate ghosts were awake!

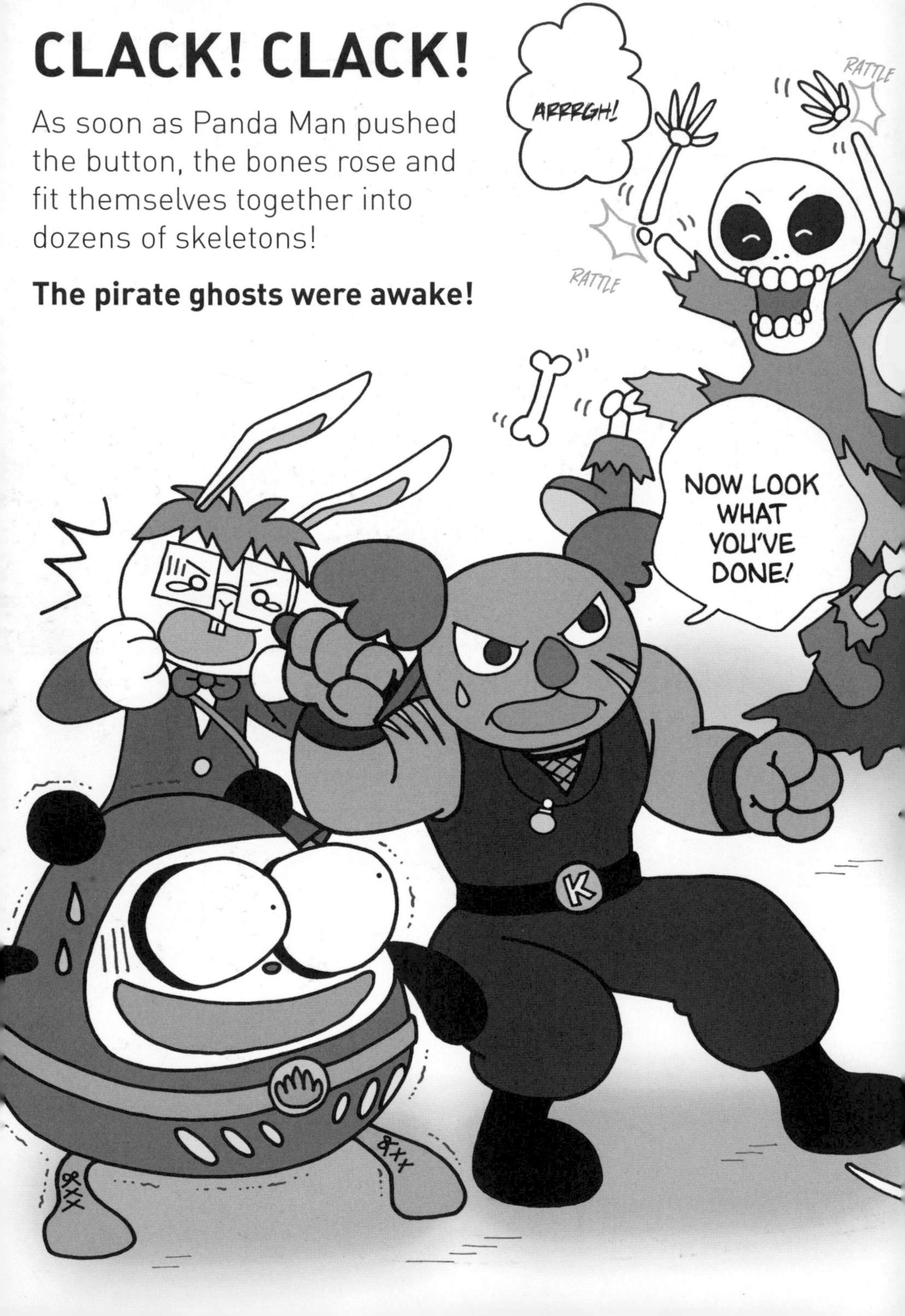

ARRRGH!
RATTLE
RATTLE
NOW LOOK WHAT YOU'VE DONE!

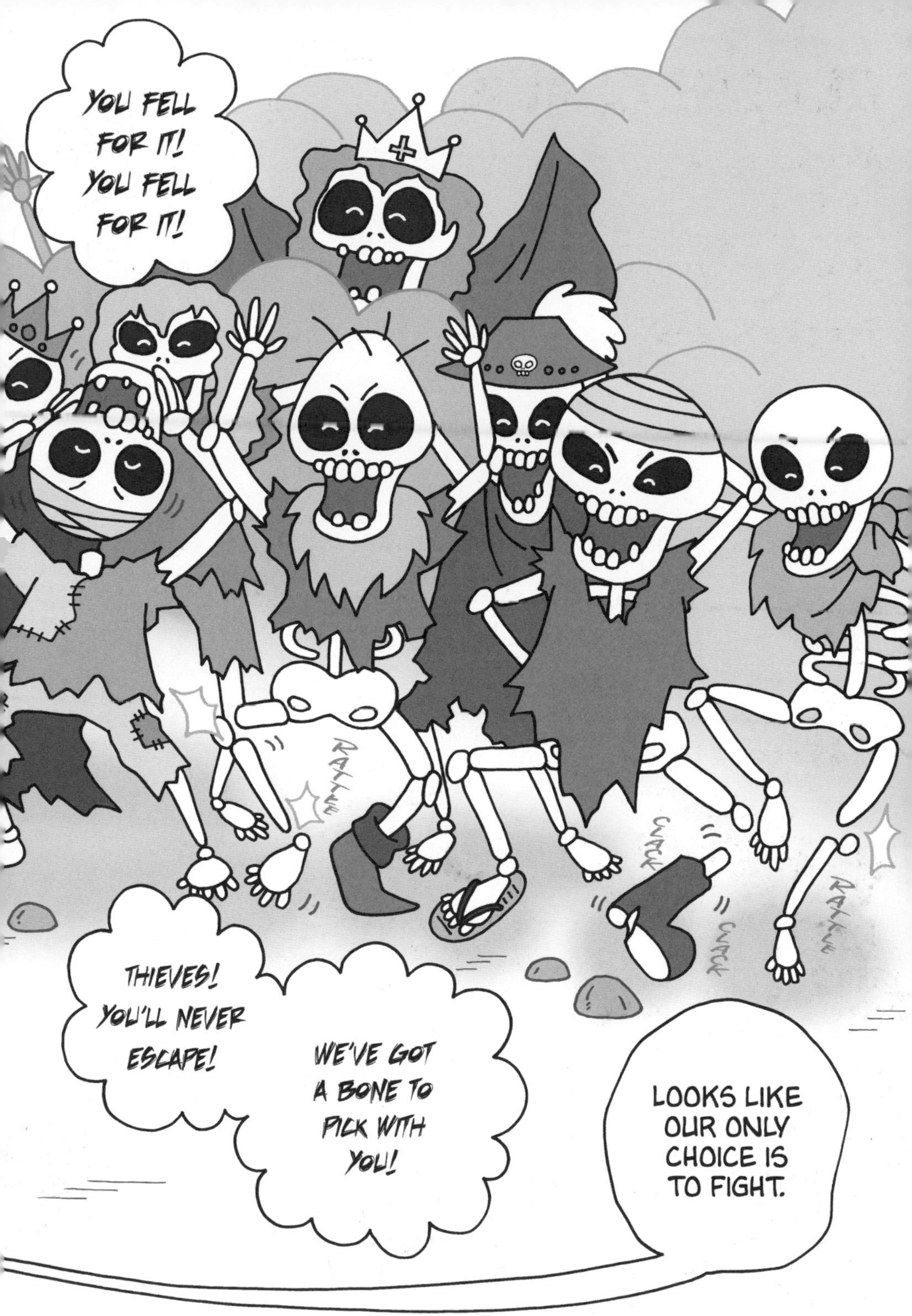
YOU FELL FOR IT! YOU FELL FOR IT!
RATTLE
CLACK
CLACK
RATTLE
THIEVES! YOU'LL NEVER ESCAPE!
WE'VE GOT A BONE TO PICK WITH YOU!
LOOKS LIKE OUR ONLY CHOICE IS TO FIGHT.

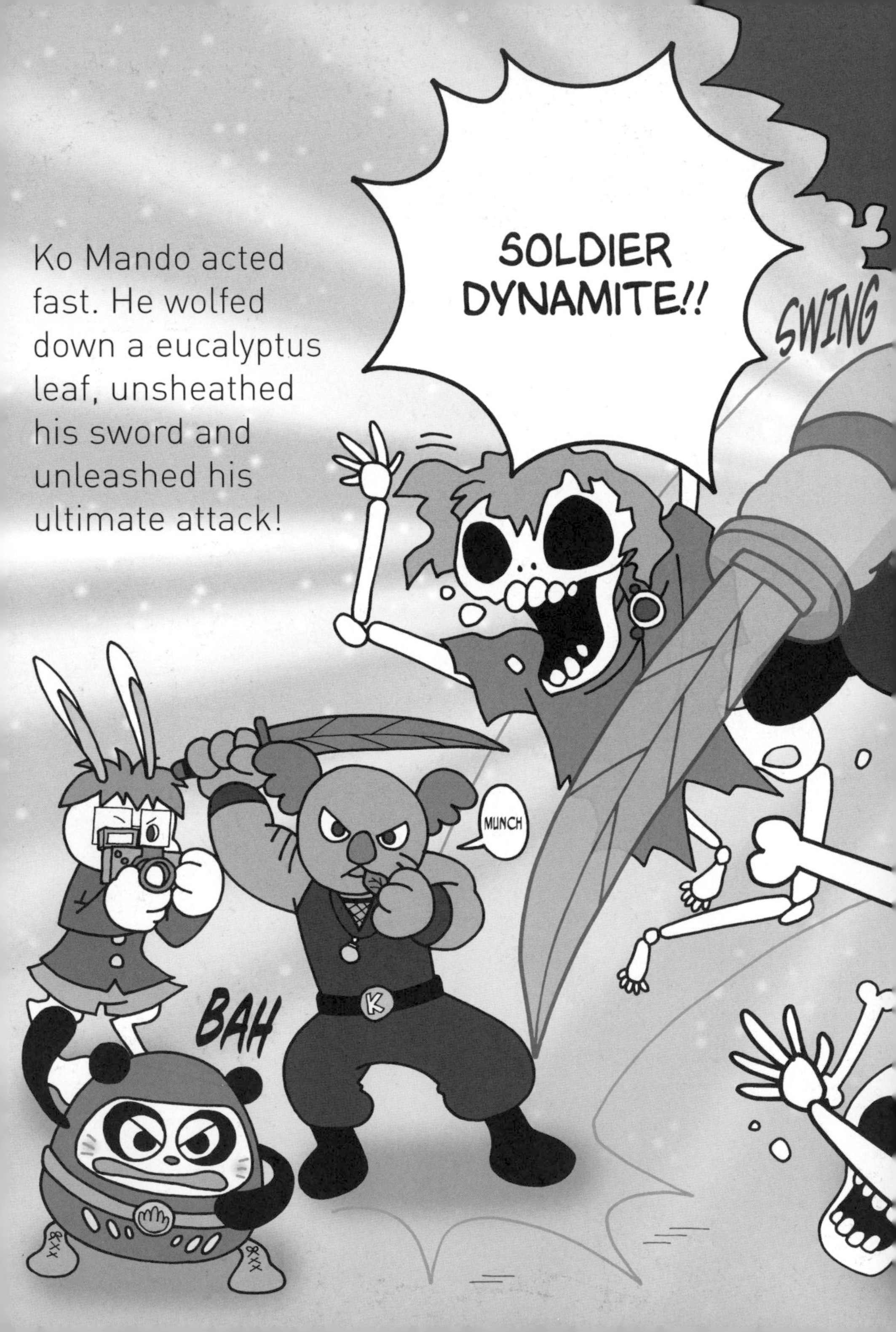
Ko Mando acted fast. He wolfed down a eucalyptus leaf, unsheathed his sword and unleashed his ultimate attack!
SOLDIER DYNAMITE!!
SWING
MUNCH
BAH

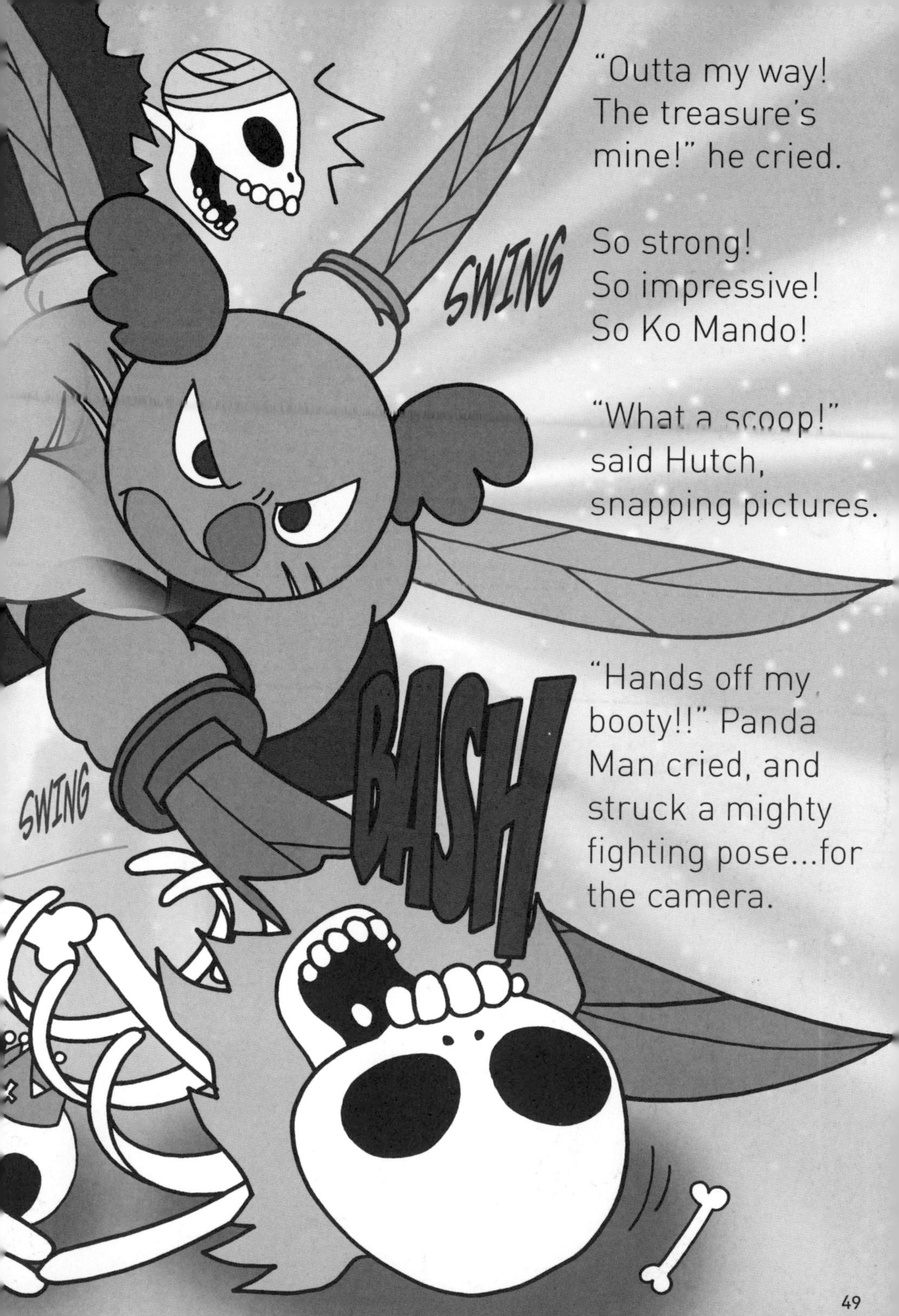
SWING
BASH
SWING

"Outta my way! The treasure's mine!" he cried.

So strong!
So impressive!
So Ko Mando!

"What a scoop!" said Hutch, snapping pictures.

"Hands off my booty!!" Panda Man cried, and struck a mighty fighting pose...for the camera.

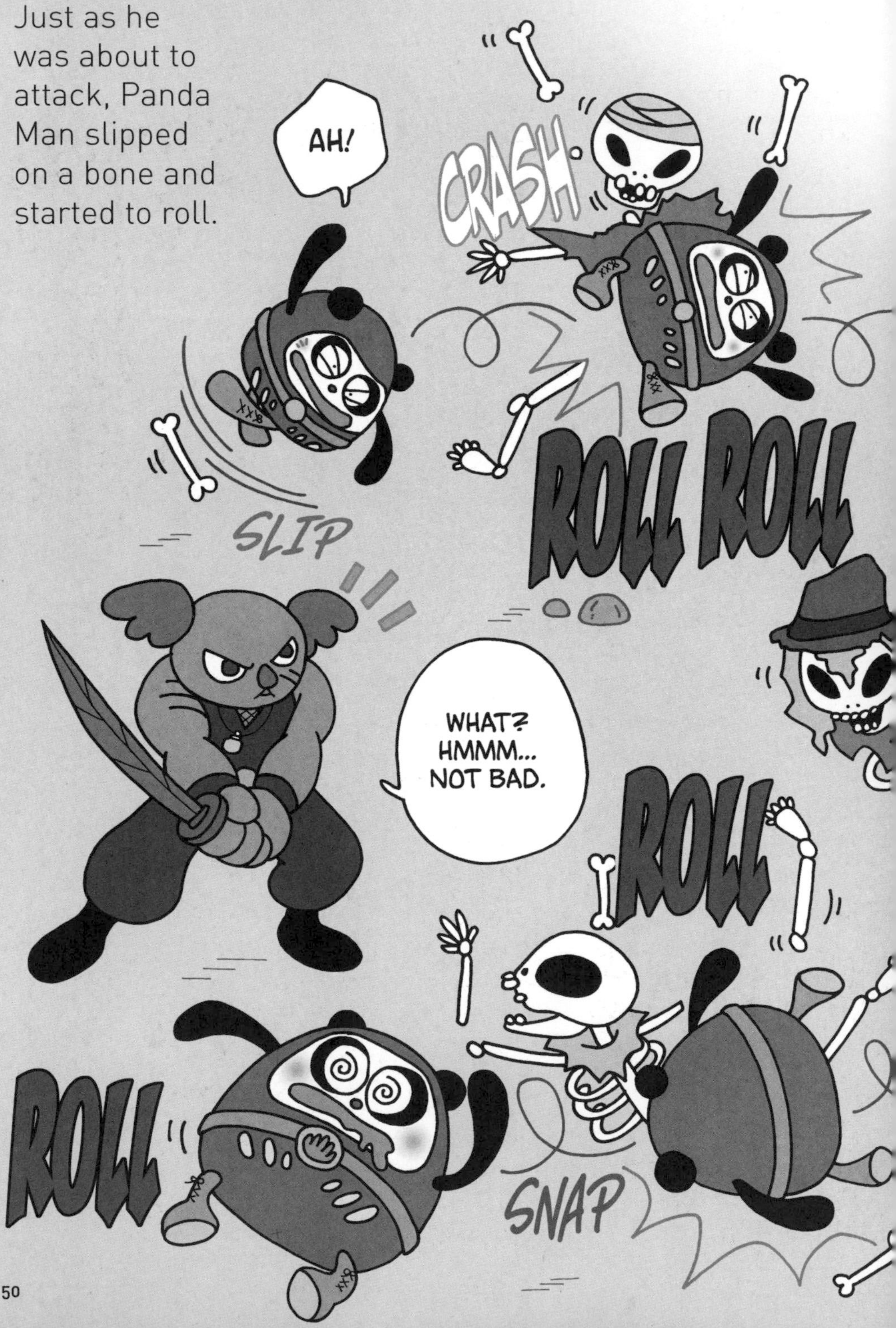
Just as he was about to attack, Panda Man slipped on a bone and started to roll.
AH!
CRASH
ROLL ROLL
SLIP
WHAT? HMMM... NOT BAD.
ROLL
ROLL
SNAP

He bowled through the pirates, knocking them completely out of joint.

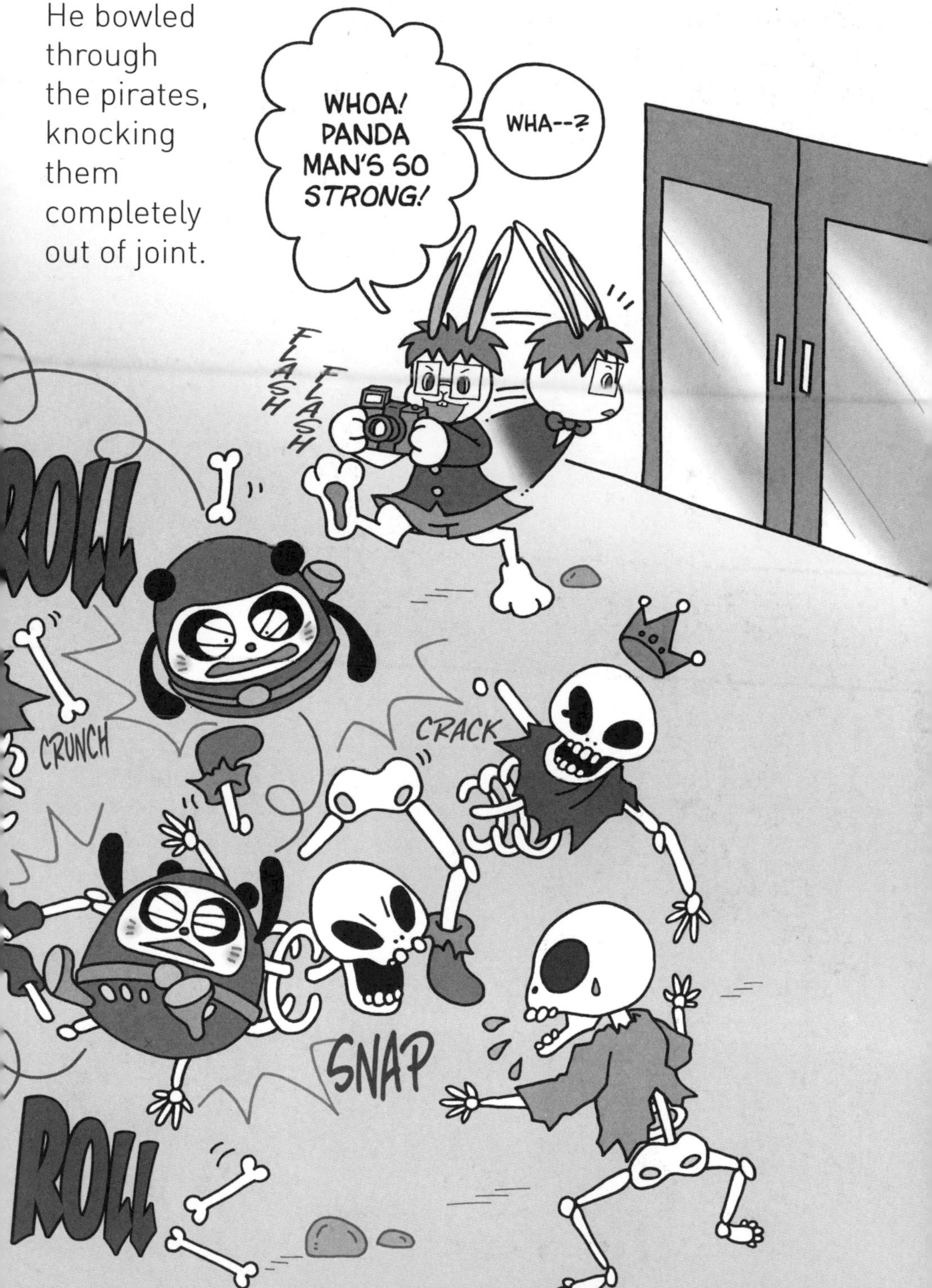

WHOA! PANDA MAN'S SO STRONG!
WHA--?
FLASH
FLASH
ROLL
CRUNCH
CRACK
SNAP
ROLL

While Panda Man and Ko Mando fought, Hutch noticed what appeared to be an exit.

The doors were a pair of mirrors, and there was a message written above them.

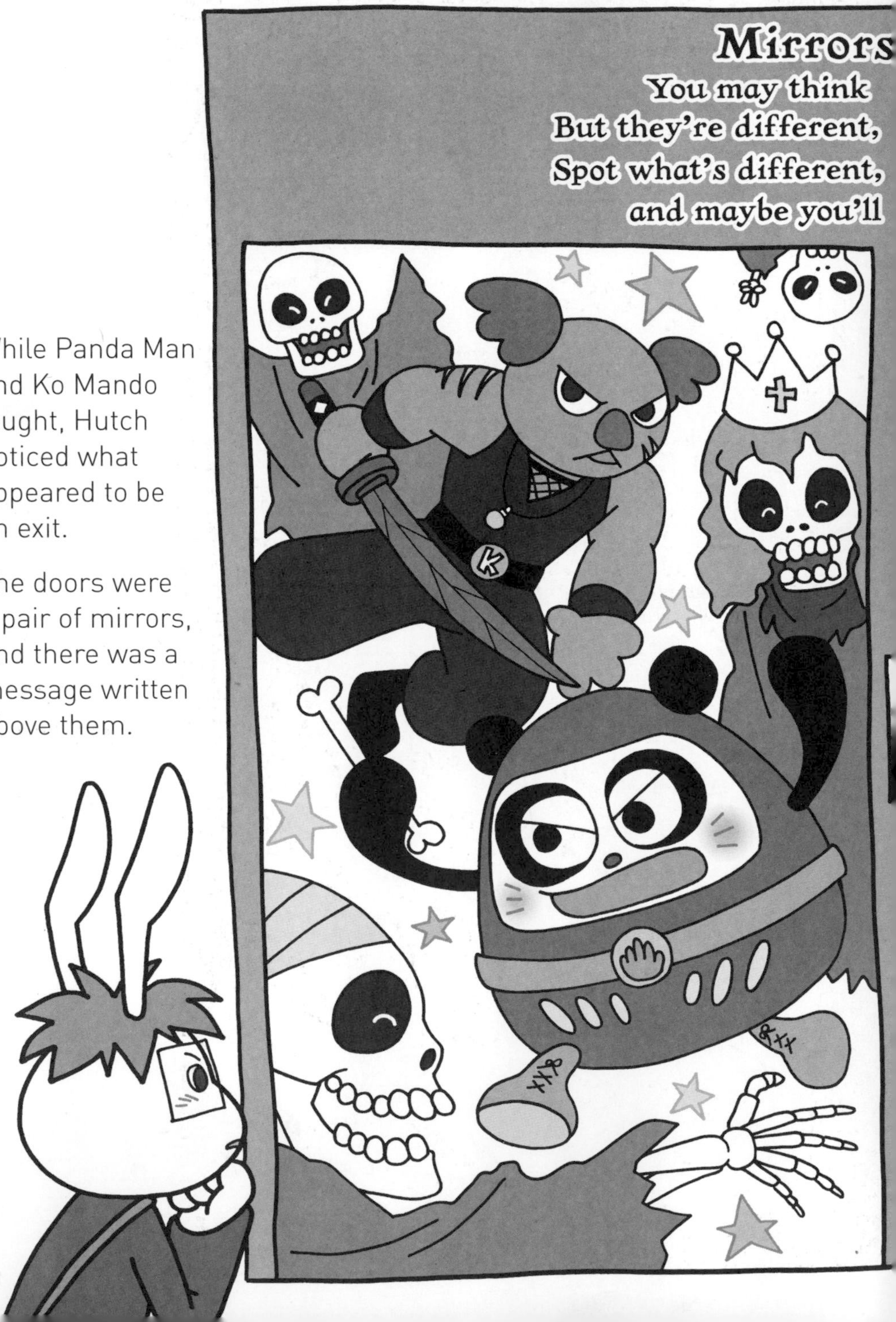
Mirrors
You may think
But they're different,
Spot what's different,
and maybe you'll

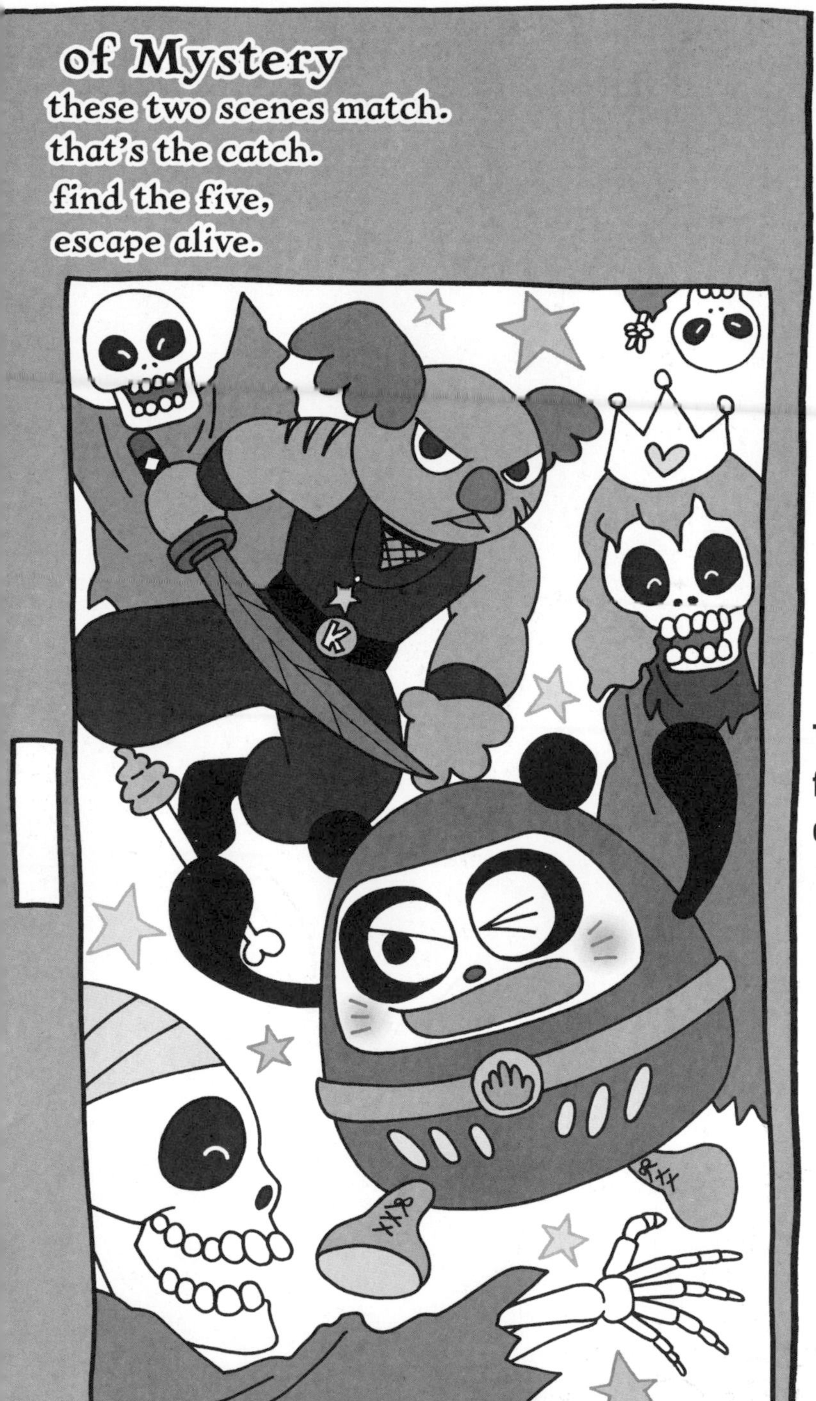
of Mystery
these two scenes match.
that's the catch.
find the five,
escape alive.

Time to
find those
differences!

The answers are:

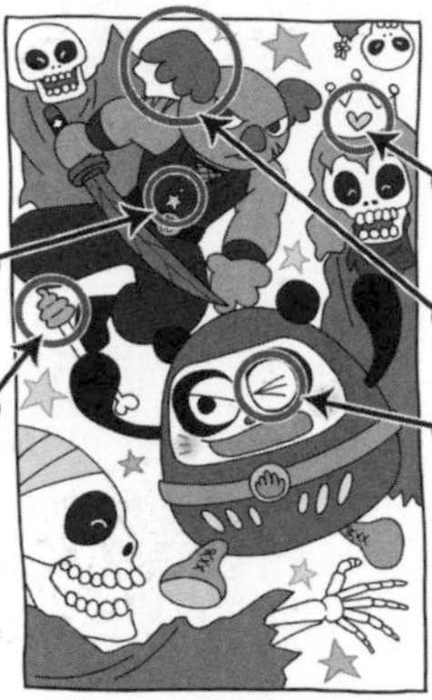
①
②
③
④
⑤

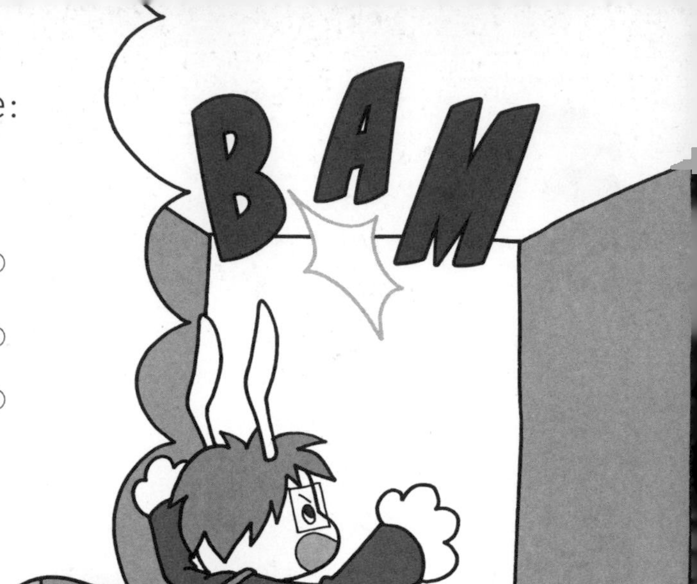
BAM

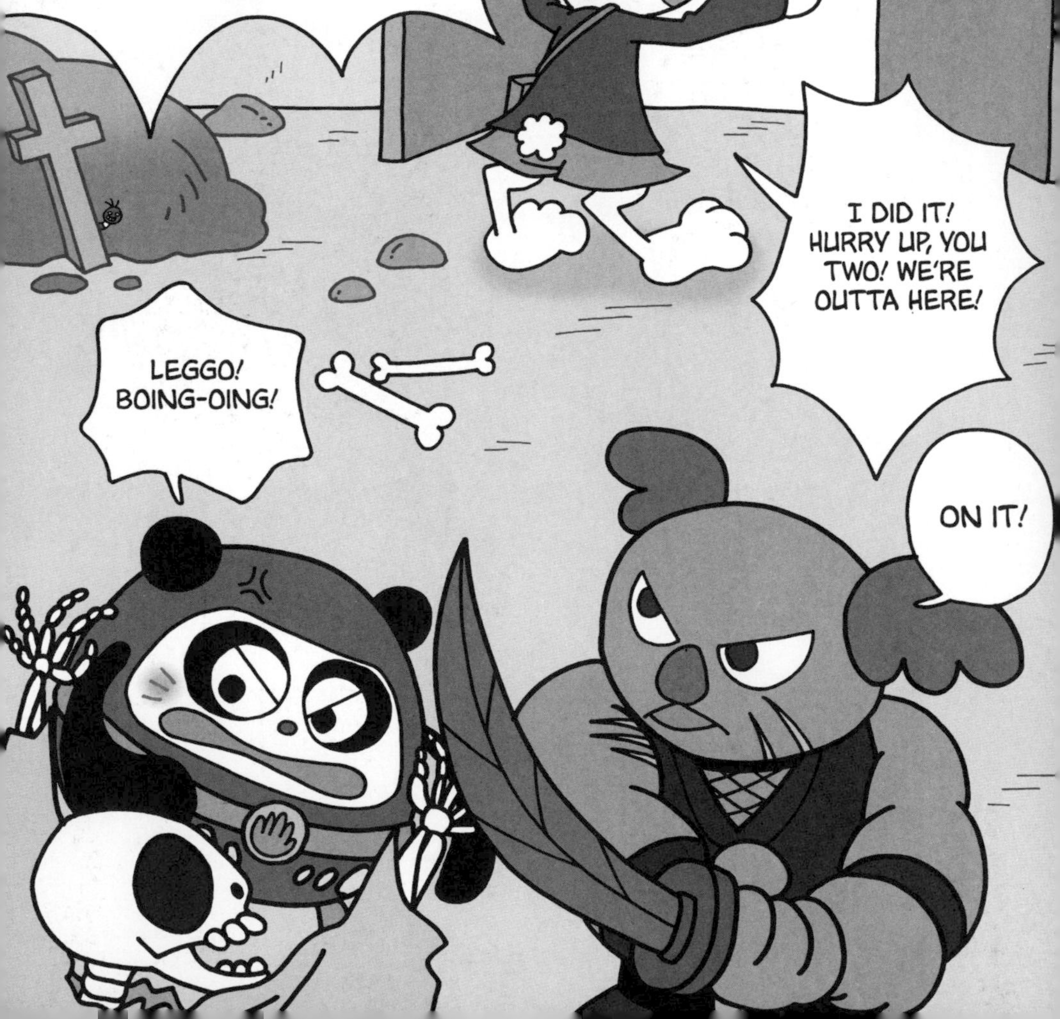
I DID IT! HURRY UP, YOU TWO! WE'RE OUTTA HERE!
LEGGO! BOING-OING!
ON IT!

When they passed through the doors, they found two mine carts.

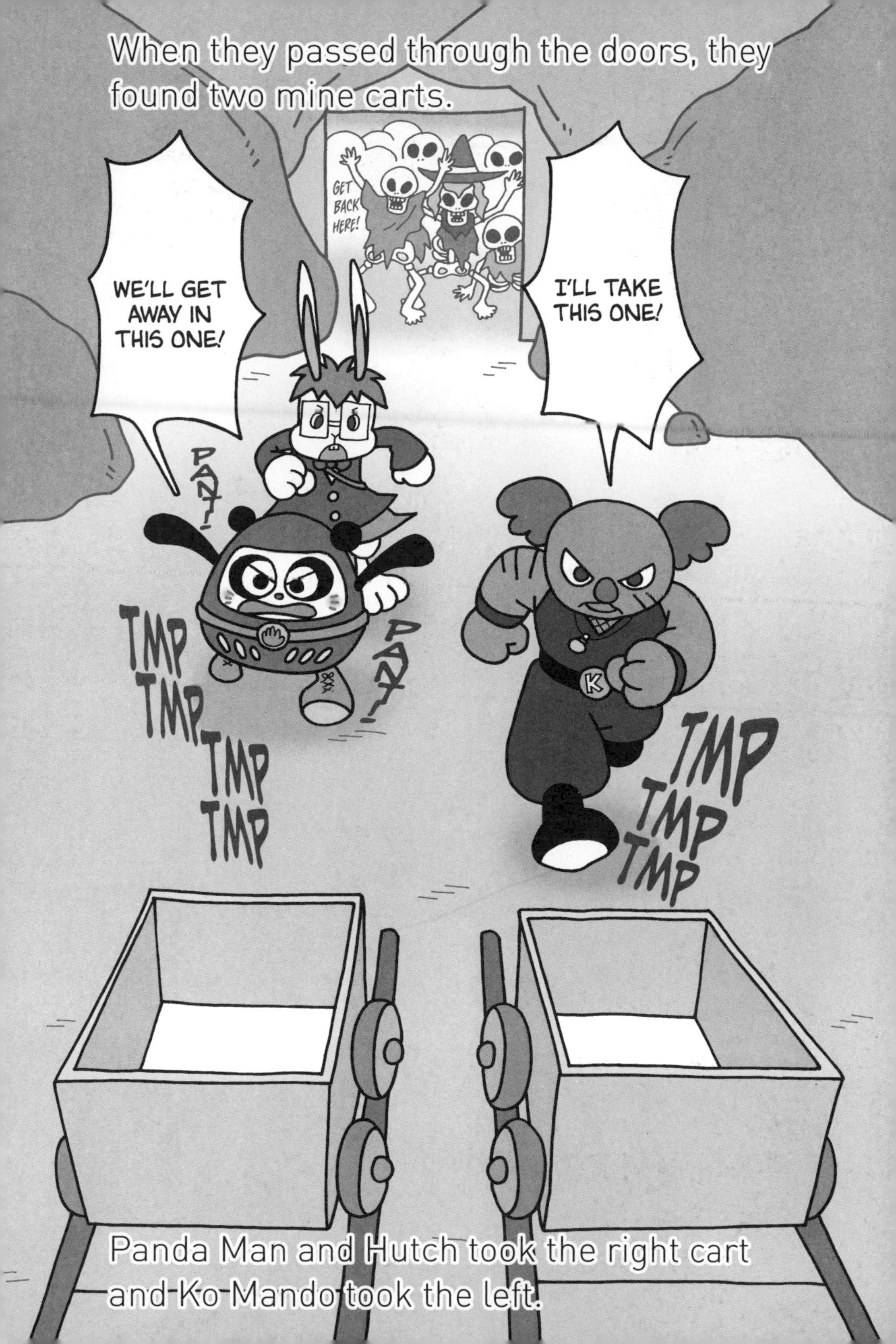
GET BACK HERE!
I'LL TAKE THIS ONE!
WE'LL GET AWAY IN THIS ONE!
PANT!
PANT!
TMP TMP TMP
TMP TMP TMP TMP

Panda Man and Hutch took the right cart and Ko Mando took the left.

Both carts took off in a flash.

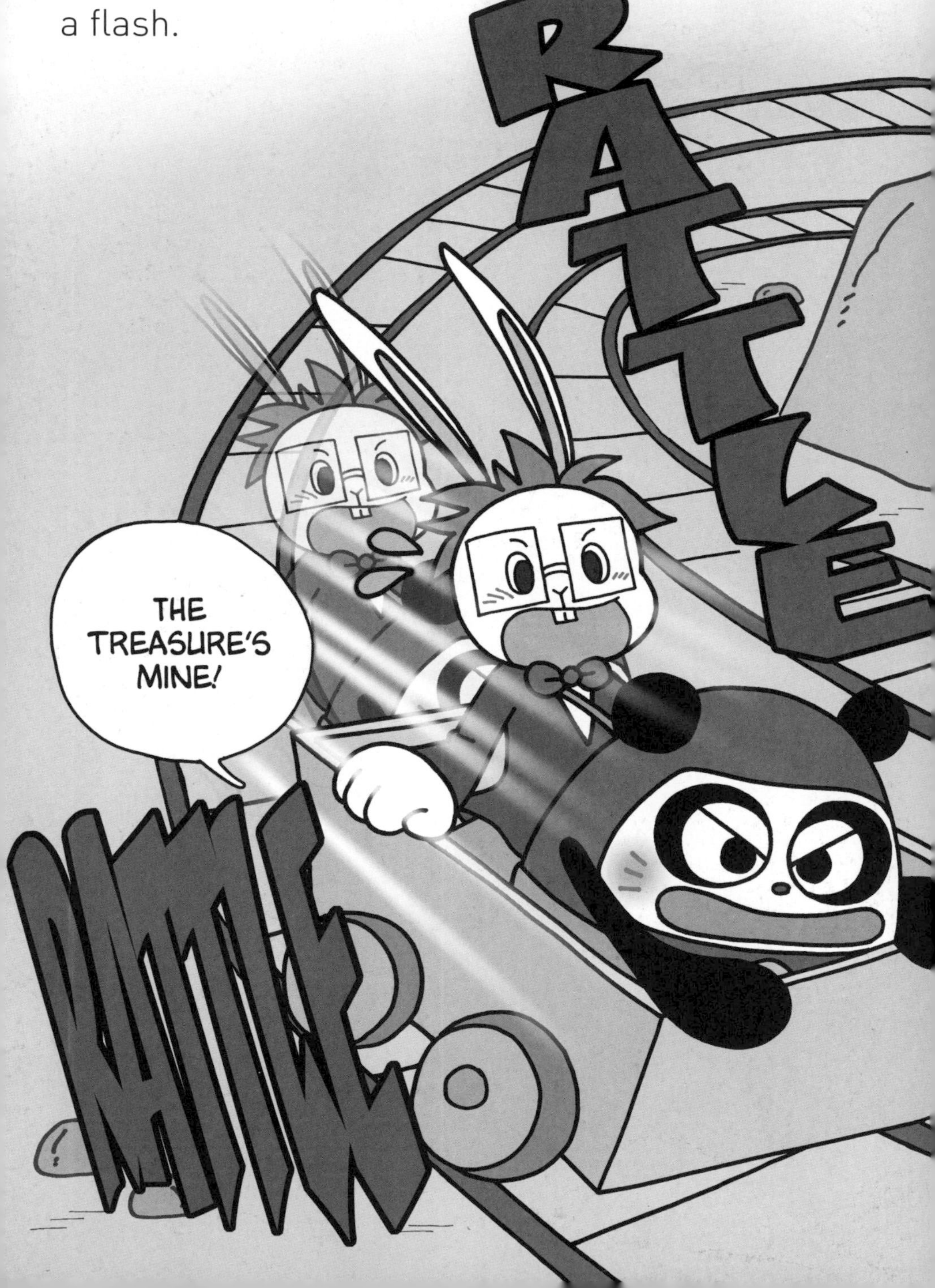
RATTLE
THE TREASURE'S MINE!

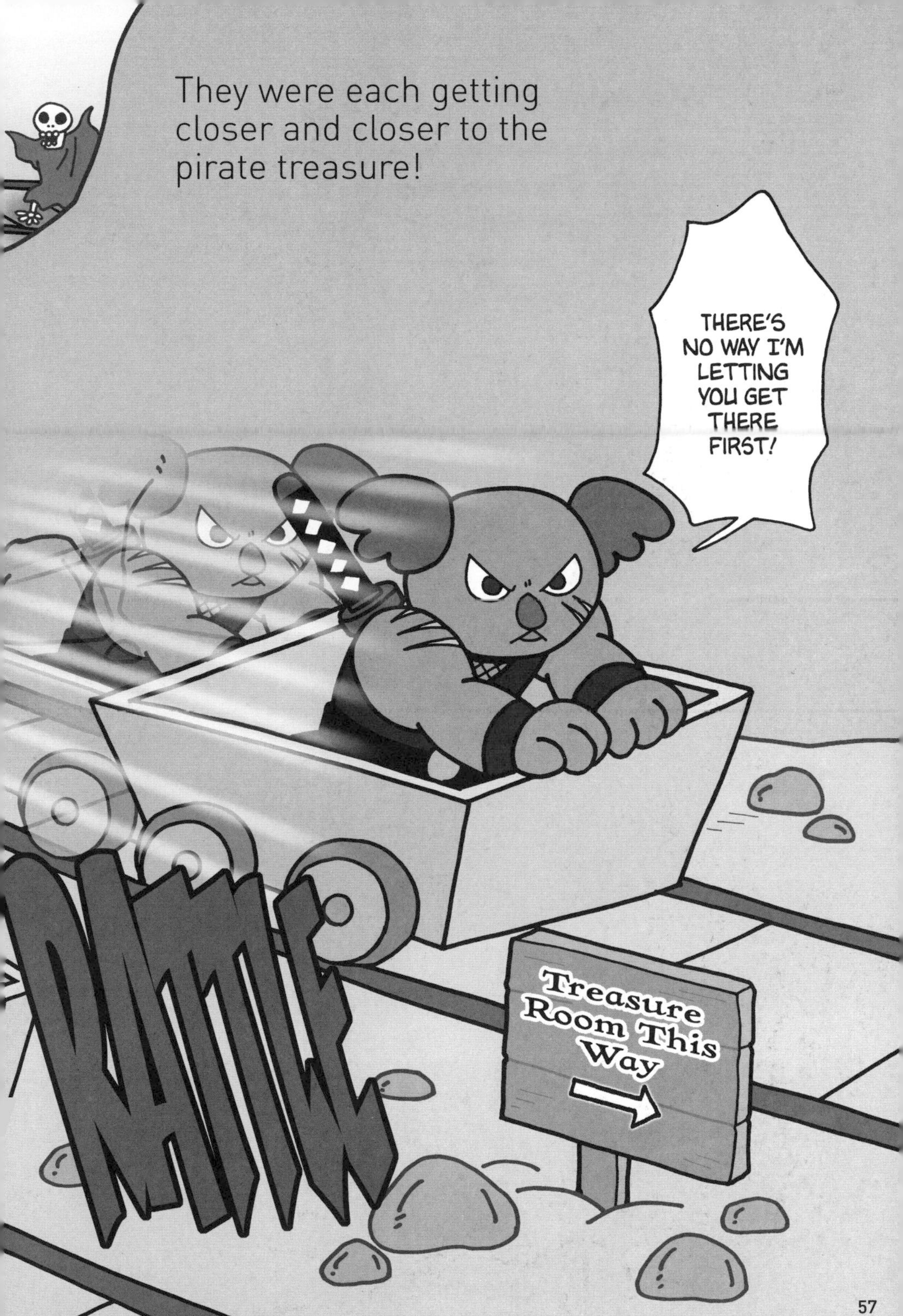
They were each getting closer and closer to the pirate treasure!
THERE'S NO WAY I'M LETTING YOU GET THERE FIRST!
Treasure Room This Way

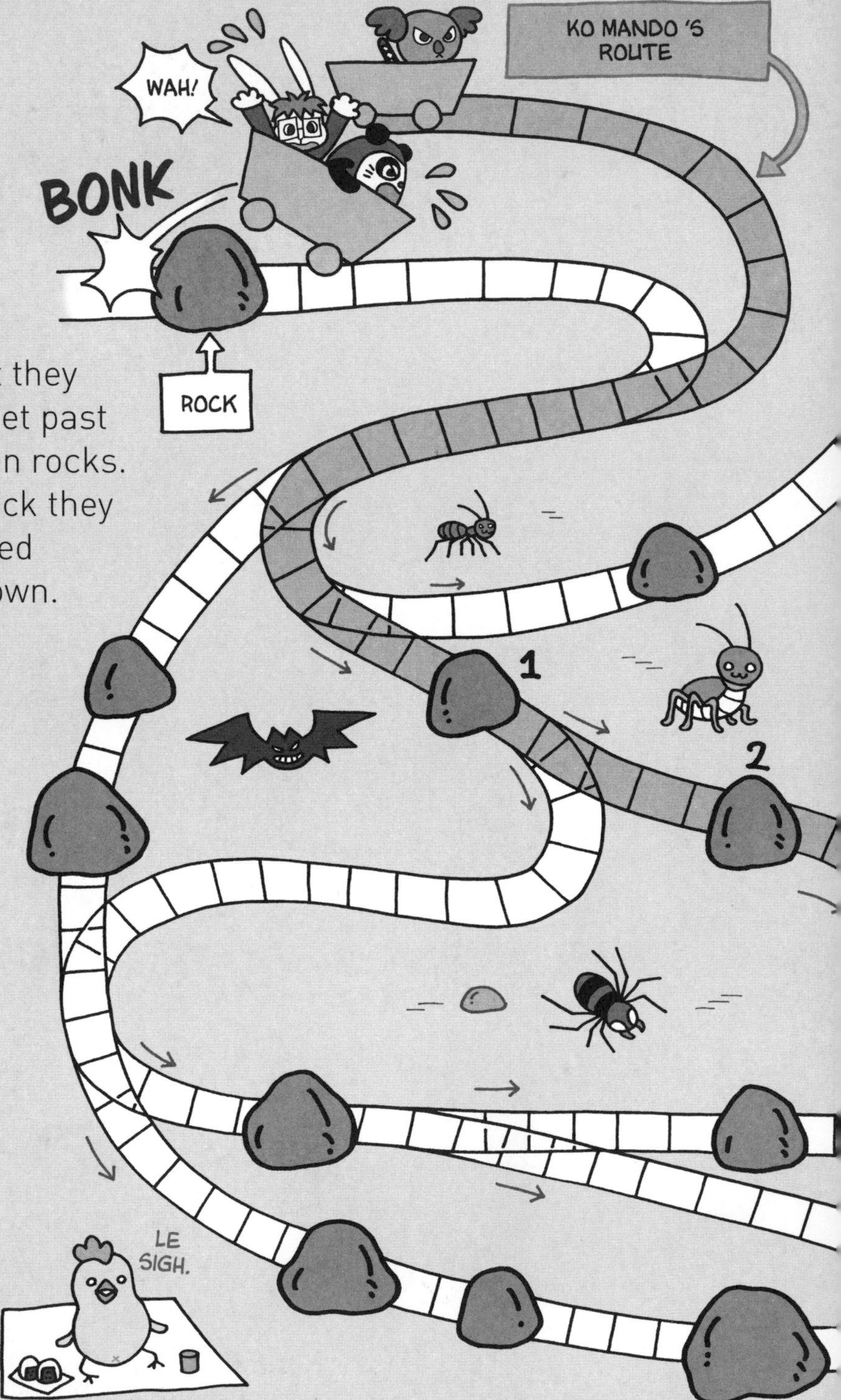
WAH!
KO MANDO 'S ROUTE
BONK
ROCK
1
2
LE SIGH.

But first they had to get past the fallen rocks. Every rock they hit slowed them down.

Help Panda Man find the path with fewer than five rocks so he can get to the treasure first!

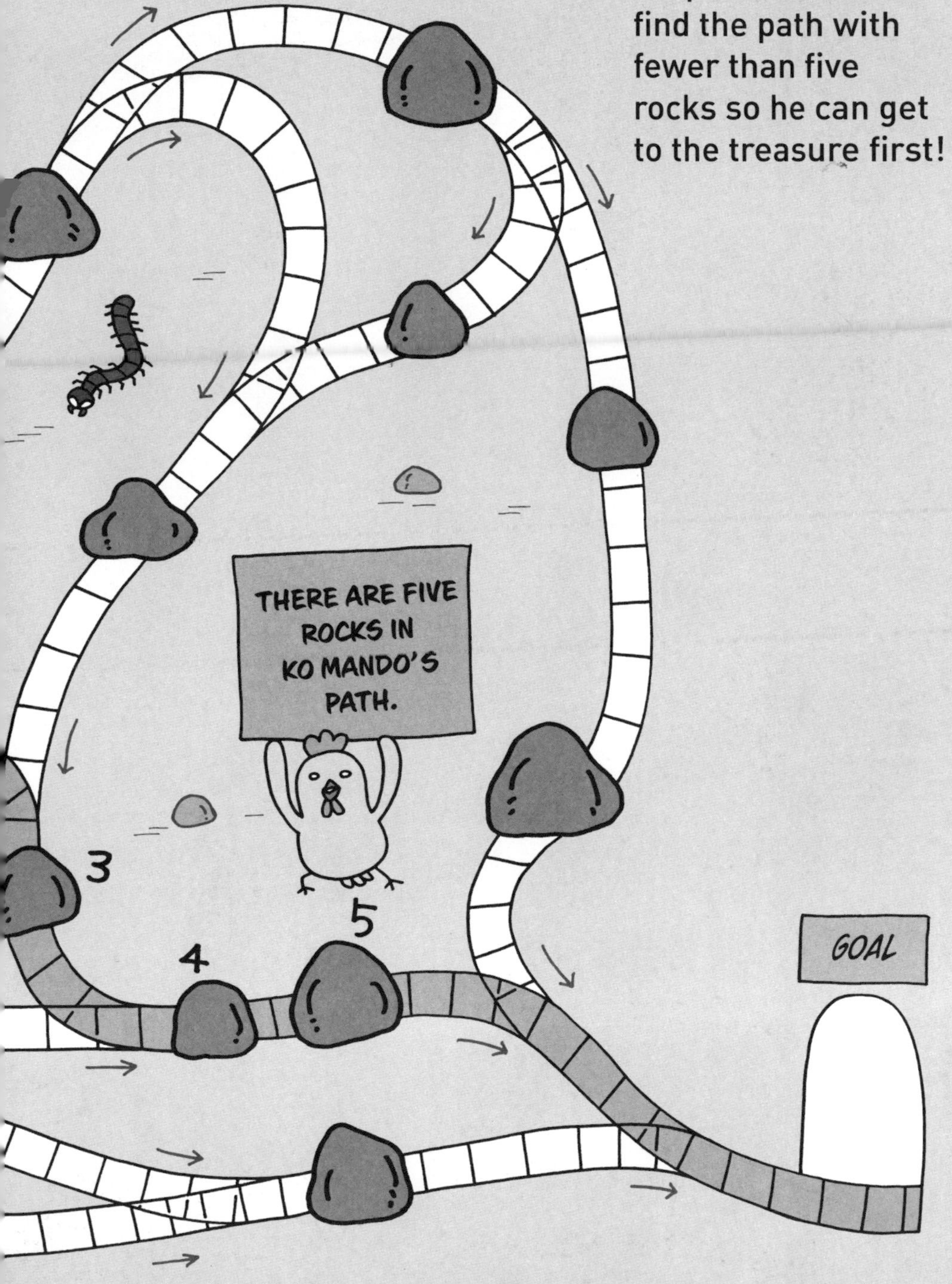
THERE ARE FIVE ROCKS IN KO MANDO'S PATH.
3
4
5
GOAL

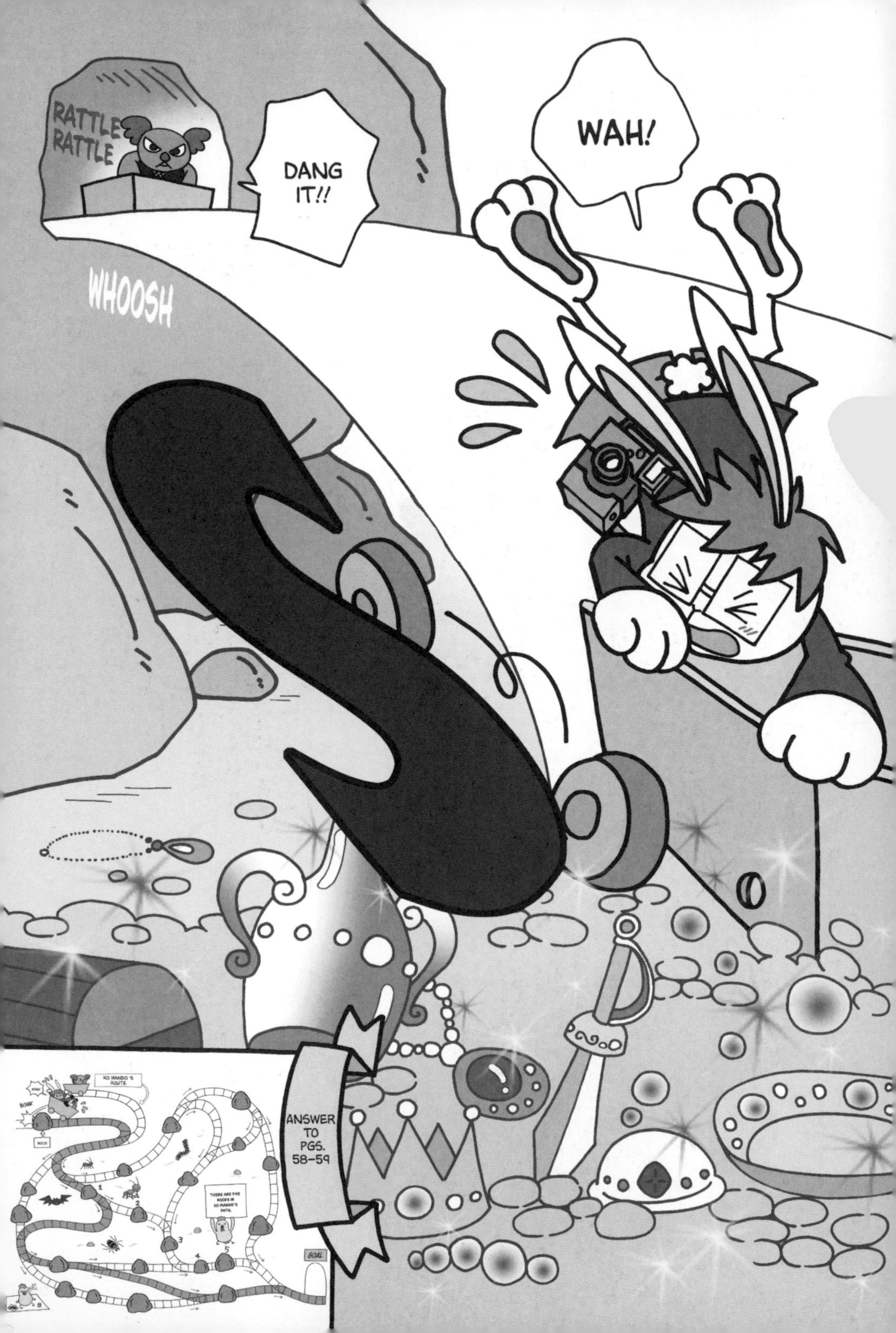
WAH!
DANG IT!!
RATTLE RATTLE
WHOOSH
ANSWER TO PGS. 58–59
KO MANDO'S ROUTE
BONK
ROCK
THERE ARE FIVE ROCKS IN KO MANDO'S PATH.
1
2
3
4
5
GOAL

They did it!!

Thanks to you, Panda Man discovered the treasure before Ko Mando!

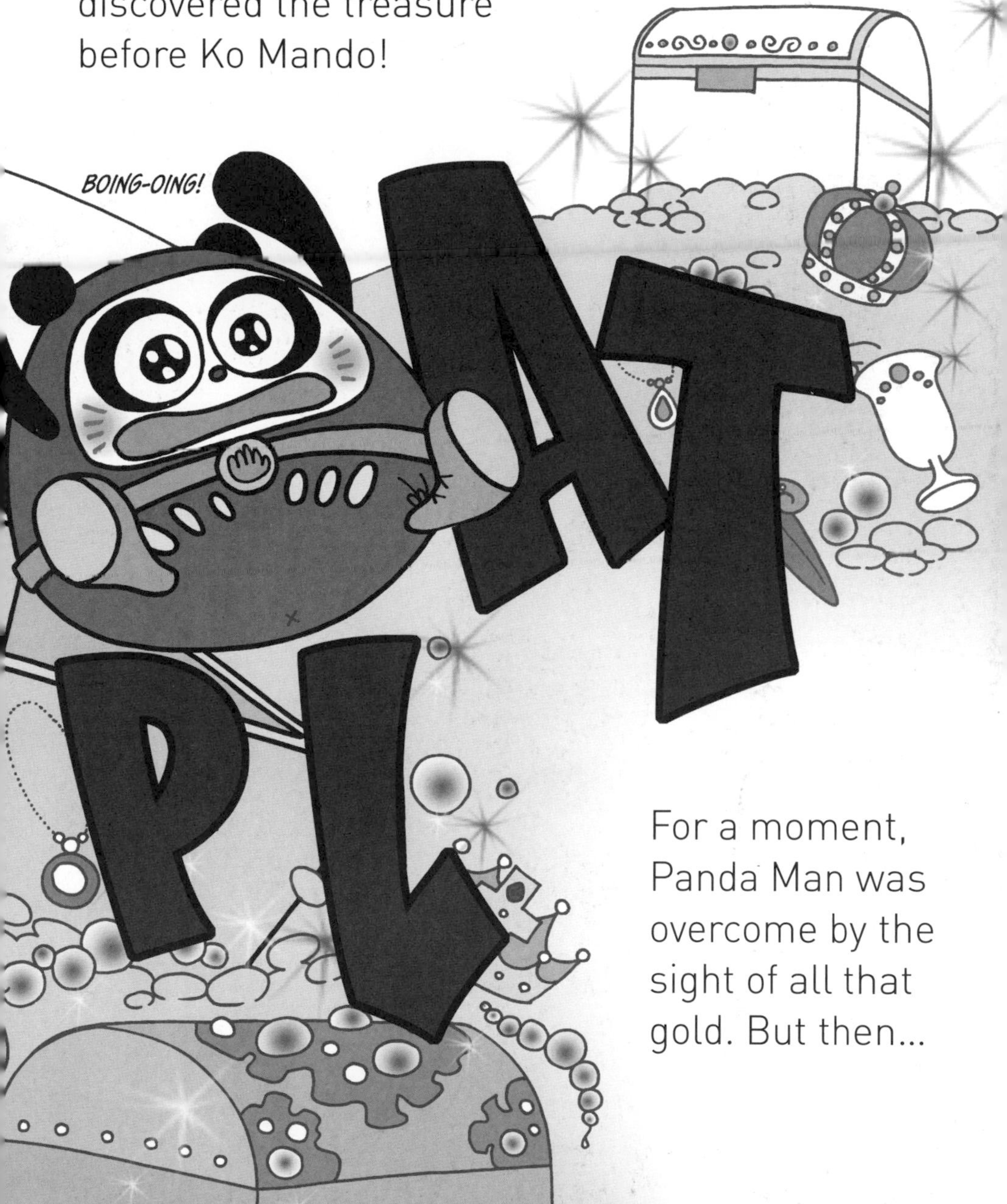
BOING-OING!
PLAT

For a moment, Panda Man was overcome by the sight of all that gold. But then...

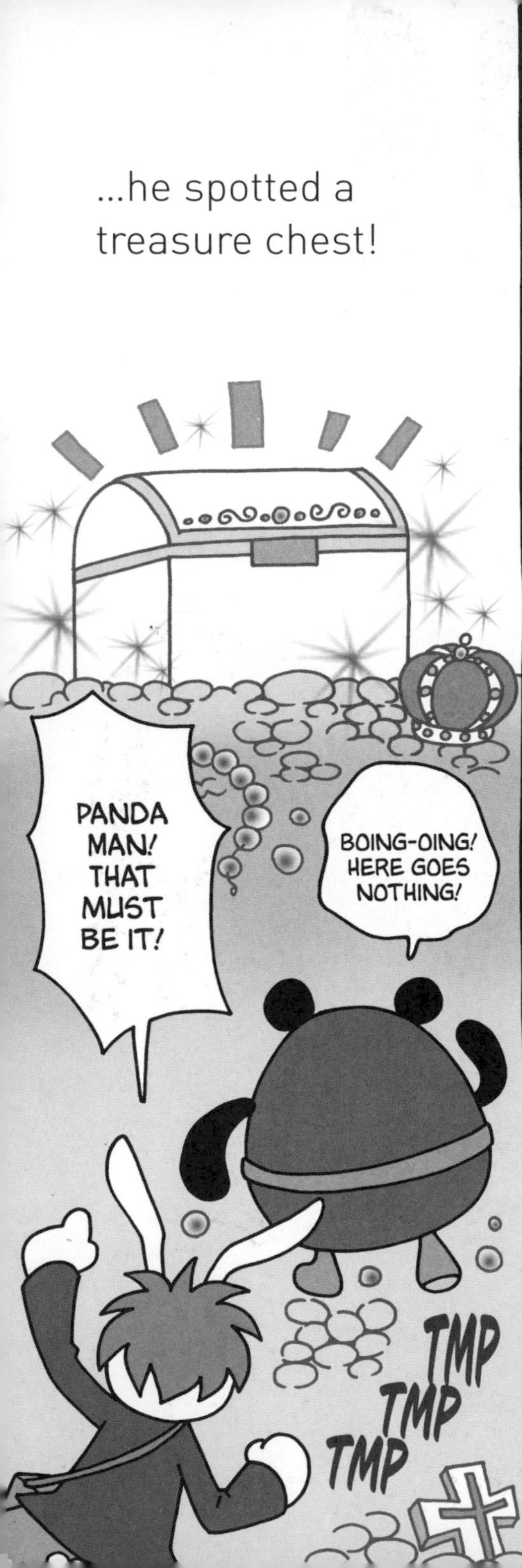
...he spotted a treasure chest!
PANDA MAN! THAT MUST BE IT!
BOING-OING! HERE GOES NOTHING!
TMP TMP TMP
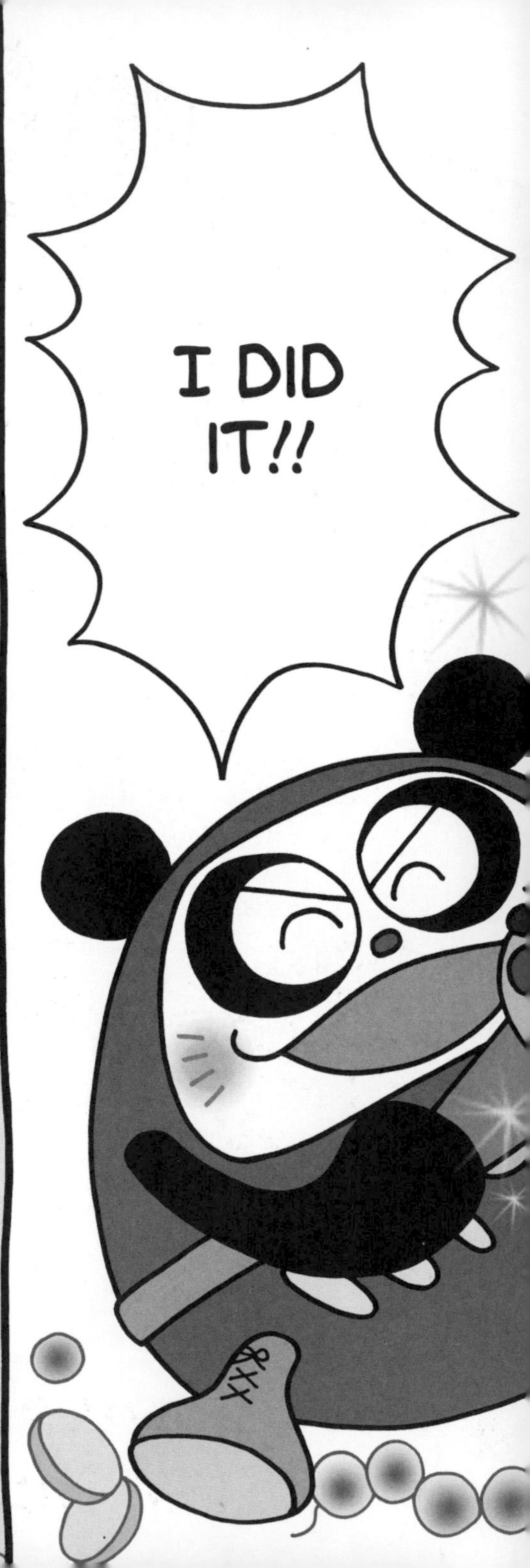
I DID IT!!

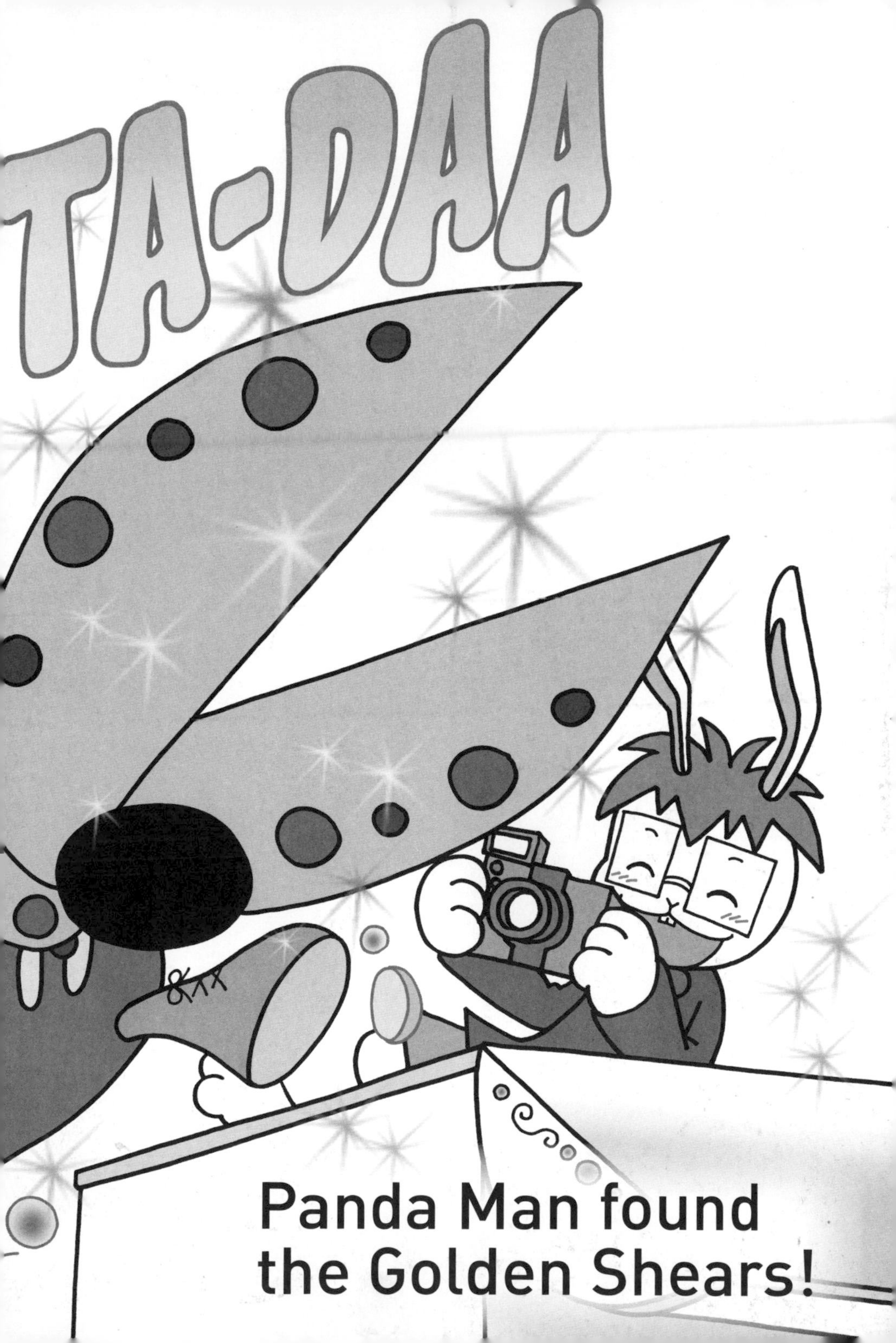
TA-DAA
Panda Man found
the Golden Shears!

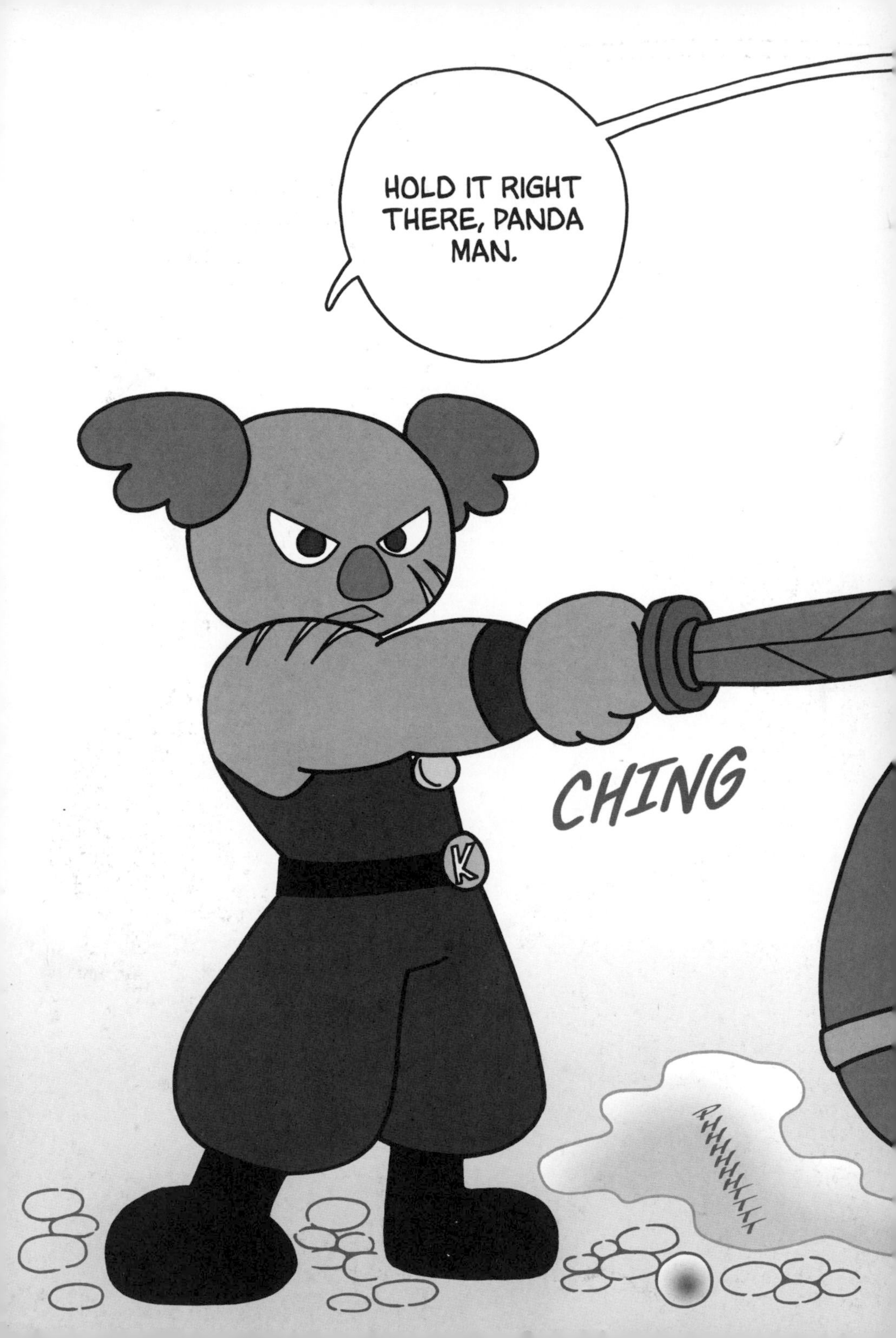
HOLD IT RIGHT THERE, PANDA MAN.
CHING

What was Ko Mando doing?

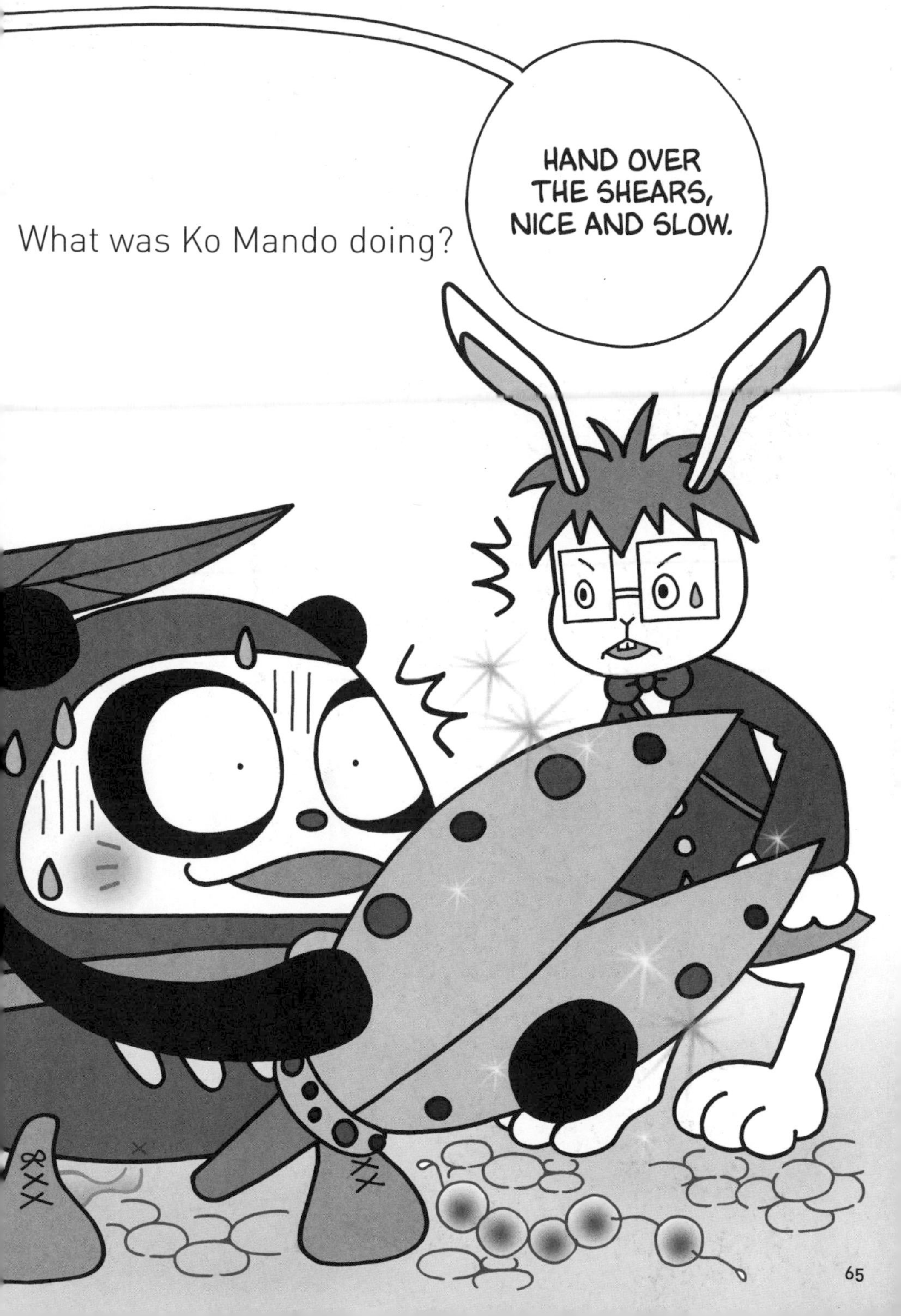
HAND OVER
THE SHEARS,
NICE AND SLOW.

"Ko Mando! How could you?" Hutch yelled. "You're supposed to be a hero!"

"Quiet!! It's not for me! It's for *them*...!"

"Them *who*?!" Panda Man cried. "Admit it. You want the prize! You're more greedy and ruthless than I imagined!"

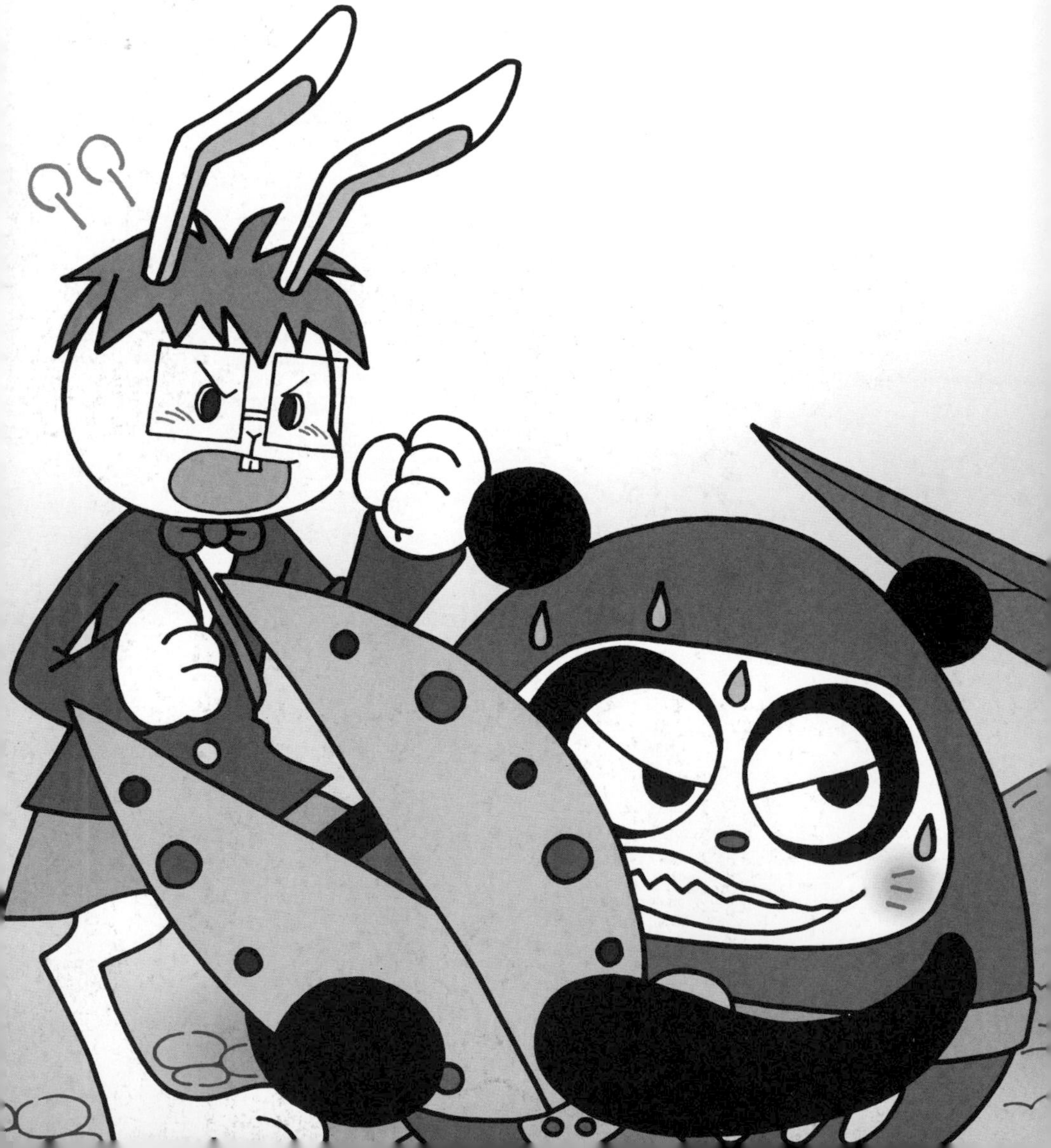

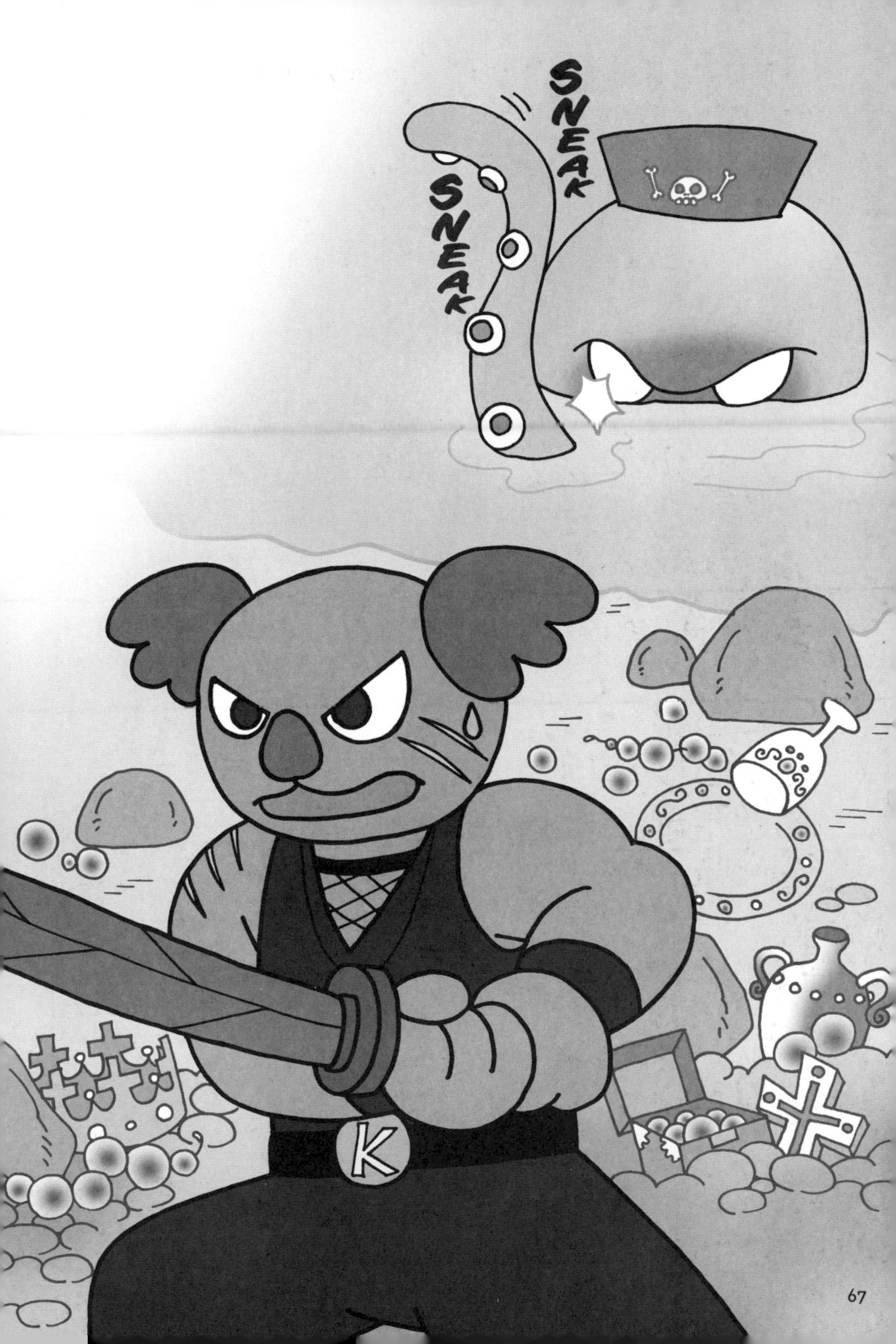
SNEAK
SNEAK

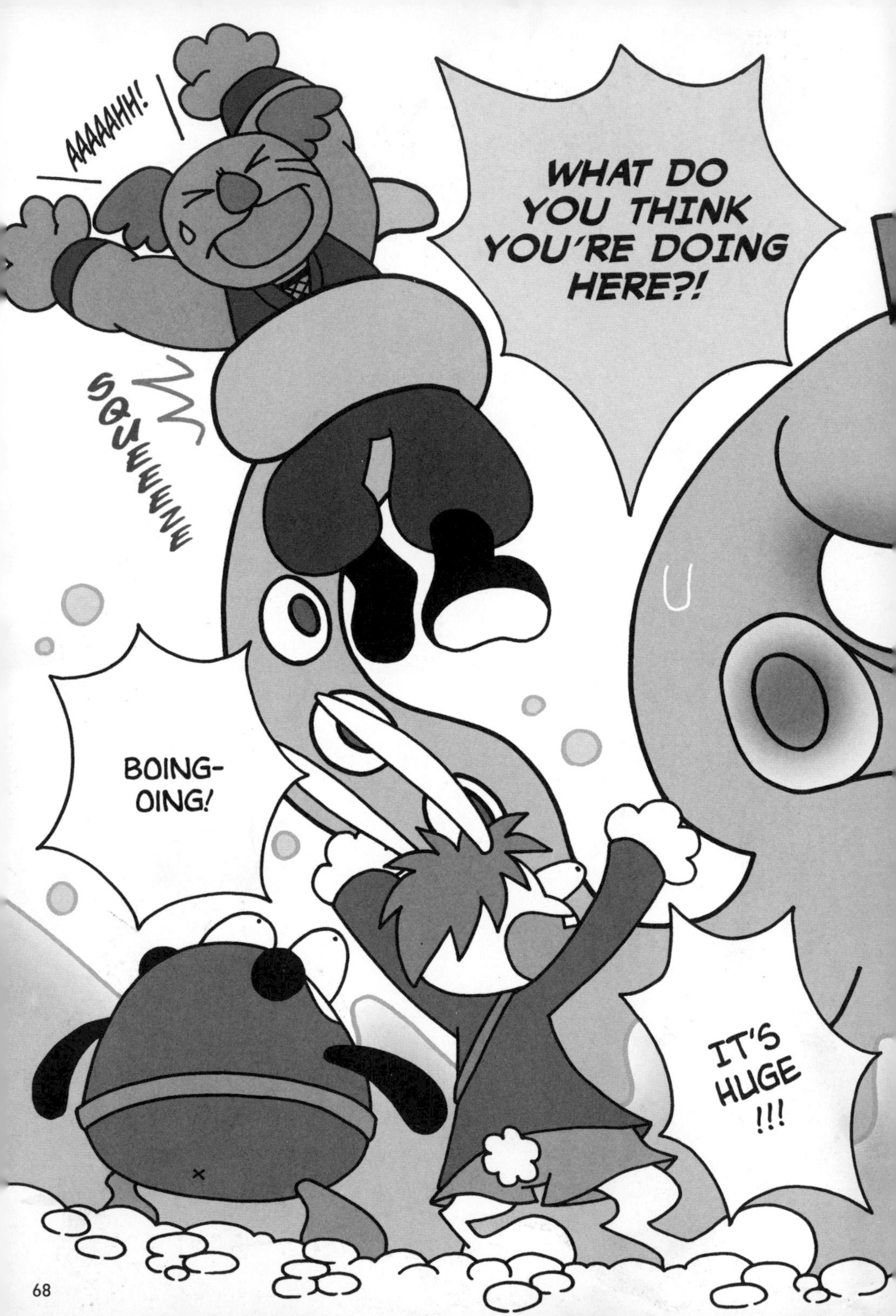
WHAT DO YOU THINK YOU'RE DOING HERE?!
AAAAAHH!
SQUEEEEZE
BOING-OING!
IT'S HUGE !!!

Suddenly, out of nowhere came a giant octopus!!

And not just any giant octopus. *This* giant octopus was the chief guardian of Pirate Island. Ko Mando was helpless in his grasp.

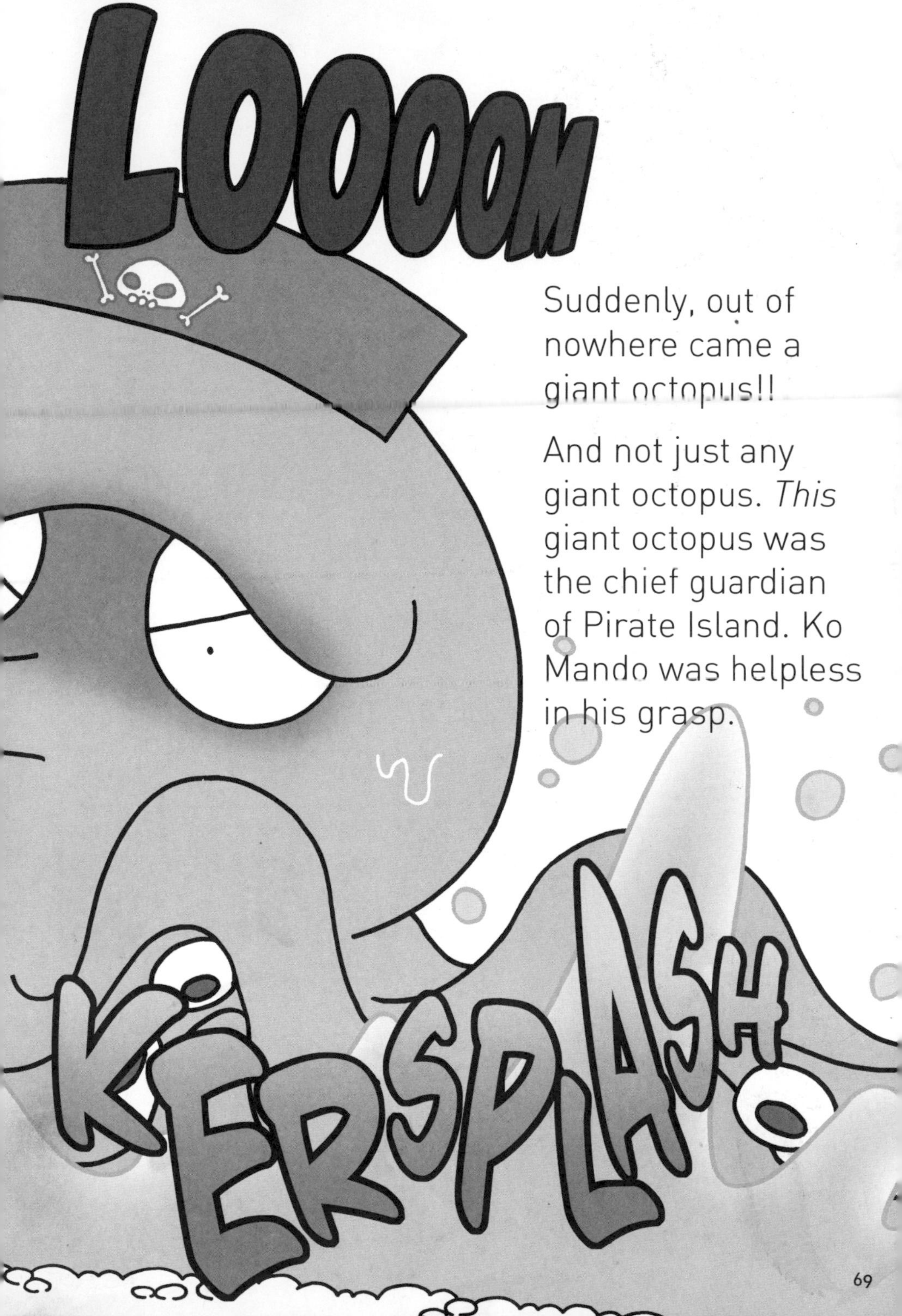
LOOOOM
KERSPLASH

BAAASH!

The giant octopus tossed Ko Mando at Panda Man like he weighed nothing more than a dried sardine.

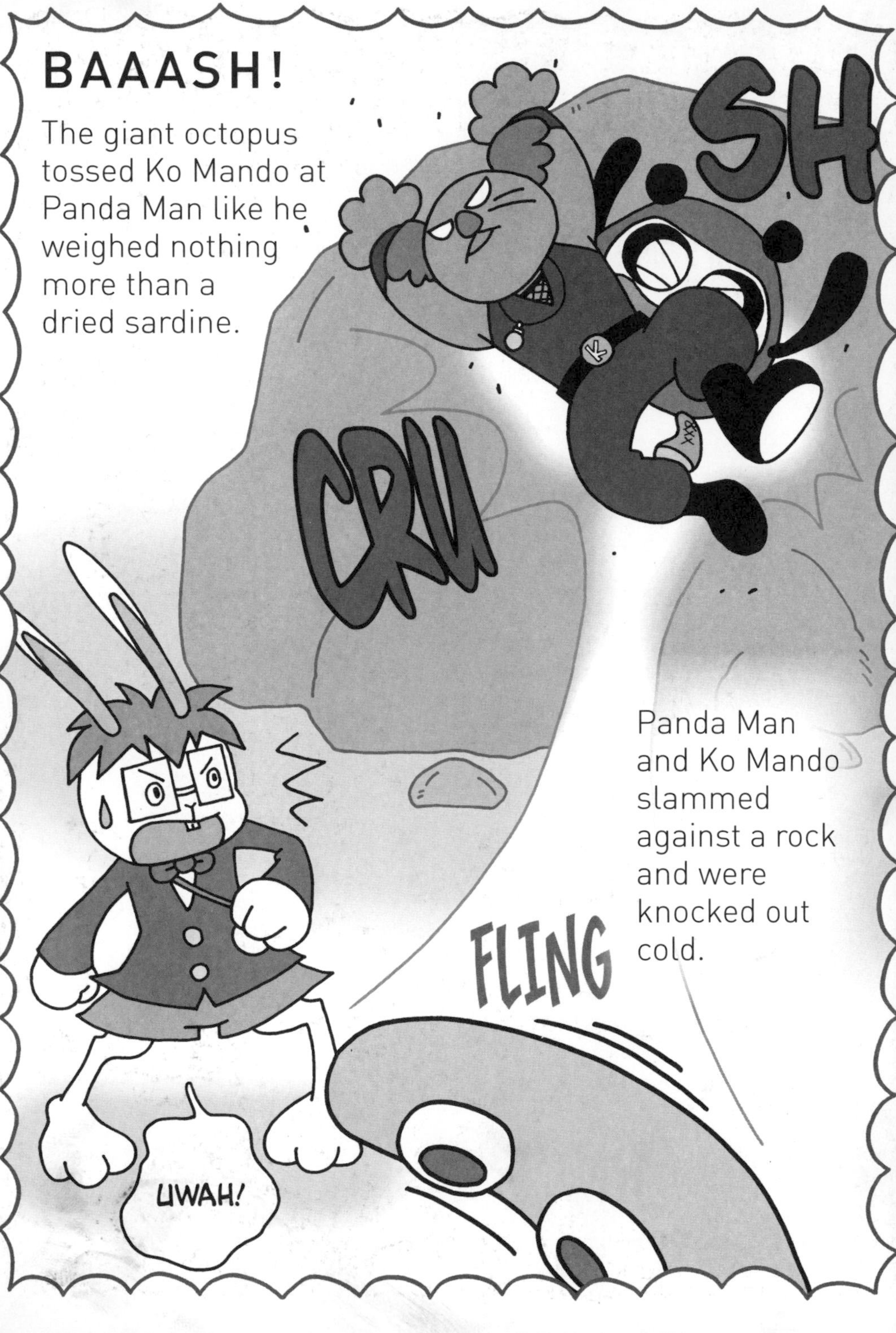
SH
CRU
FLING
UWAH!

Panda Man and Ko Mando slammed against a rock and were knocked out cold.

The octopus closed in, spewing ink as it slithered. Ko Mando wasn't moving, and Panda Man's eyes were blank. There was nothing either of them could do.

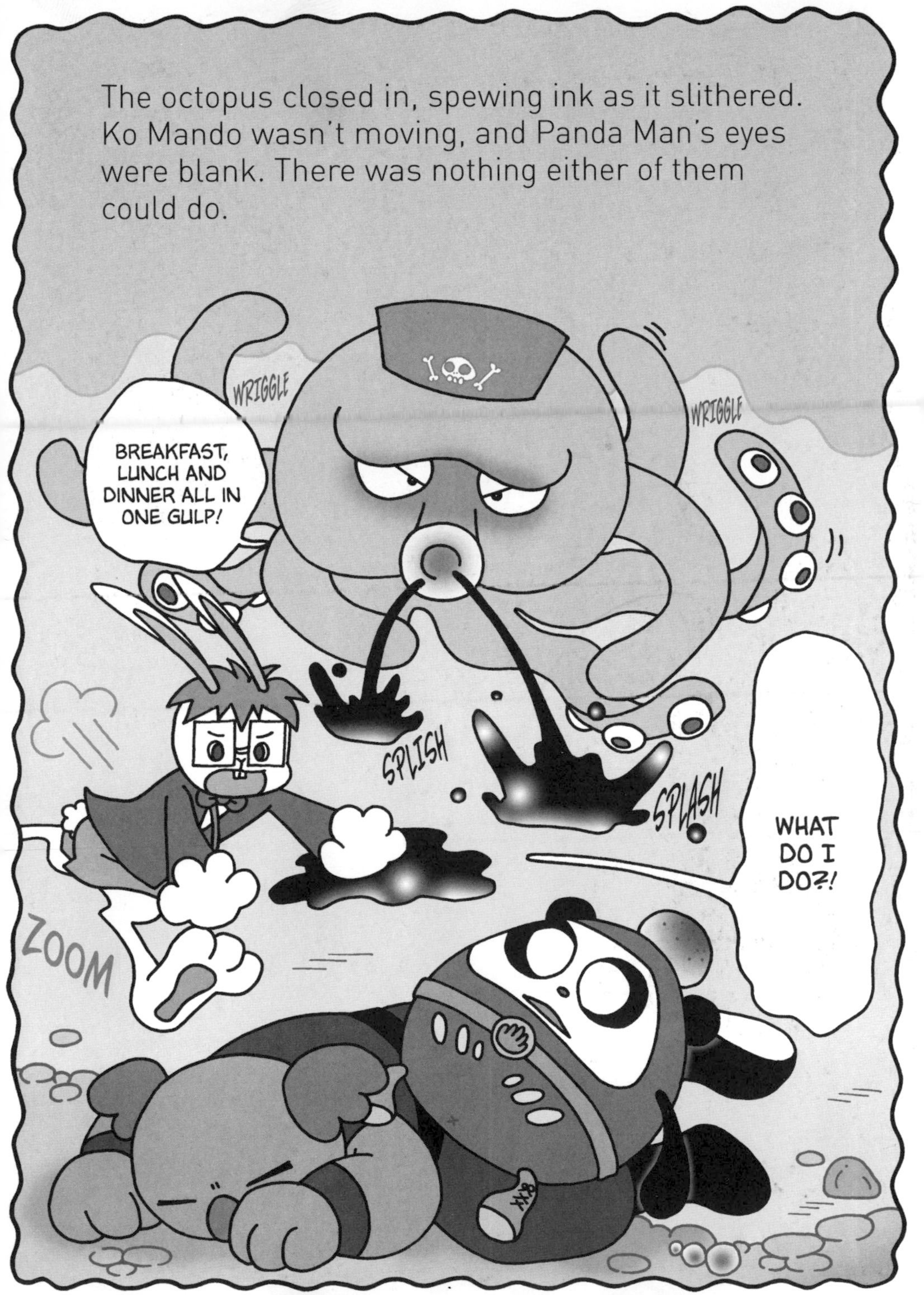
WRIGGLE
BREAKFAST, LUNCH AND DINNER ALL IN ONE GULP!
WRIGGLE
SPLISH
SPLASH
WHAT DO I DO?!
ZOOM

But there was something Hutch could do.
"Oh! I'll check the *Really Big Book of Heroes*!" he cried. "Let's see...It says here that when Panda Man's eyes go blank, they have to be drawn back in!"

Hutch scooped some octopus ink onto his ear and went about drawing in Panda Man's eyes.

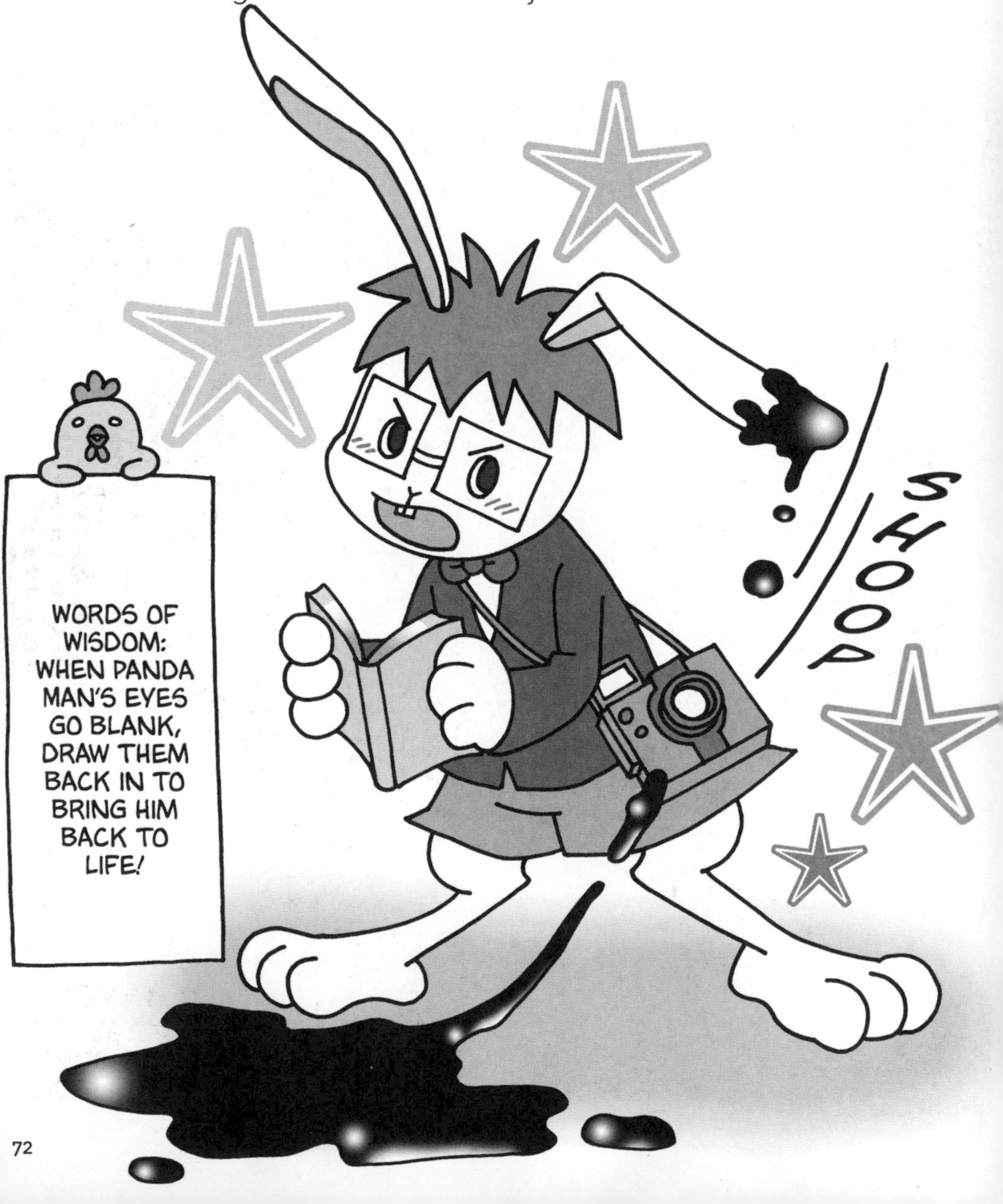
WORDS OF WISDOM: WHEN PANDA MAN'S EYES GO BLANK, DRAW THEM BACK IN TO BRING HIM BACK TO LIFE!
SHOOOP

You can draw Panda Man's eyes in too!

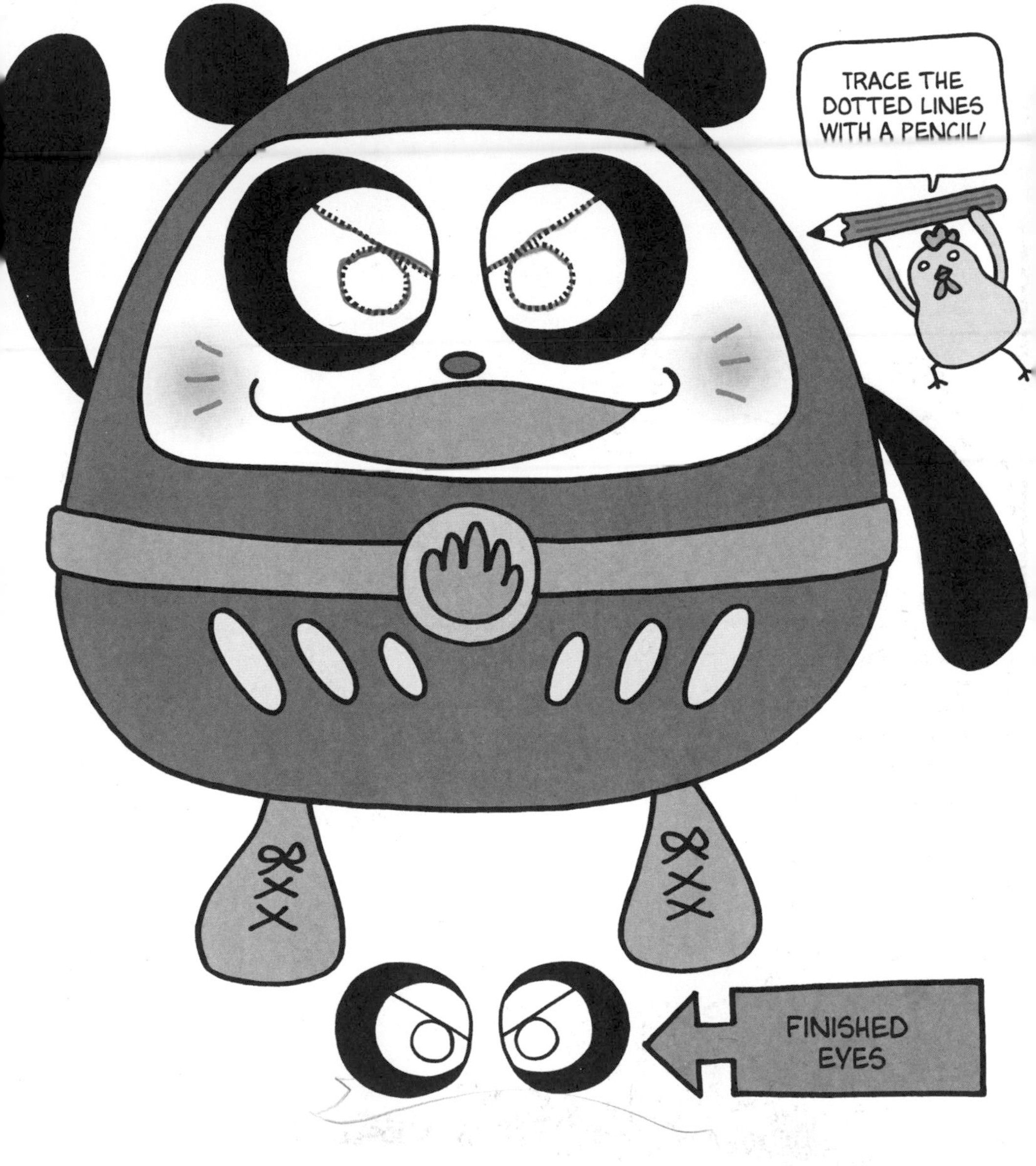
TRACE THE DOTTED LINES WITH A PENCIL!
FINISHED EYES

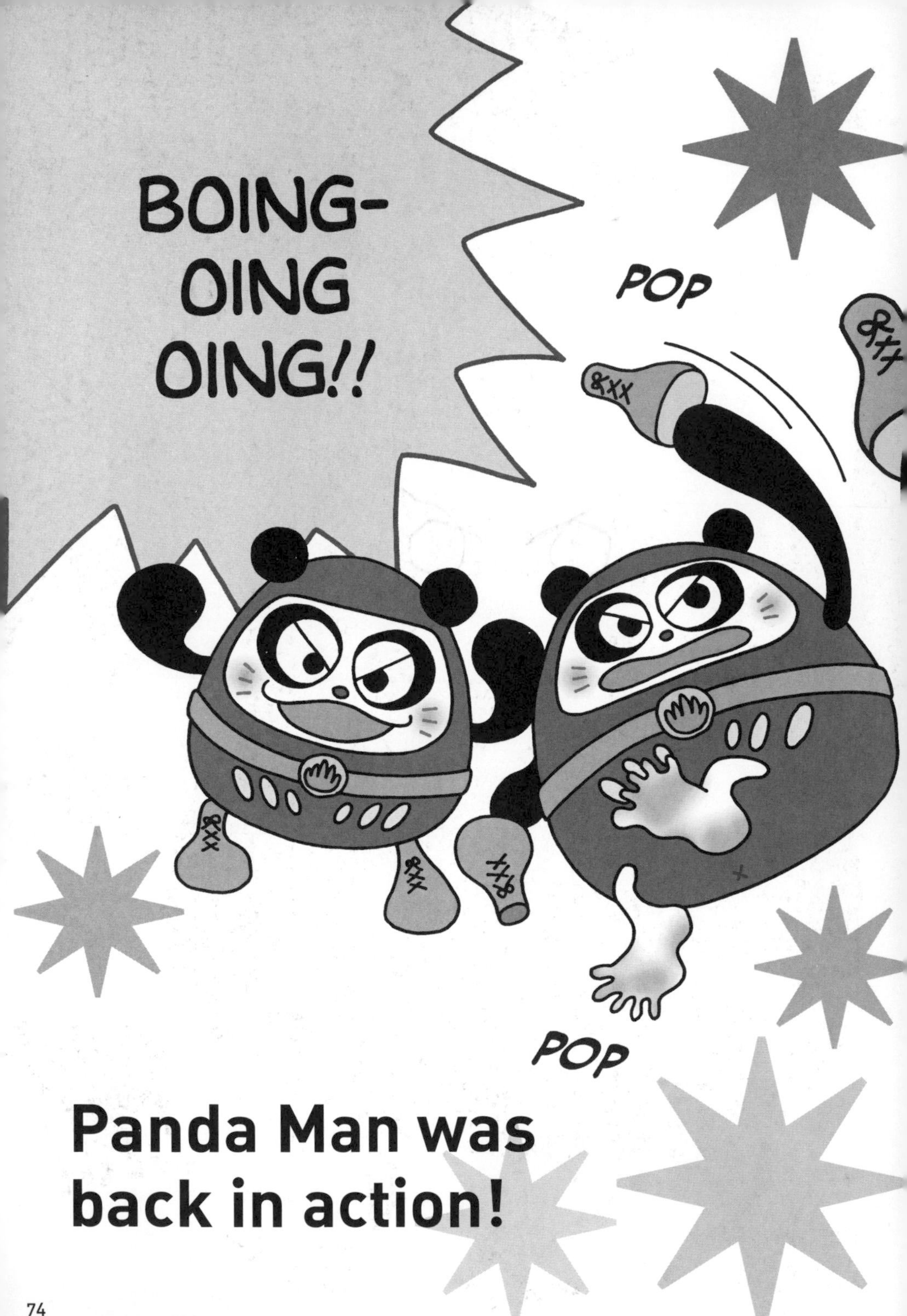
BOING-
OING
OING!!
POP
POP

Panda Man was back in action!

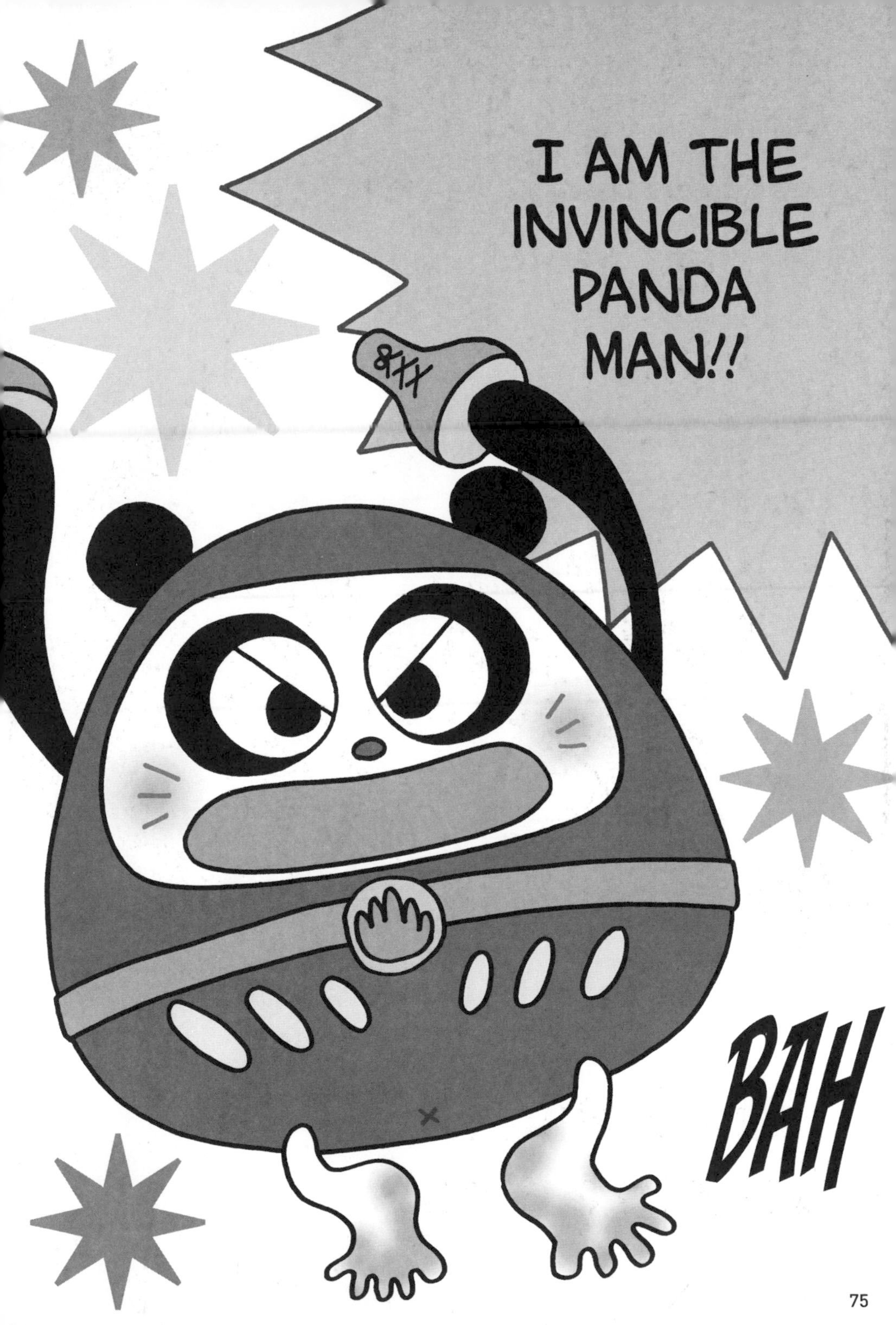
I AM THE INVINCIBLE PANDA MAN!!
BAH

TWISTED STINKY FOOT SCREW!!
JIGGLE
He unleashed his ultimate attack!

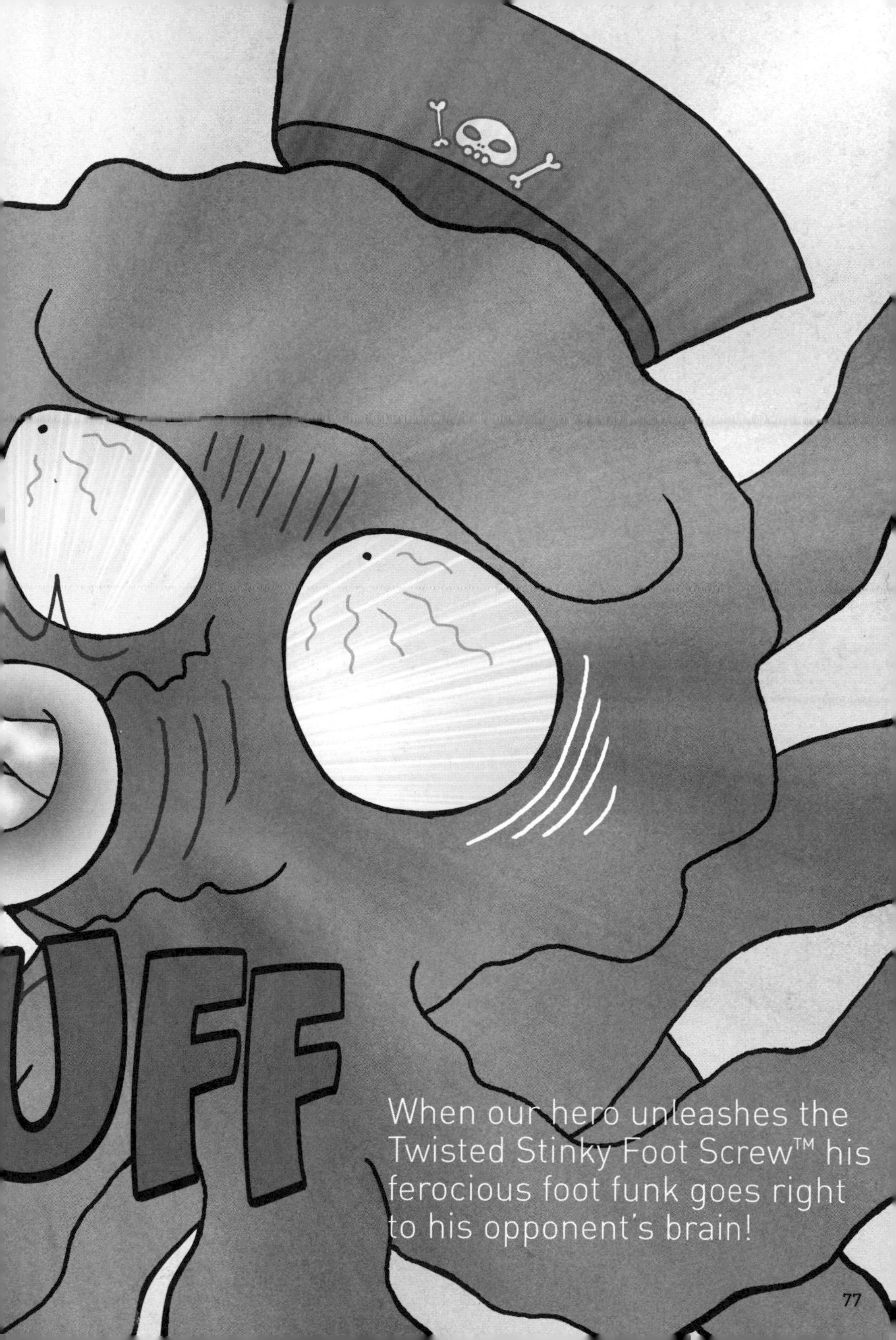
UFF
When our hero unleashes the Twisted Stinky Foot Screw™ his ferocious foot funk goes right to his opponent's brain!

Completely helpless, the octopus swam into a wall. And that was the end of that.

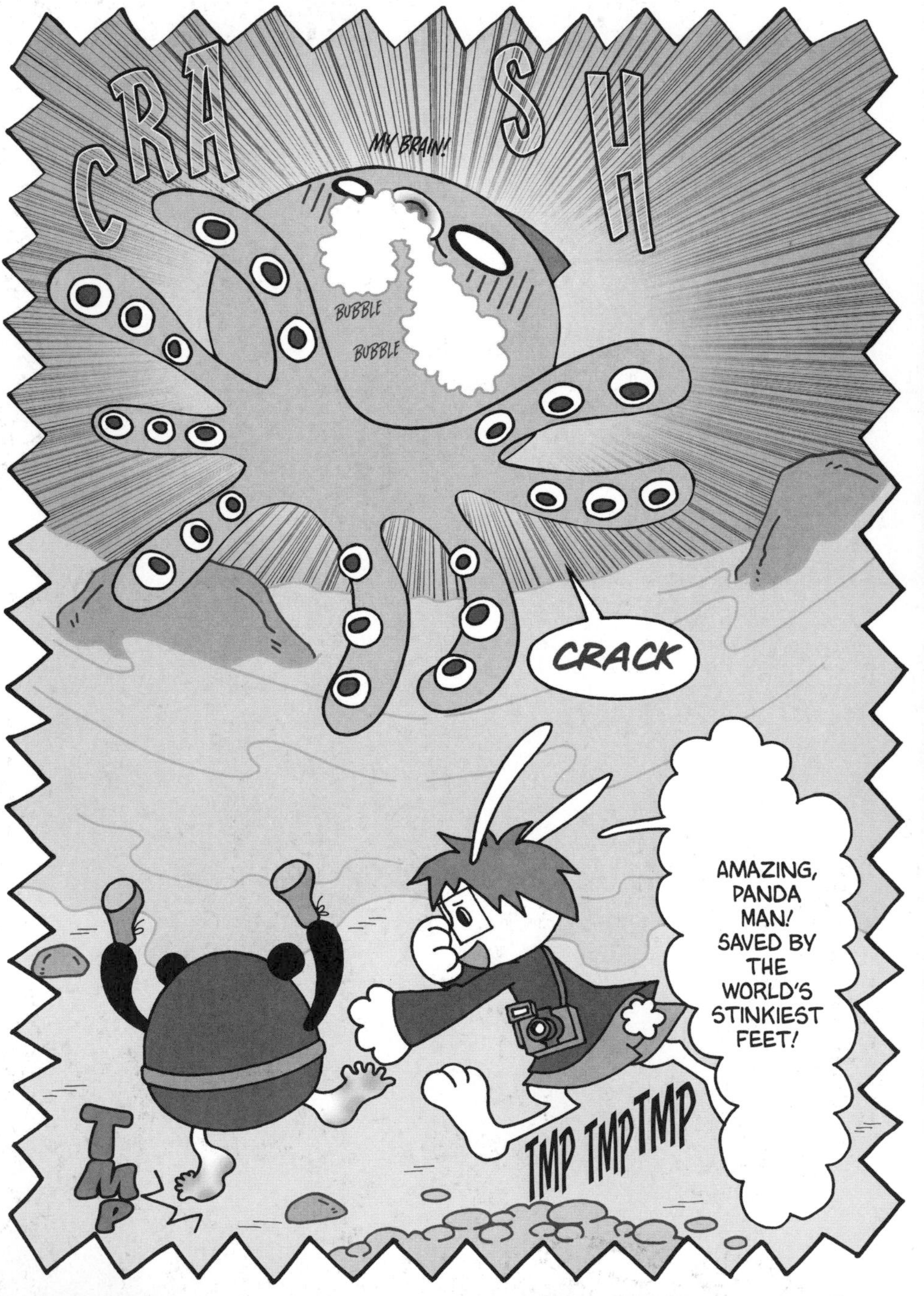
CRASH
MY BRAIN!
BUBBLE
BUBBLE
CRACK
AMAZING, PANDA MAN! SAVED BY THE WORLD'S STINKIEST FEET!
TMP TMP TMP
TMP

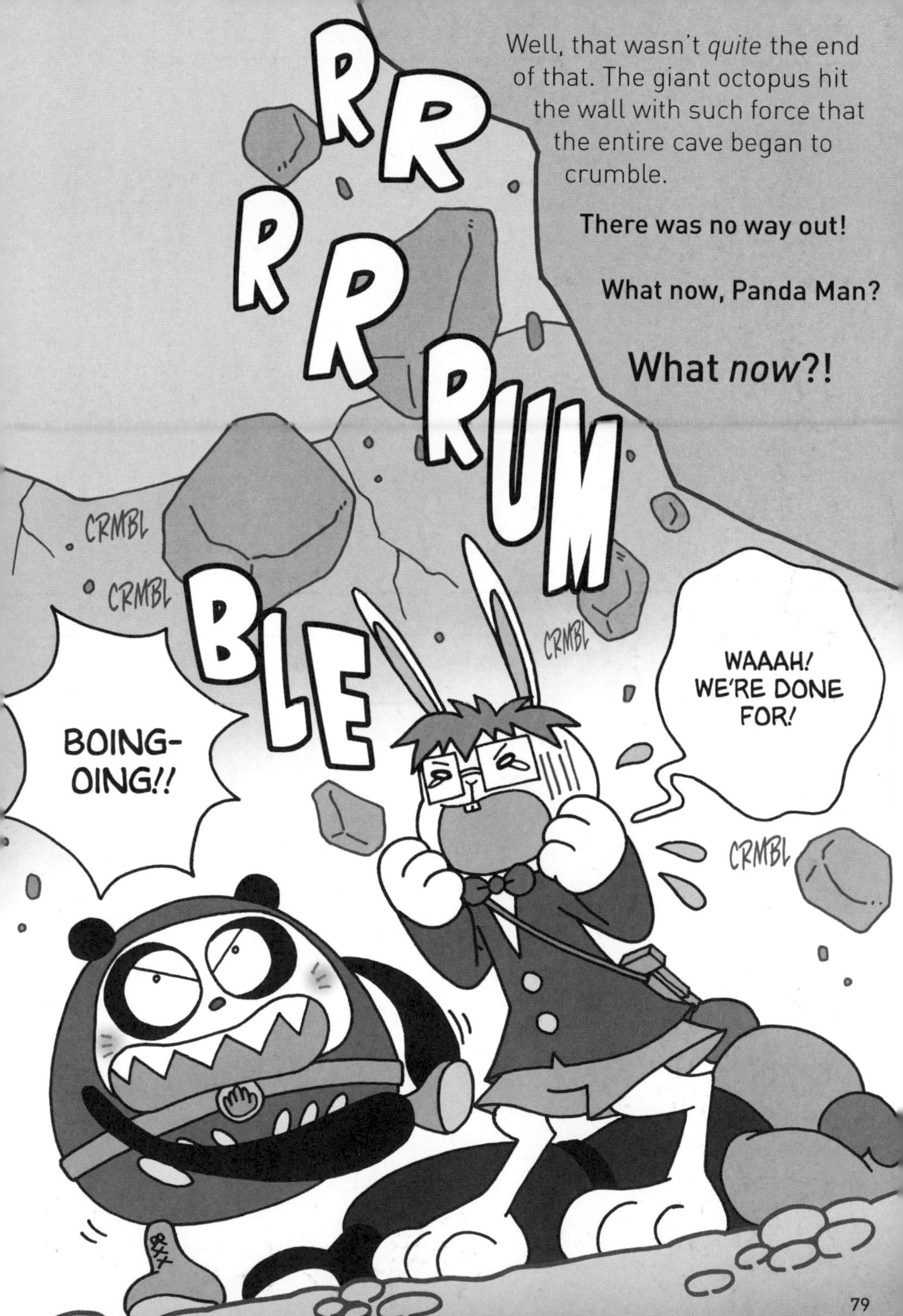
Well, that wasn't *quite* the end of that. The giant octopus hit the wall with such force that the entire cave began to crumble.
There was no way out!
What now, Panda Man?
What *now*?!
RRRRRUMBLE
CRMBL
CRMBL
CRMBL
WAAAH! WE'RE DONE FOR!
BOING-OING!!
CRMBL

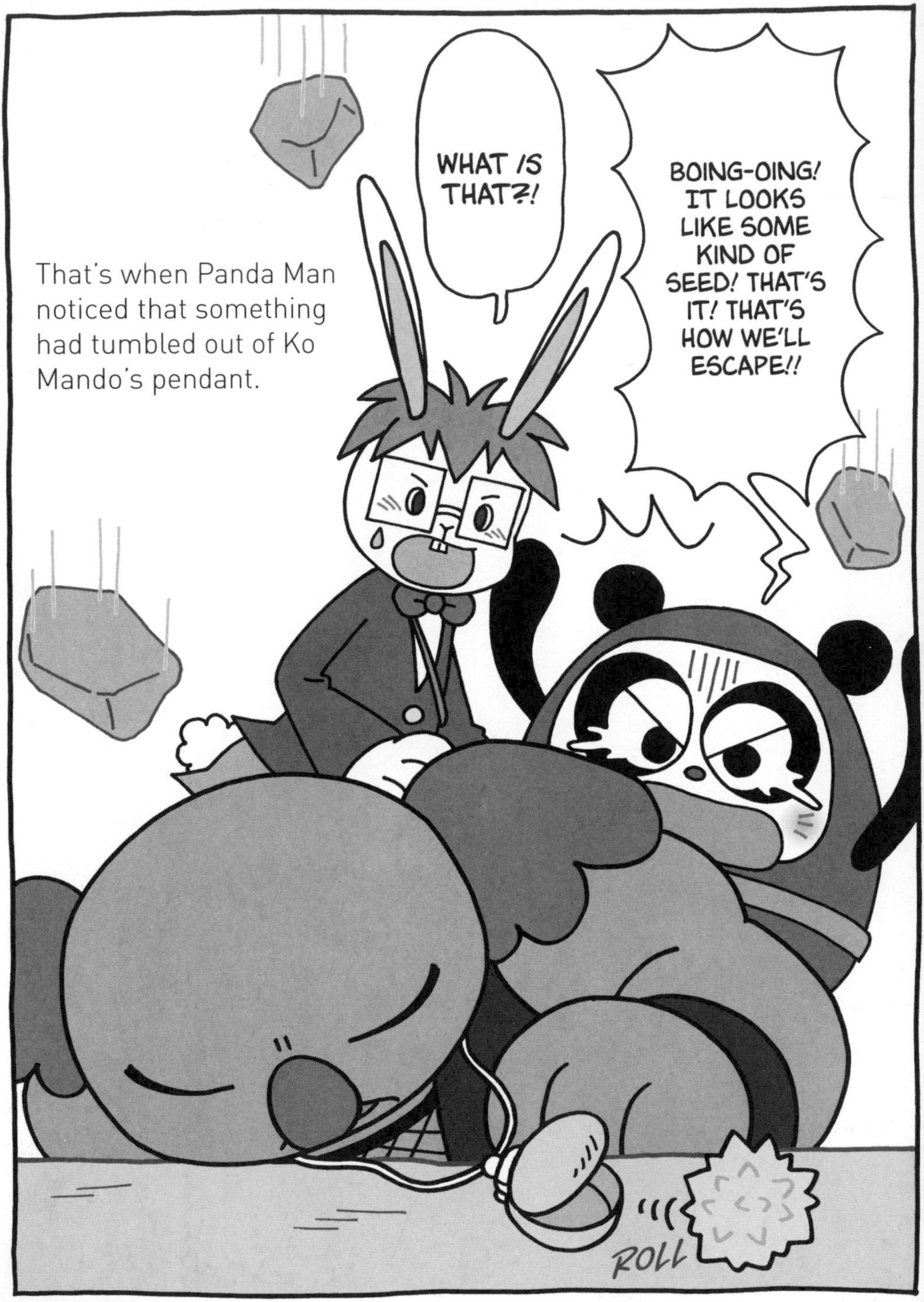
BOING-OING! IT LOOKS LIKE SOME KIND OF SEED! THAT'S IT! THAT'S HOW WE'LL ESCAPE!!
WHAT IS THAT?!
That's when Panda Man noticed that something had tumbled out of Ko Mando's pendant.
ROLL

Panda Man waved the Golden Shears over the seed with all his might. Except for the might he saved for chanting the Golden Shears chant.

Instantly, the seed sprouted and grew and grew and grew...

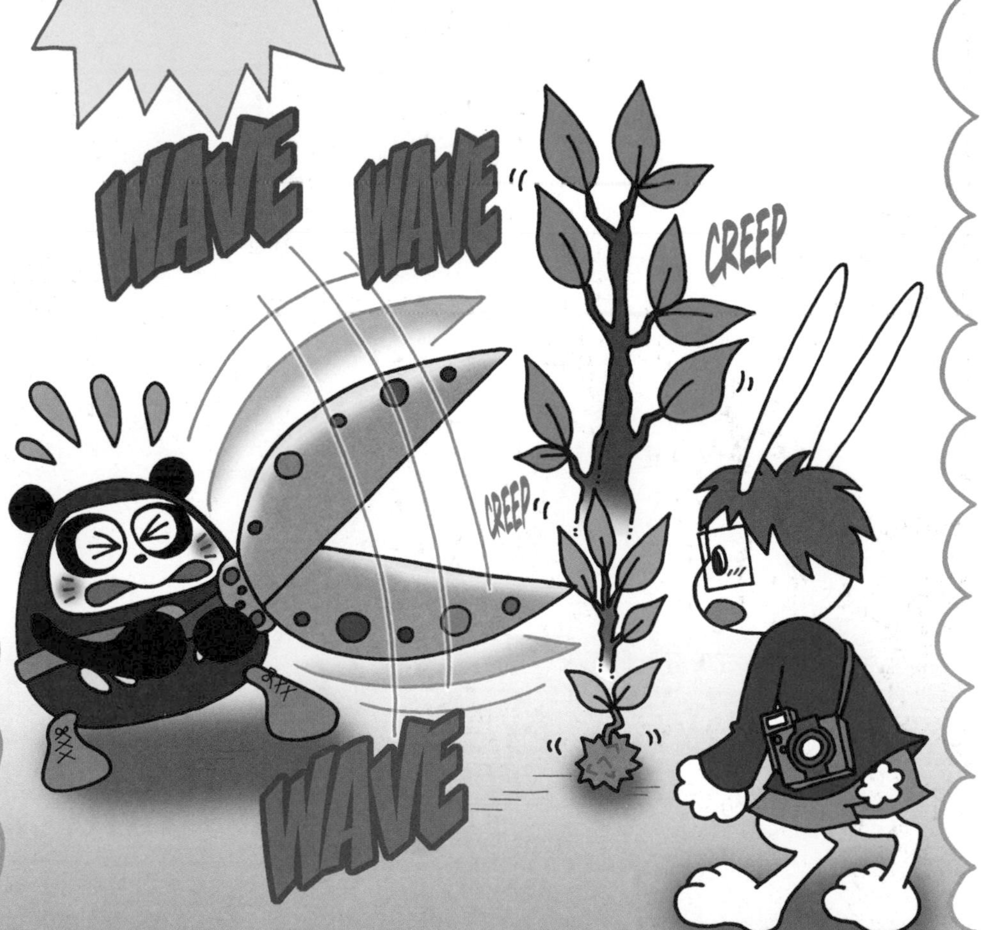
GROW! GROW!! OR I'LL CHOP YOU IN HALF!!
WAVE
WAVE
CREEP
CREEP
WAVE

GROW!
GROW!
GROOOOW!
WORLD'S BEST
KA-POW
...until it burst through the roof of the cave!

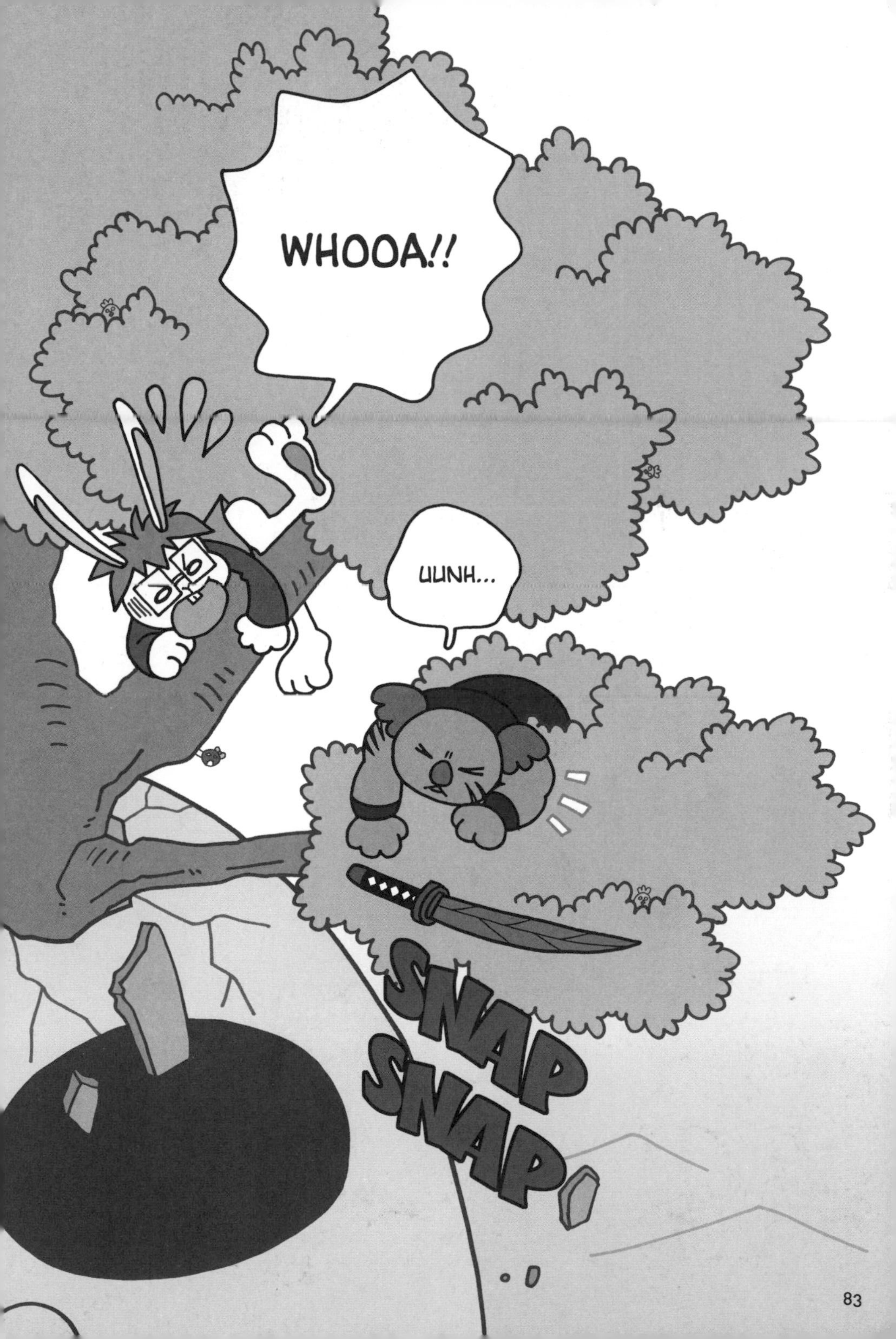
WHOA!!
UUNH...
SNAP
SNAP

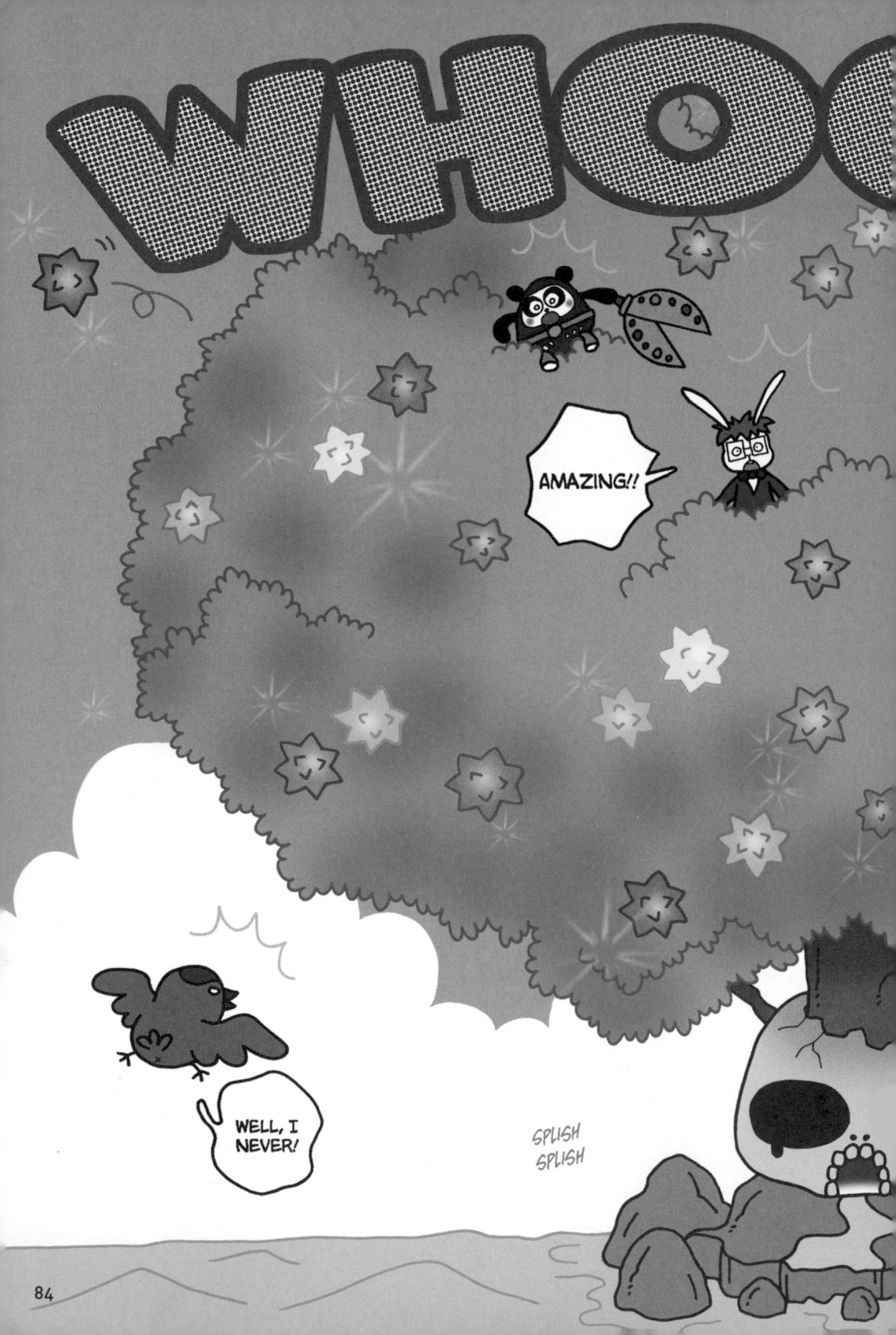
WHOO
AMAZING!!
WELL, I NEVER!
SPLISH SPLISH

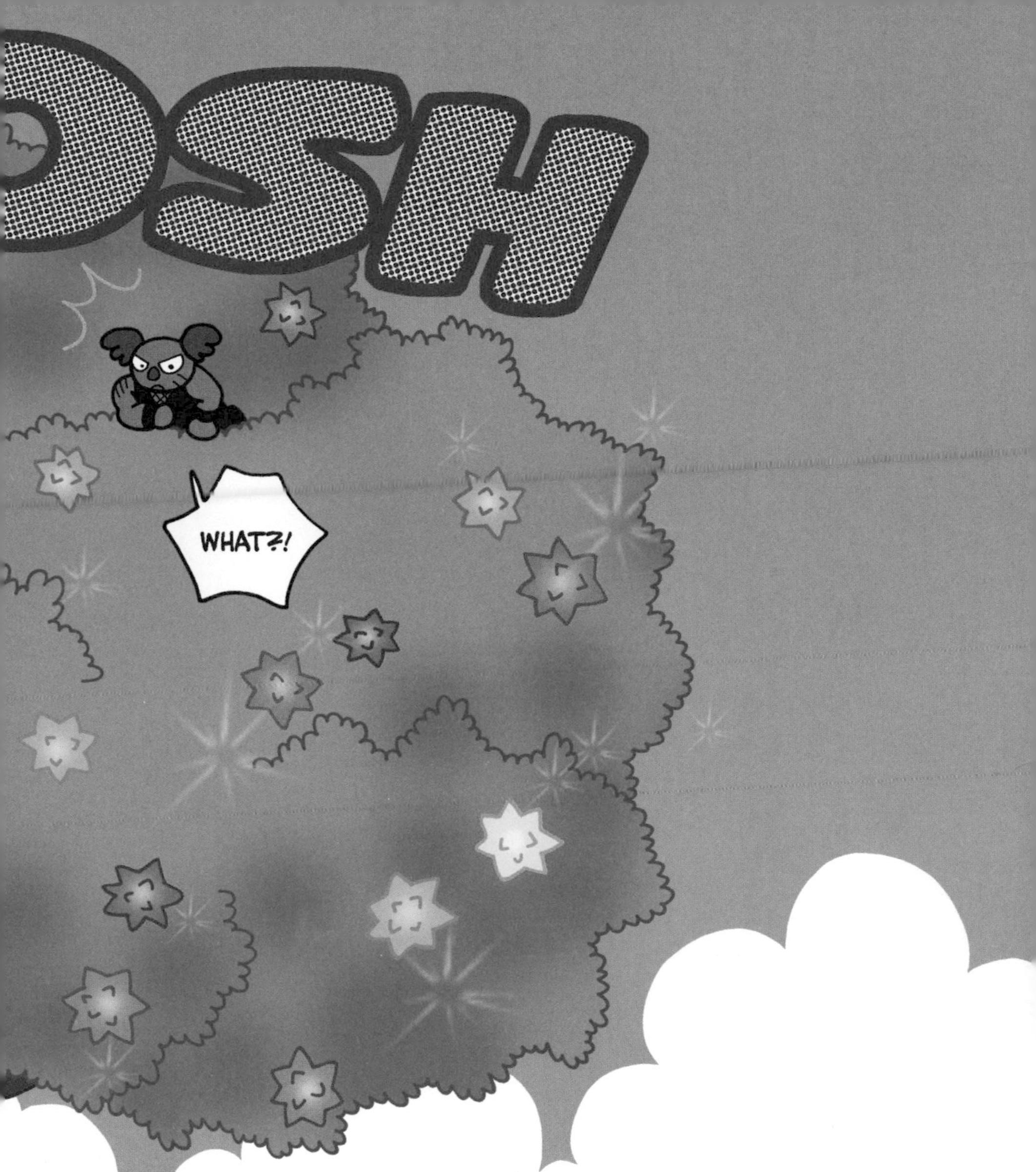
DSH
WHAT?!

The tree was fully grown and bursting with strange, colorful fruit. "Boing-oing...! What's this?" Panda Man cried.

"It's...it's the world's sweetest fruit," said Ko Mando in amazement. "The fruit of the confetti tree."

"Confetti tree?" Panda Man asked.

"Yes. This is the fruit that will save my village." Ko Mando replied.

"Boing-oing? Save your village?"

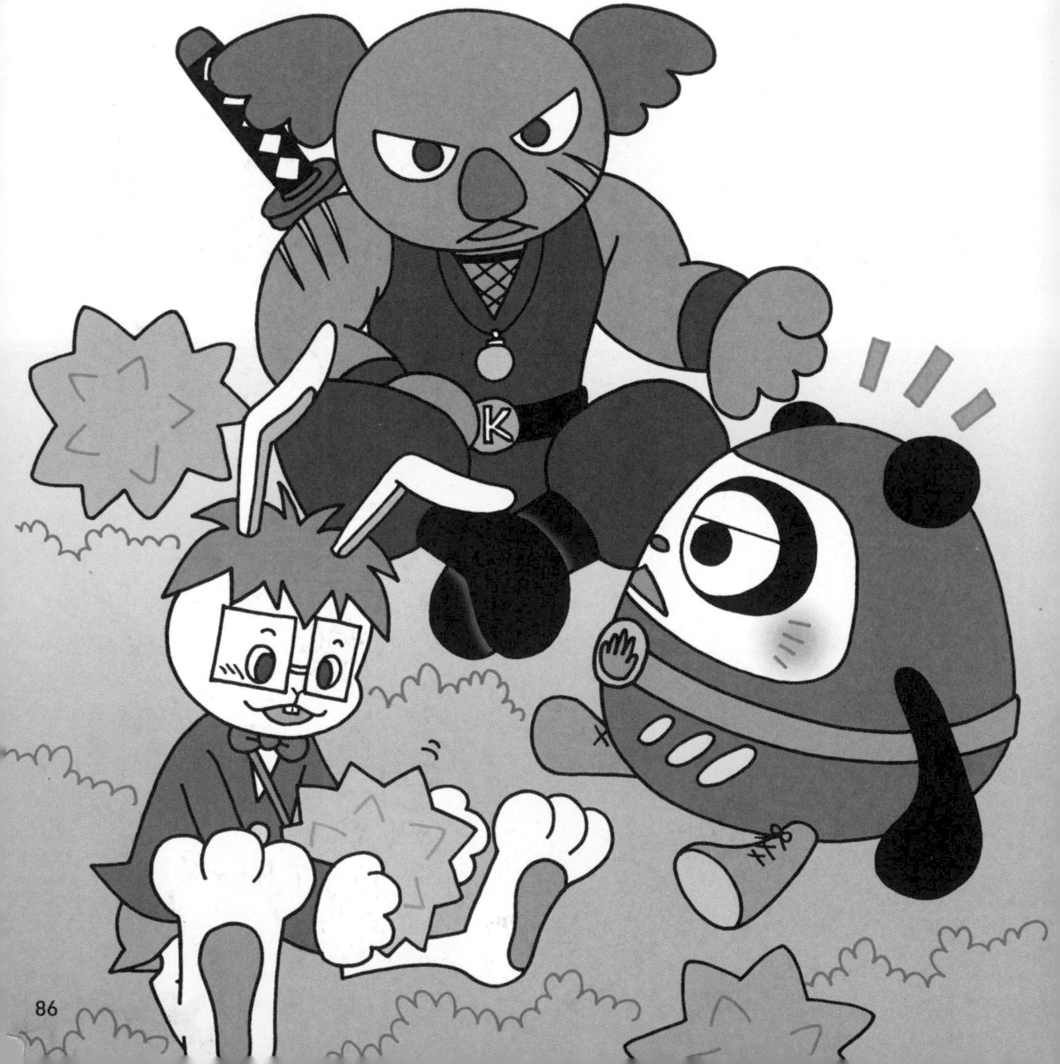
K

"Almost everyone in my village has Sandman Fever," Ko Mando explained.

"It's a terrible disease that makes you sleep all the time. My strength and training kept me from getting sick, but the rest of the villagers weren't so lucky."

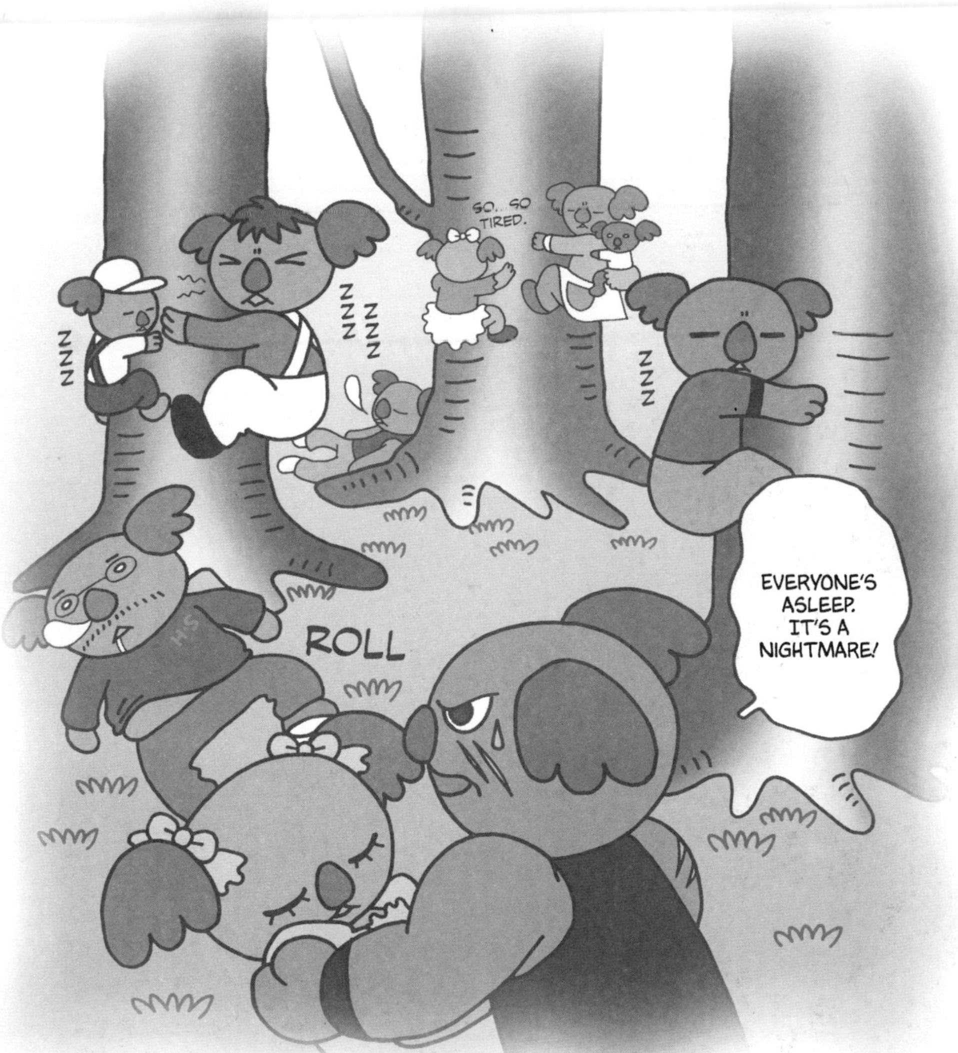
SO... SO TIRED.
ZZZ
ZZZ
ZZZ
ZZZ
ZZZ
ROLL
EVERYONE'S ASLEEP. IT'S A NIGHTMARE!

"The only cure for Sandman Fever is the fruit of the confetti tree," Ko Mando continued. "There are very few confetti trees in the world, but I managed to find this single seed.

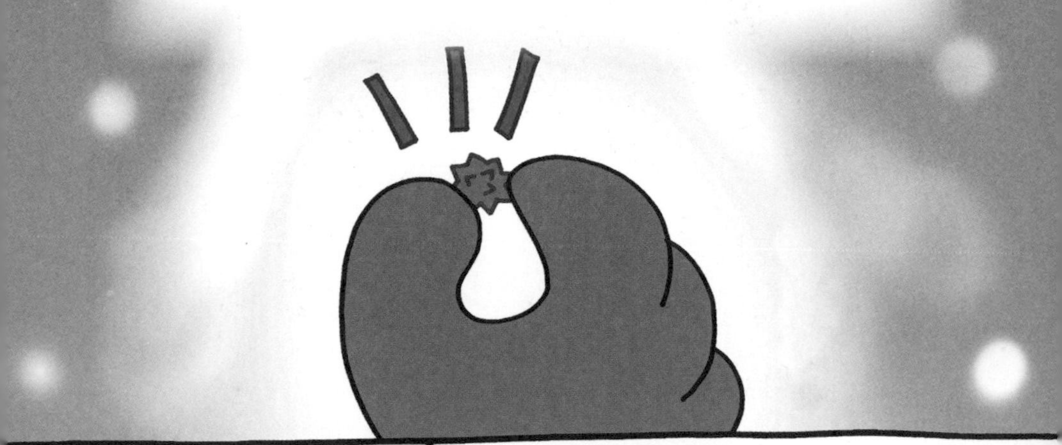

"I couldn't save my village with it alone, but I knew there had to be *something* I could do. I read everything I could find, and then I learned about the Golden Shears! I had my answer!

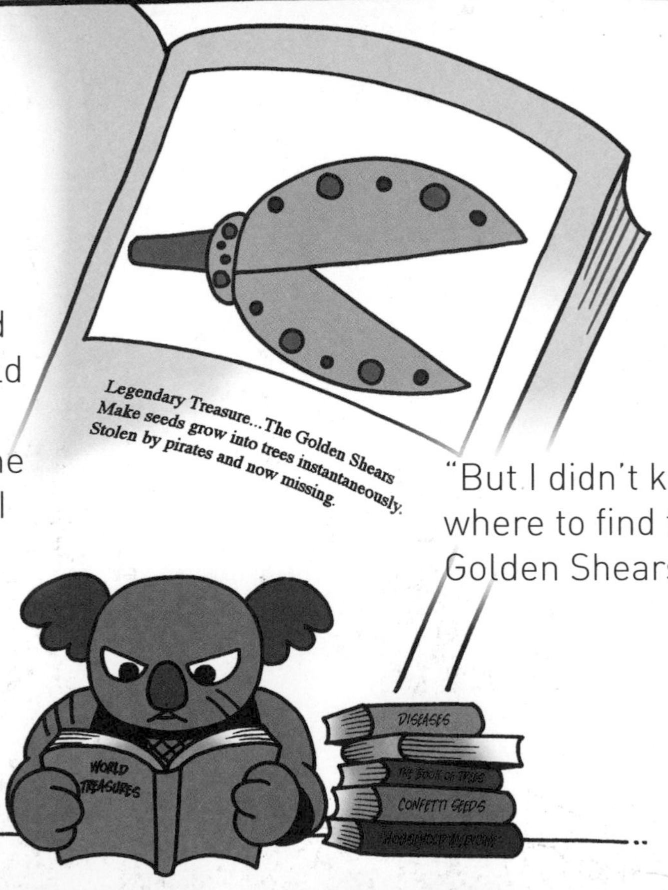
Legendary Treasure...The Golden Shears
Make seeds grow into trees instantaneously.
Stolen by pirates and now missing.
WORLD TREASURES
DISEASES
THE BOOK OF TREES
CONFETTI SEEDS

"But I didn't know where to find the Golden Shears."

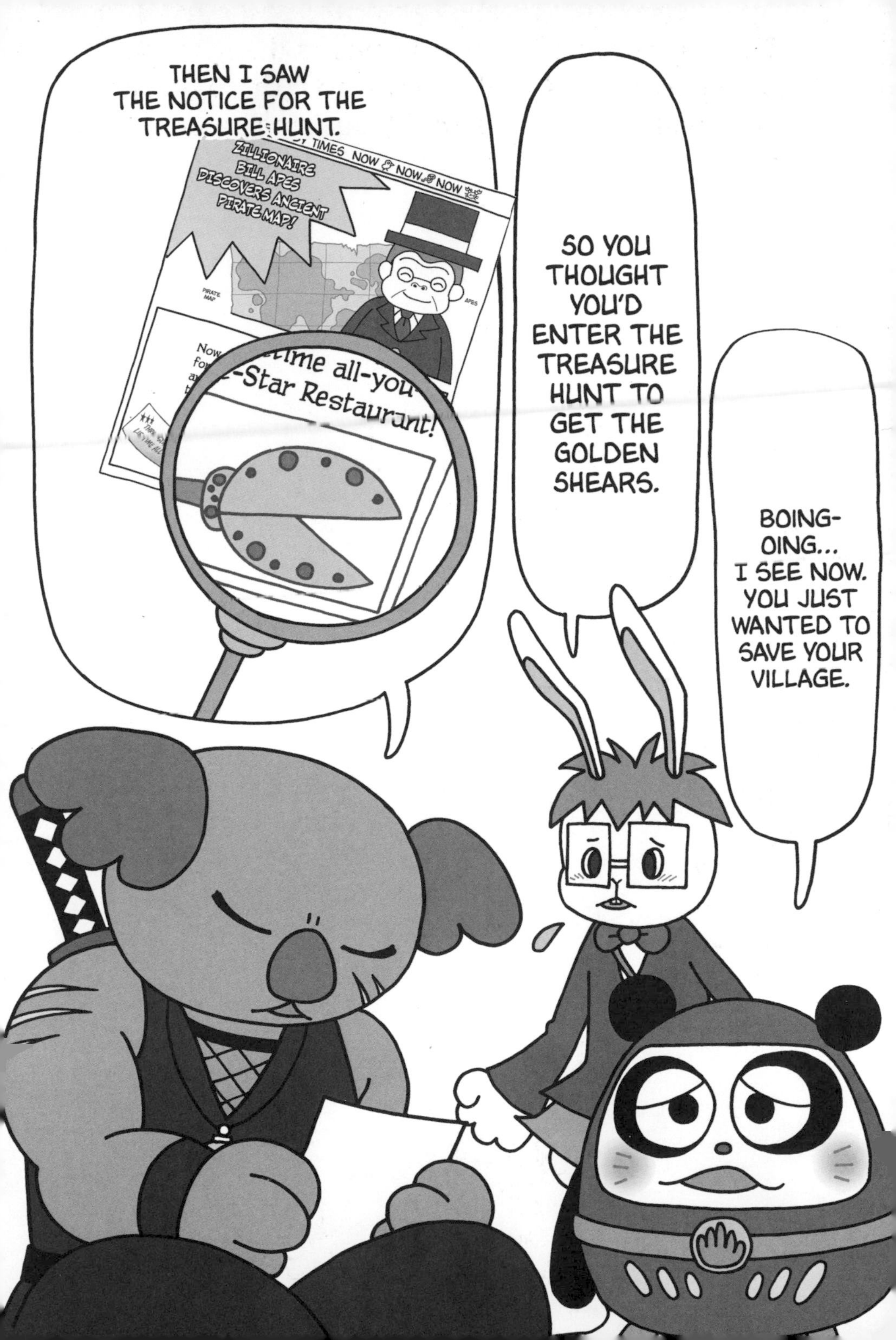
THEN I SAW THE NOTICE FOR THE TREASURE HUNT.
TIMES NOW NOW NOW
ZILLIONAIRE BILL APES DISCOVERS ANCIENT PIRATE MAP!
PIRATE MAP
APES
-Star Restaurant!
SO YOU THOUGHT YOU'D ENTER THE TREASURE HUNT TO GET THE GOLDEN SHEARS.
BOING-OING... I SEE NOW. YOU JUST WANTED TO SAVE YOUR VILLAGE.

"And now, thanks to you, Panda Man, I have enough confetti fruit for everyone." Ko Mando smiled.

"You really are the **world's greatest martial artist**."

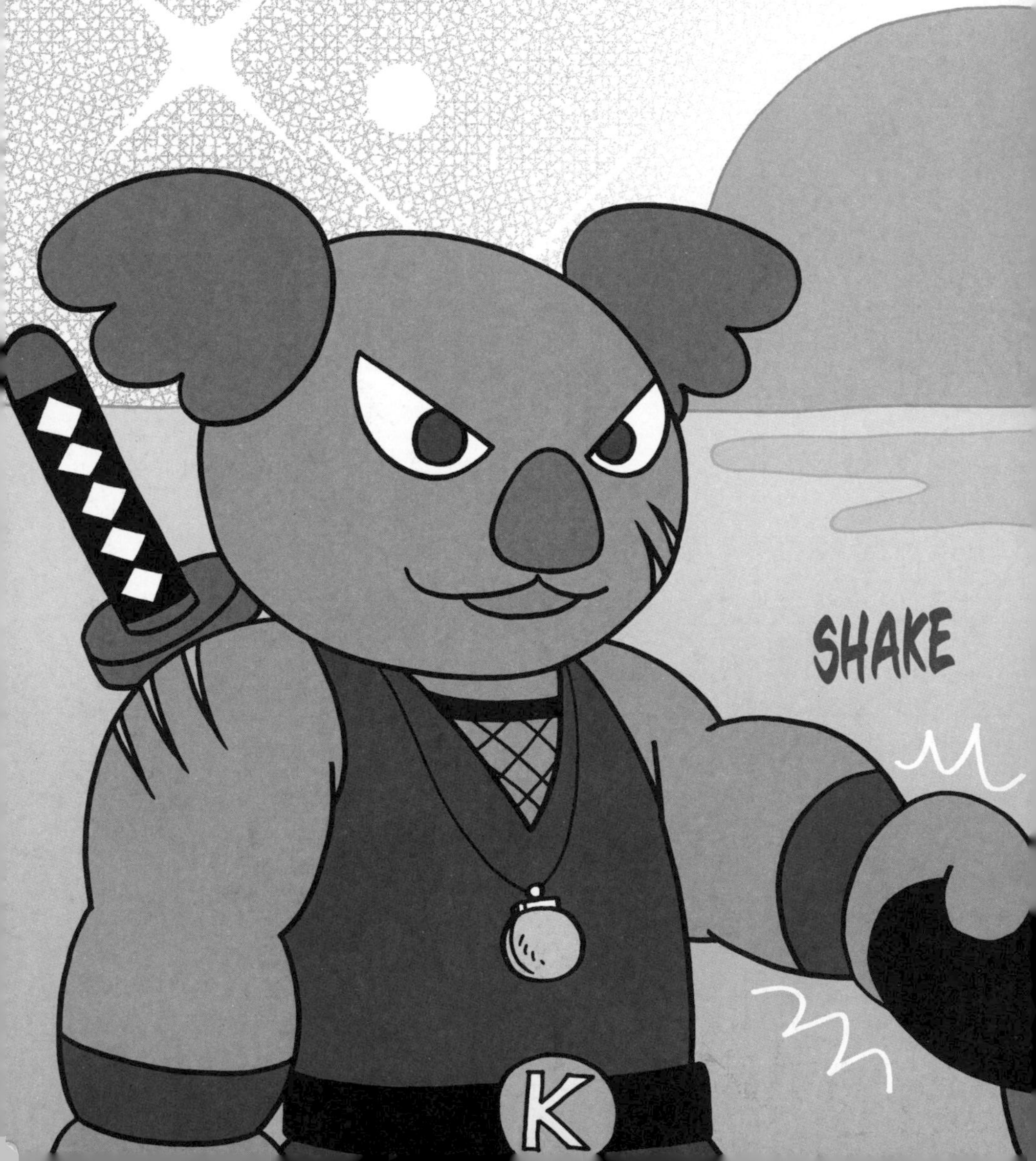
SHAKE

"And to think, this whole time I thought you were just a major pain in the boing-oing." Panda Man said.

"But you really are the **world's greatest swordsman**!"

With their misunderstandings resolved, Panda Man and Ko Mando became fast friends.

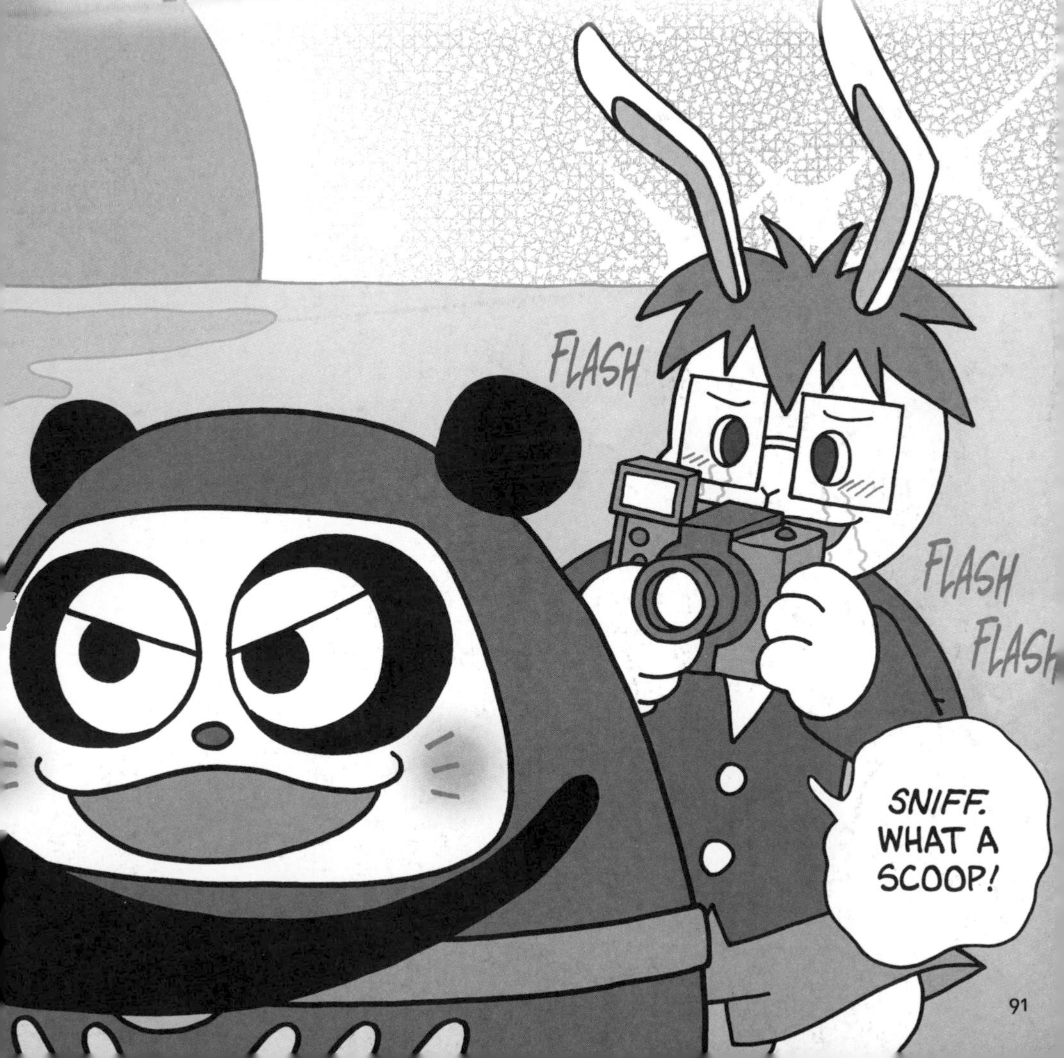
FLASH
FLASH
FLASH
SNIFF. WHAT A SCOOP!

At that very moment they noticed that the Golden Shears had shattered and were worthless. Growing the confetti tree had used all of their power.

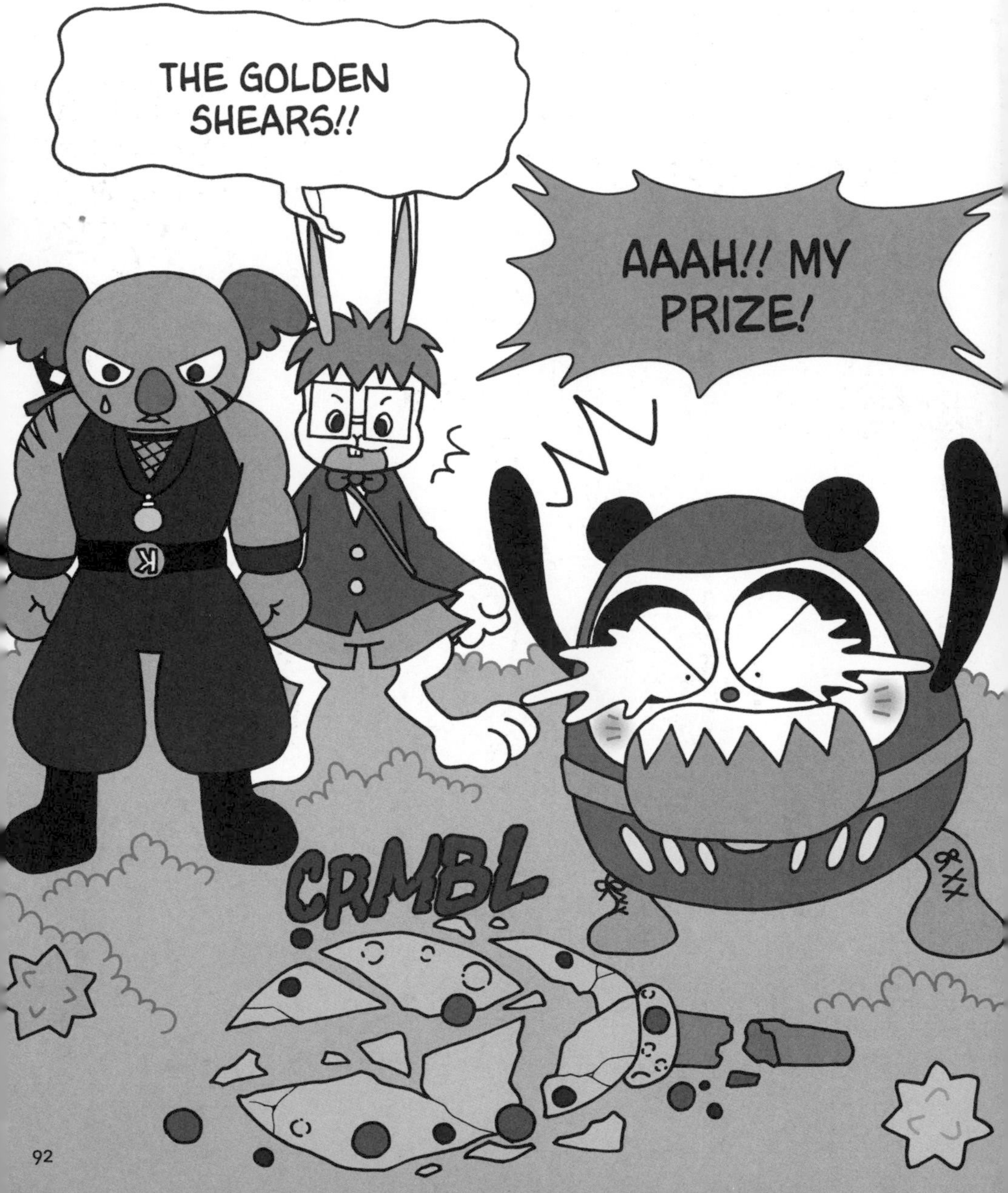
AAAH!! MY PRIZE!
THE GOLDEN SHEARS!!
CRMBL

The next day, the paper announced the news.

Panda Man was probably somewhere crying all alone...

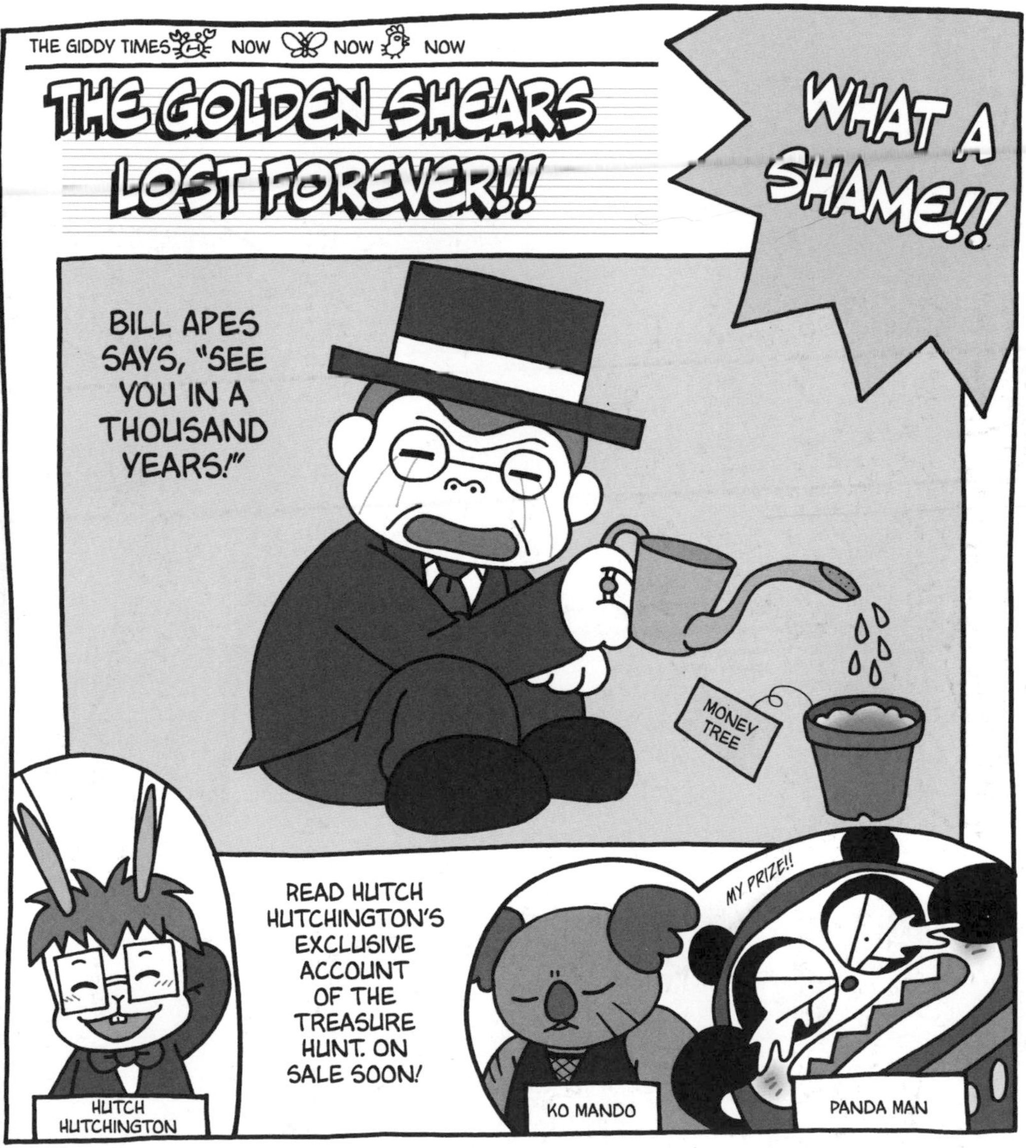
THE GIDDY TIMES NOW NOW NOW
THE GOLDEN SHEARS LOST FOREVER!!
WHAT A SHAME!!
BILL APES SAYS, "SEE YOU IN A THOUSAND YEARS!"
MONEY TREE
HUTCH HUTCHINGTON
READ HUTCH HUTCHINGTON'S EXCLUSIVE ACCOUNT OF THE TREASURE HUNT. ON SALE SOON!
KO MANDO
MY PRIZE!!
PANDA MAN

As it turned out, Panda Man was far from crying. And he was far from being alone.

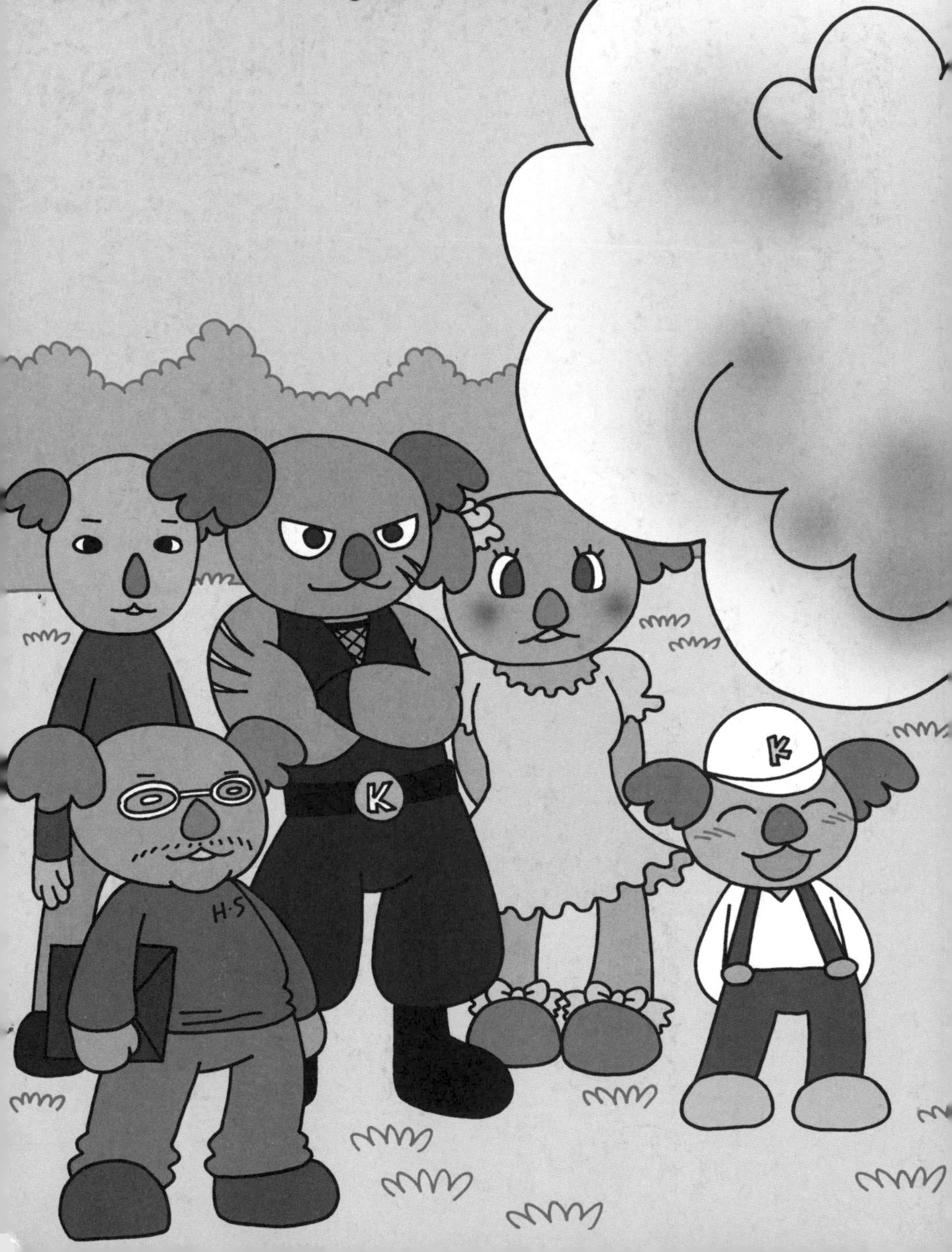
K
H·S
K

He was in Ko Mando's village, stuffing his face with the world's sweetest cotton candy, made from confetti berries, of course.

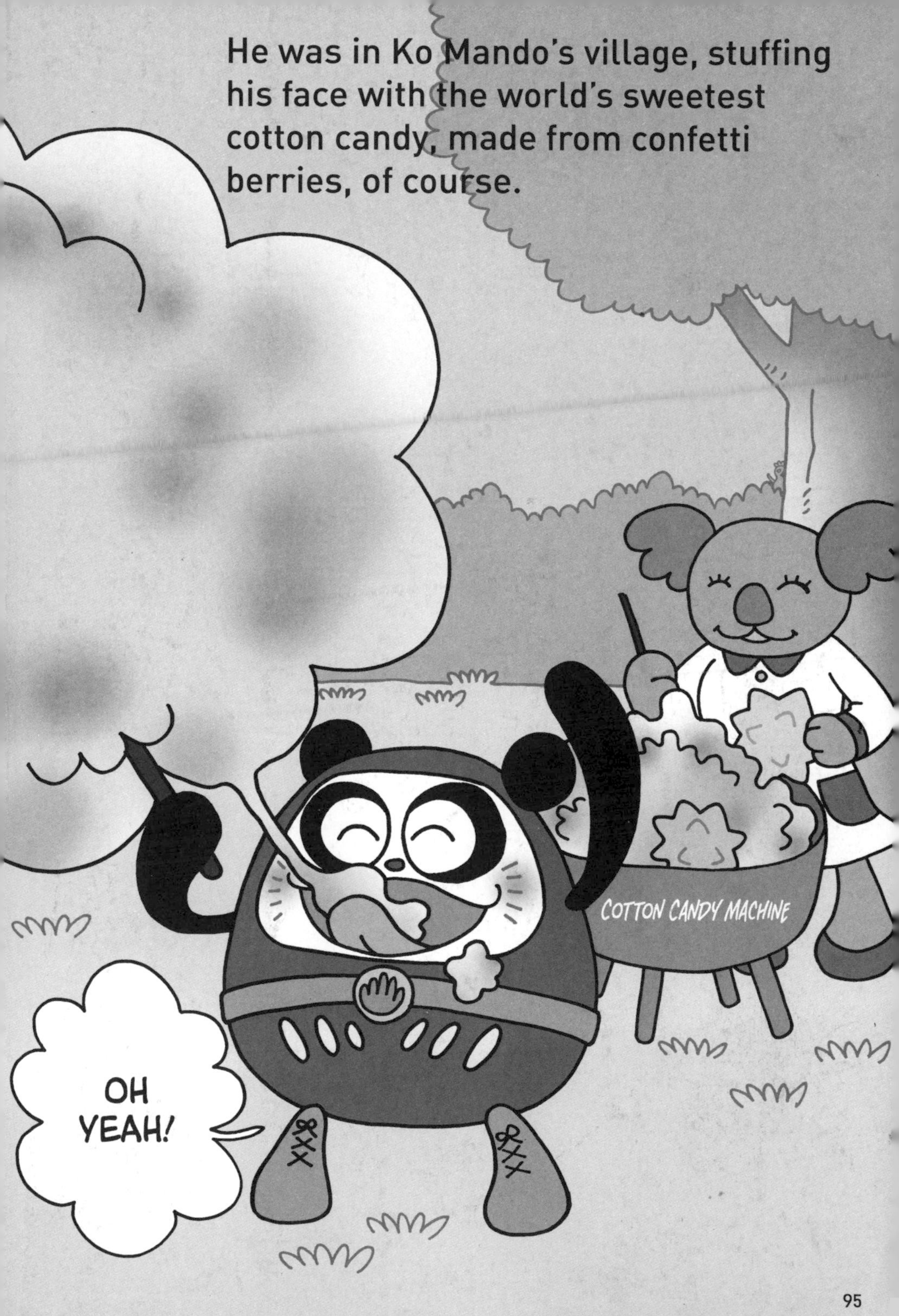
COTTON CANDY MACHINE
OH YEAH!

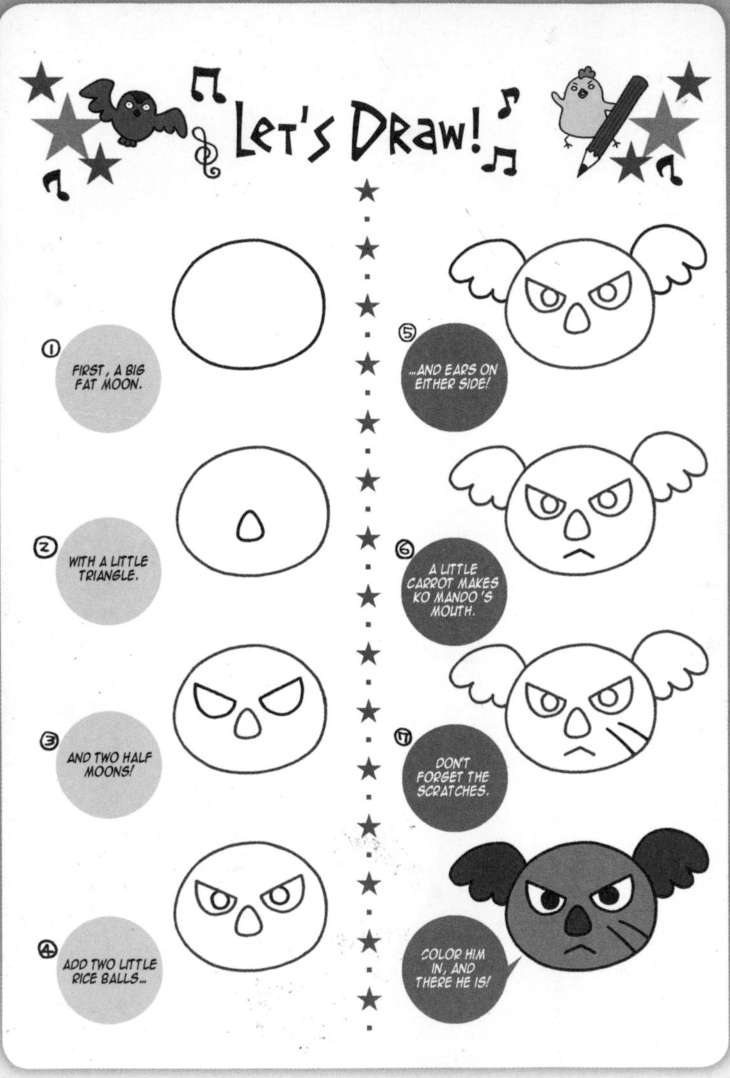
LET'S DRAW!
① FIRST, A BIG FAT MOON.
② WITH A LITTLE TRIANGLE.
③ AND TWO HALF MOONS!
④ ADD TWO LITTLE RICE BALLS...
⑤ ...AND EARS ON EITHER SIDE!
⑥ A LITTLE CARROT MAKES KO MANDO'S MOUTH.
⑦ DON'T FORGET THE SCRATCHES.
COLOR HIM IN, AND THERE HE IS!

Panda Man and the Treasure Hunt

VIZ Kids Edition

Story by Sho Makura
Art by Haruhi Kato

Translation: Katherine Schilling
Touch-up Art & Lettering: John Hunt
Graphics & Cover Design: Frances O. Liddell
Editor: Traci N. Todd

First published in Japan in 2008 by SHUEISHA Inc., Tokyo.
English translation rights arranged by SHUEISHA Inc.

Printed in China

Published by VIZ Media, LLC
P.O. Box 77010
San Francisco, CA 94107

10 9 8 7 6 5 4 3 2 1
First printing, January 2011

www.vizkids.com